FINDING IT-666

The Beast

By Cordelia Malthere

Book One

ISBN:978-0-9931450-1-8

It-666: The Beast

First instalment of a saga which consumed my nights away.
Her compelling story had to be told.

First, I had nightmares about It-666, as I dreamt of her crucified
upside down in the middle of my bedroom.

First, I could not come to terms with her and that
recurring nightmare.

Until, Seeing the four walls bleeding around her words
which spoke for her,

One morning I decided to write them down.

Until, Seeing her tongue was ripped apart , that she was crying
her blood inside out for everyone,

One morning I decided to write the story of her life...

I never looked back.

I feel Free.

Cordelia Halthere

Dedications,

1996,

Door 103 Noel Road opened in the Angel,

To your beautiful welcoming smile,

To your all-embracing arms,

K Y Lawman,

RIP,

You made me feel

Truly Adopted.

I will cherish your memory,

Forever.

Verse 1. Finding It

Autumn 2012

He checked one last time upon the mirror. He hasn't been followed. He had managed to lose them on the way. It was tricky but he did it. Parking his black Peugeot 306 under the cover of the trees, he fetched his pocket camera from the glove box and muttered between his teeth,

-Dirty son of a bitch, this is it. What are you bloody hiding in those woods, in that bunker of yours? Let's find out...Bud, wake up Bud, you're coming.

Behind him something moved, the head of a black and white Great Dane appeared between the driver and the passenger's seat, gazing at him with eyes full of expectation.

Stroking the dog's forehead, he whispered firmly,

-Mission, Bud, mission, no running about.

He opened the door and walked warily to the low concrete building before him. His dog strayed on the side, relieving itself upon a tree, before joining him.
He pressed a button in his pocket and a red light coming from the car illuminated the space in front of him, revealing booby traps and hidden wires he had not seen in the darkness of the night.

-Follow close Bud.

He made his way to the side of the building, and followed an almost invisible trail upon the ground leading a few metres away from the building, with no grass growing upon it and covered by crisp copper leaves. It led to a grid, barely hidden from sight. He smiled before it, frowning his blond brows,

-Sadly too human, everyone has to go to the toilet. Unfortunately for me, safest way in.

He removed the grid and jumped in, leaving his dog on guard at the manhole. He looked surprised at the spacious tunnel before him. He barely had to bow his head. Just a small gutter trailed in the middle, relatively clean, flowing refuse water at his feet, indicating that the building was not occupied at present. He breathed a sigh of relief, his job will be a tad easier for it. Mentally counting his steps, he knew when he reached underneath the bunker. He climbed upon a small ladder and was out by the first manhole, whispering as he stood in a large round room,

-That was painless.

He looked around him, his eyes adapting to the darkness and realised that the entire room was covered by strange black magic symbols from wall to floor. He took his camera and collected a few pictures. Suddenly, a suspicious thought rose within his mind at the rich redness of the markings. He approached with his gloved fingers and touched one line, flaking slightly under the leather. He muttered,

-Holy shit, its blood, Bastard. If it's human, I am going to make sure you answer for it.

He collected carefully a few samples, from different symbols, and put them in the large pocket of his mac. His attention was caught by a trap door right in the middle of the large floor pentagram. Full of curiosity, he knelt by it and lifted it with great care. It was far too dark for him to see anything, but something seemed to shimmer slightly down there. Taking his flash light, he inspected the hole. What he saw took him by surprise. He felt revolt and total disgust. The stench of it overtook him, and he turned away from it, livid and sick. Trembling, tears running uncontrollably from his eyes, he decided to hoist the cage from the hole, he had to ascertain if it was a dead body or someone still alive. The cage was surprisingly light and his own sheer strength sufficed to lift it. He pulled it to the light and sad eyes blinked at him, considering him with surprise.

His throat knotted itself as he took a good long look at the human within the cage. At first he could not say if he had before him a man or a woman. It was young, barely alive, laying on its side awkwardly. One of the hips was at a bad angle, dislocated, and one of its arms was dark with bruises and misshapen, most probably by multiple fractures. It had no hair, its head shaved completely, and cut badly, everywhere. The creature had a frighteningly skeletal aspect, starved to skin and bones. How long was it left in that cage, in that hole, in its own piss and shit? Disturbed by the sight of the being in front of him, he could only feel deep sorrow. He finally found his voice and asked in a whisper,

-What is your name?

The creature's eyes twinkled kindly and its dried mouth made moves but no sound came, too dehydrated to be able to talk, most probably he thought. One of its hands moved upon the floor and its finger traced in the red blood lines a short word,

-It.

Verse 2. Code 666

He nodded sadly, and told the naked creature within the cage,

-Well, It, you in a cage will not do. I will ask questions later and get you out of here.

The human smiled to him, its eyes full of sudden hope, closed and tears appeared running down its dirty cheeks. They reopened and saw him, attempting to open the cage.

He had found the lock, it was small and hidden in one top corner of the cage. It required a five digit code. Great, he thought, he did not have time to spend guessing a code and taking the whole cage was logistically impossible through the manholes. He pulled an army knife, lifting the bottom leg of his jeans. The being within the cage, full of fear tried to helplessly move back but couldn't and shivered all over. He gave an acknowledging nod and reassured,

-Not for you, It, the knife is for that damn lock. We have to make a move as soon as possible. I am as much of a hunter as a hunted.

The human moved suddenly and its hand reached out to the sleeve of the man, touched it briefly calling for his attention. He was surprised by the gesture and looked attentively at the scared being within the cage, and asked gently,

-Are you trying to say something, It?

It nodded and pointed to its name traced upon the blood, then to its left foot and finally to the lock. He smiled and stated,

-So you kept your surviving wit about you, It. Right, so the code is I-T, and if you put your foot so I can see it better, I will know what you meant.

The being obliged and with great physical pain exhibited the bridge of its foot. It was marked by 666, forming a kind of a pattern, with their tips touching. It was not a tattoo, it had been deeply stamped upon It, probably by a hot iron. He considered the mark, dreading its implication, and muttered,

-Fuck it. I don't believe in any of that shit. If that caused your ordeal, human, you are in front of an unbeliever, therefore safe hands. Let's get you out, It.

He put the proposed code upon the lock: I-T-6-6-6. He smiled widely as a clicking noise announced the unlocking of the cage. He opened its door and presented his arms to It, helping the naked human out,

-Come here, poor thing, no more shit hole for you.

He realised that the being was a young woman, so damaged that she was unable to stand or walk. He carried her away within his strong arms, headed for the manhole and exited the bunker as fast as he could. His dog waiting for him, wagged its tail at his emergence. As he pushed the body of It before him, the dog turned around her, smelling her and pushed her with its nose to make her react somehow. The woman moved weakly, showing her face, trembling. The dog licked her pale visage, crying slightly doing so. He took the little human within his arms once more and told his dog,

-Yep, I know, she bloody needs a good clean, but I don't think that your tongue will do, Bud. I don't know how you are going to both fit in the car but we will figure it out.

He walked quickly to his Peugeot, his Great Dane in toe. He opened the back door of his car and laid the woman upon the back seat, wrapping her in a large tartan blanket, saying kindly,

-Here, It, the ride is not going to be pleasant but I think you have seen worse than being unsafe in the back of a speeding car.

The woman blinked and smiled, nodding. He put his dog in the boot of his car, and drove away from the place

Verse 3. Calling Earth

Upon the highway, he grabbed his phone and dialled, looking anxiously at his mirror. He was still not followed, maybe he could call his night a clean sweep, or maybe with the unusual package, he had in his car, he should wait until dawn to declare it so. An annoyed feminine voice answered his call,

-What the hell is up now?

-Caro, it's me.

The exasperated voice stated,

-I know it's you, Walter, there's only one arsehole that can possibly wake me up in the middle of the night! Twelve fifteen, are you drunk out of your mind again?

His lips grinned slightly as he tried to smooth the temper of his ex-wife,

-Caroline, it's an emergency. I need you at your clinic Asap.

The voice snapped,

-Go to the ER! I haven't got the au-pair girl tonight. I can't leave Micky on his own. As you are still talking, I am sure you will survive.

-It's not for me, Caro. Hunting trip gone bad. ER is a no go. DIY job required, non-disclosure. Take Micky with you.

-I will be there in half an hour. What can I expect?

Walter smiled knowingly, the caring Caroline was now on the line, listening attentively. Somehow he knew he could always count on her. He announced,

-Minus twenty, hen, right A broken, right H dislocated. No water, none whatsoever. Mute. Appalling to see. I cried. I think it's a brink case, Caro.

His ex-wife sighed, closing her eyes, and asked,

-Was it in the trail of P? A leftover?

-Yes, another one. Left but not over. I stepped into the dish, hopefully on time, this time. Your opinion is required to determine this last point.

Caroline whispered,

-Walt, we can only do our best. I will get everything ready, when can I expect your package delivered?

-Speeding my way to you, Caro. 45 to 1.

The phone hung up on him. Walter looked at the package at the rear, worryingly. It had not made a sound nor moved. He tried to talk to see if the young woman would stir, just to reassure him,

-It, are you alive down there? Are you still with us upon Earth?

Her hand appeared from beneath the blanket and tapped upon it in a rhythmic fashion. To his amazement he realised her fingers were saying something in Morse code. He asked, slightly bewildered,

-I am sorry It, you will have to repeat that, your wit lost me in translation. I don't see a lot of young people knowing their Morse code at the tip of their fingers nowadays.

He saw the fingers tapping again their message,

-I am fine, enjoying the few extra inches of stretch upon my body,

Walt. Keep your eyes on the wheel, safe delivery to Caroline sounds good.

He looked ahead of him grinning wildly, thinking he had a hell of a package in his back seats, an intriguing being which had already gathered information from one small call. He wondered if Caroline was that loud and checked if he had put his phone on loud speaker by inadvertence but this was not the case. He rose his eyebrows and looking at the poor girl intently from the rear view mirror asked,

-Mute but not deaf it seems. Were you born mute or was it torture? You know Morse code very well, do you know sign language too?

The car was reaching his destination fast. A long silence answered first the puzzled Walter, as the young thing had closed her eyes lost in the mist of her thoughts...Sorrowful thoughts about humanity and her own self in the midst of it.

Verse 4. Affect & Effects

-Walt, I know both. I can't use signs right now, being invalid. I am not a real mute but I lost my will to speak out loud very early on.

At long last 'It' had answered him as he was pulling inside the car park of the clinic belonging to the brother of his ex-wife Caroline, with her weak fingers moving fast upon the cover. Walter could not help thinking that the torture question had been avoided by her somehow, very sensitive matter he guessed especially if it happened 'early on'. He sighed sadly at the idea of a child being tortured. It was sickening him deep deep down. His anger rose to the fore and he muttered out loud,

-Bastard, bastards, bastards...

'It' looked at him, cocked her shaved eyebrow and with half a smile, coughed calling his attention back to her as she tapped upon the cover some more, and pulled her tongue to him,

-I was tortured, but it did not render me mute. I have still got my own tongue and language. Please do not curse for my sake.

Walter looked absolutely baffled as he parked the 306. She knew what went on in his head, his very thoughts, and was trying to answer those.

He stepped outside of the car and went to open the back seat door, his jaws clenching with slight fright, the girl was reading his mind, he could swear it. As he picked her up in his arms, he whispered his question,

-Did you read my mind, just now? Can you read minds, It?

She nodded positively to him, and her fingers morsed upon his hand,

-Please, Walt, stay with me. I am scared to death everywhere. I am a freak.

He turned to see his ex-wife arriving with a hospital trolley, half running by her brother the tall and awe-inspiring Dr Gabriel Purallee and he muttered back to 'It',

-It depends on her welcome. I am not always very welcomed around here. I am considered as a troublemaker.

Gabriel stood by him as he finished his last word, smiling knowingly and gave him a silent nod, before saying,

-Give us a brief. You can leave her with us. Non-disclosure is understood, we will keep her safe. We will keep you updated upon the package.

Walter staring at Caroline which he found as beautiful as usual, pleaded,

-Does anyone of you two know Morse code? She is communicating with it and is completely distraught. She wants me to stay and translate for her. Her name or un-name is 'It', just plain and simple 'it'. I am not a psychologist but I guess that the package is fully damaged physically and internally, on an emotional level. May I stay with It?

Caroline gave a surrendering glance to Gabriel who warned,

-Walter, my sister is profoundly tired, exhausted from her twenty-four hour shift of only four hours ago. Micky is sleeping tight in one of the clinic's bedroom. I will not have you playing mind games on her, nor tolerate any signs of temper. Do I make myself clear? If so, put your damaged package on the trolley and follow us quietly.

Walter felt like a monster for a split second, remembering an inebriated night which he could never forget. He shivered and although years had passed, it seemed there was never enough water to flow under his bridge to wash away the pain, his own and the ones of Caroline and his son. He bowed his head in a subdued agreement and looking at the concerned green gaze of It, deposited her with his up most care upon the trolley. He saw the little hand grabbing his, and tapping upon it in fast Morse,

-Thank you, Walter. Look after me, I will look after you. I saw your troubles. Make it past. Make It pass.

He looked baffled again, grinned as he let himself addressing his thought to It-666, silently while running alongside the trolley,

-You've got a freaking mind about you, It. I don't know what to make of it, but I am tagging along, anyhow. I will make sure you are okay.

The being smiled at his thought and sent him hers,

-Telepathy is faster than Morse. I think you can cope with a hell of a lot, Walt. Mind intrusion should not freak you too much. Our secret.

Her trolley entered a deserted A & E room. Walter cocked his brows full of surprise towards his ex-wife,

-When I said secrecy, I didn't think you would be that effective, Doc.

Gabriel replied sternly for his sister who was giggling,

-With you, we never know what to expect, from a politician with his arse pelleted to a stag hit by your latest drink driving. We used a little magical medical word to close the clinic and seclude it. We made time and space to what was coming from you.

Walter couldn't help thanking his dodgy past behaviour for it gave an incredible sudden sanctuary for his latest package: It-666 and whatever It meant. He enquired further, teasing,

-Gab, I have seen you cross with a baseball bat, and I can hardly imagine you like a 'Wizard of Oz' look alike Glinda, waving a magical wand and clearing the path for me. What was the trick to protect the clinic from my own infamy?

Gabriel gave a wide smile to him and replied,

-Come, Walt, my magical bat wand is in my office, if you have any wish to see it, Bro, to keep you nice and calm, I will fetch it for you. I won't jeopardise my establishment for you. The medical word to restrict our clinic was 'meningitis'. Little Micky plays the part of the carrier of an outbreak. Simple, what you bring to me, I will keep between us. You loved my sister and I loved yours till her untimely death. Hunting trip gone bad meant for us. It's been a month since you went hunting last. I want you and need you to trail P. You can't lay Wendy to rest, I accept that because I can't either. I have strong coffee waiting for you on the reception desk. Then wash your hands thoroughly and help us with your latest arrival, 'It' sounds unusual.

Walter gave a bear hug to the black man before him retaining his tears, and whispered,

-Thanks, Gab. Meningitis...Jeez, the package I have in store for you is mind boggling. We will have to put our brain cells together to work 'It' out.

Verse 5. Stating It-666

In the emergency room, Walter drew all of the curtains closed with caution, and looked worryingly back to the trolley where It was, immobile, wrapped in the tartan blanket. When he saw Gabriel about to lift her to put her on a bed, he intervened,

-Let me Gab, she is a pile of broken bones.

A dark glance welcomed his concern, as Doctor Purallee stated, lifting It to the bed,

-Back off Walt! I know more about dislocated hips and broken arms than you do. I mend them and repair damage often done by careless arseholes who have a tendency to cause them, a bit like you. I don't think you can argue your case with me about your hands being safer than mine, Bro. I made a profession of caring. You made a life to throw caring far away from you. I thought I told you to get and drink the coffee and gather some of your wits about you. Go, and don't wake little Micky up. He will think he is having a nightmare, and that the Bogeyman is coming for him. You're dishevelled and you smell like shit. Did you waddle in bloody sewers again?

Walter's face shifted from extreme worry to deep sadness in a split second, taking in the full blow of Gabriel's comment. His blue eyes dived upon his own hands and he whispered,

-I am sorry. I didn't mean to offend you, Gab. I stayed clear from any drink for six days, not to ruin the hunting trip. Is my coffee spiked with medicine? However I did walk in a sewer but it was cleaner than the shit hole where I found It. She was left in a cage in her own mess. The stench comes from her.

Caroline couldn't help smirking, and told,

-You never were a man that would bring something normal like a bunch of flowers, like nicely scented red roses. We spiked your coffee, a little Alka, it won't harm you, bring me some too, I need to stay awake to tend to your new delivery.

When Walter left the room, Caroline turned to her brother and admonished him in a secretive voice,

-Gabby, lay off a little. It was six years ago. He broke down at his twin sister's death. He threw things, broke everything, there was no aim, no intention. Walt has never lifted a finger against me and Micky before then, and has not since. I want you here because I am too tired to deal with anything especially from him, and you have a way with him. He listens to you. Now, let us look at It. Somehow I am dreading it, but even smelling like hell, it cannot be as bad as the day we had to remove all those pellets from Henrickson's arse.

She started carefully removing the blanket from the young woman, and turned livid at the sight of It. She went to a small hand sink and threw up.

Purallee stood there without a word to say. When Walter came back in the room, Gabriel's tearful black eyes met Walt's blue ones for an explanation. Understanding, Walter went to Caroline and held a white towel for her. He poured her a glass of water and presented it, as he told,

-I warned you, Baby, I cried. It is as bad as one human can get physically. I am not even sure if she can make it. I need you to be strong to be able to tell me.

He then went to It, taking a patient white overall upon a hook and carefully started to cover her with it. Gabriel came to help dressing the young woman, saying as he held the broken arm gently within his caring hands,

-Let me help. Describe how you found her Walter, and tell me all you know about It. Caro, if you are recovered from your initial shock, get me the drips we have prepared, It will need the three of them. Then get me antiseptic wash, for she is going to have a thorough clean before we can put any bandages upon her. Last but not least It will need nappies, she will not be able to walk for at least a couple of month. She is going to need physiotherapy and re-education.

As Gabriel put his fingers upon her wrist measuring her pulse, It-666 moved her fingers upon his wrist tapping a message in Morse, smiling shyly. Walter making the bow at the back of her neck to hold her patient's tunic, translated,

-Doctor Purallee, It is thanking you from the bottom of her heart. She is sorry to be an appalling and sickening sight.

Gabriel nodded, looked gravely at the young woman and asked again,

-Walter, I need to know more about It. Her pulse is unbelievable. Did you speed on the highway, Bro? She may have had a longer lifespan in her cage rather than in your damn car.

Walter gave the Doctor his coolest look before arguing,

-I was scared to be followed, because I was earlier on this evening. It didn't mind the speed at all. She liked the car as she was able to stretch a little.

Gabriel clasped the finger of It-666 upon an ECG to measure her heart rate further and scolded,

-Walt, do you know that you're always half true and half fucking paranoid? Do you know that most of the time Caro and I have to deal with your worst half? Cage's measurements, in situ description, patient first reactions, help me help you, Bro. Did you take any pics of It as you found her, so we can bring down that son of a bitch?

Walter emptied the content of his mac's pocket upon a nearby table, the camera and blood samples. He confided with a confounded shame,

-It was in his bunker, the one deep in the wood. As I arrived I was focused. I took pictures of the main room. It has all those damn symbols upon it. Yet it lacked the black mass paraphernalia of all the other rooms, he used for human sacrifices. The round room was empty, only the floor pentagram, largest so far, and the other drawings are there which I suspect are made of blood. There was a trap in the centre of the pentagram and that is where It was, in her cage, in a hole, in her own piss and shit. At first I thought she was a cadaver. As I lifted the cage, a metre long at most on all sides, It stared at me surprised. Gab, I know I should have taken pictures of her in situ, like that, but it was the furthest thing in my mind. All I could think at that moment was to help that human in distress and remove It from that shit hole. If taking pictures would have crossed my mind at that point, by decency I think I would have abstained.

Purallee's voice rose, he took the camera and started taking pictures of the young skeletal woman,

-Decency: look at her fucking state! The son of a bitch has to be stopped somehow. Evidence, you had them in front of your eyes. The woods are his property, for Christ's sake! Wendy is dead and buried because of him, my fiancée, my life to be is gone in dust. I don't want him to destroy others in his wake, all his human sacrifices, and look at yourself Walt, you're a wreck since Wendy is gone. Gather evidence, display them, build the case as strongly as we can, and bring him to justice that is all that we can do. Bro, you vowed to avenge Wendy, I did too so we could sleep at night, so she could rest in peace, I need you to be fully aware and efficient upon the matter. There are many young women lives at stake upon it.

It-666 looked startled by the flashes harassing her, she tried to move hurting herself doing so. Walter grabbed her within his arms, securing her from falling onto the floor and tried to soothe her as well as reasoning with Gabriel,

-Schhh, it's okay It. Gab, cease it now! I mean it. Don't scare the shit out of her like that. She lived in darkness for god knows how long. Any pictures can be taken later, when she understands what we are doing, why and with her consent. We don't mean bad, It. We don't.

Caroline removed the camera from her brother's hands, put it back upon the table, and made him look at the heart rate results pointing at them then commented,

-I don't think it is a good idea to raise our voices around her or to startle her with flashes right now, her heartbeat is racing through the roof.

Gabriel giving a quick glance at the result, swore,

-Fucking hell, it's far too high to be normal, did you bring me the broken one, Sis? Fetch the one in the other room, we will do the measurement again. Now, I am sorry It for over-reacting upon your appalling state. I wish I could comprehend where horrors came from in the human heart and eradicate them.

Walter holding It-666's left hand reassuringly, pointed to her left foot and stated,

-I think for her ordeal, it has all to do with her mark, Gabriel, branded on her foot.

Purallee took a good look at the bridge of her foot and put it down immediately, as if he had burnt himself somehow seeing her triple six mark. He couldn't believe his eyes, thinking that his worst nightmare had finally taken a human shape. He gave a bewildered look at Walter,

-Holy mother fucker, Walt! What did you fucking bring in my clinic? Shit, man, bloody hell! All of a sudden I prefer Bambi ran over by you, and plucking bullets from a man's arse! Holy crap, It was under a pentagram made with blood, has a heartbeat to sky-rocket you to the moon, and the bloody mark of the beast on it. It's in my bloody damn clinic, you must be having a laugh, man! What's the hell is that? What the hell is going on?

Walter stood confronting the tall Doctor and shouted, tears coming to his eyes, pointing all the while to the skeletal woman,

-This is 'It', for Christ's sake: A fucking human being who had the bad luck, I am pretty sure of it to be born at the wrong time, wrong day, wrong month and wrong year. It was enough for others who thought it significant to mark her like a bloody beast and treat her like so. You want to know what the hell that is? It's a human in need, an appalling picture of what lack of reason can do and result of beliefs gone horrendously too far. Her state is similar to the one we saw in our history books of the victims of the holocaust. You want to know what is going on. Let me tell you, if you can't bloody see someone that needs your help any more just because it has a mark with some cultural or religious significance you are one of those 'good' self-assured 'convicted' of their convictions men who let horrors happen. Yes, the poor bloody thing was called It-666. My heart tells me an error was made somewhere; seeing a human treated like that, it tells me to help and do something. Obviously I made a mistake coming here. I always thought you had the soundest heart. I just heard horrors from it, Gabriel. Sorry to bring an injured and abused human into your clinic instead of Bambi or an arse.

Caroline sat on the bed by It and looked gravely upon her ex-husband, stating,

-Walter, she is staying here. She can't be moved around like that in her state. It will kill her.

It moved her fingers and Caroline gave her a pen and pad from her blouse pocket. The young woman scrambled a few words,

-Just kill me. I had my lot of suffering. End me please.

Caroline passed the note to her brother, after reading it. Walter knelt by Caroline and laid his head upon her lap, crying silently, his mind invaded by It's plea,

-You have done enough. You're a good man. Please, kill me. You are a hunter, you said. I will be forever tracked and hunted. Get your gun, and make me pass away. I want it to be you rather than to be thrown to the dogs.

Walter's upset grew louder, and sobbed heartbreakingly,

-Where have all the good people gone? Where are our hearts? Do we use them? No, no, no, I don't want to kill It. She can be saved. It doesn't have to be that way. One human shouldn't suffer such harrowing cruelty.

His ex-wife stroked his soft blond hair and whispered,

-Come, you had a long night. You're getting distressed by it all. We will look after It-666.

Gabriel touched Walter's shoulder reassuringly and stated,

-Brother, if you want to see a good heart, look no further than in front of your nose, at the mother of your son. I think she is right about you getting distressed, and she is also extremely tired. In Micky's room, there are two more beds, both of you get your rest. Let me deal with It-666. As I can still feel my heart, as you made such an eloquent plea for It, I will look after your human in need, Walter.

Caroline helped Walter up, who glanced at It-666, sending his thoughts to her while walking away from the room,

-Help from Gabriel is the strongest one you can get, It. Just don't invade his brain with your suicidal thoughts or demands, because he might just answer them. If it's what you want, euthanasia is softer than a gunshot. I am no killer, It. I will look after your life but not your death. Think it over and see you tomorrow if life is your choice.

The young woman waved him goodbye from her only good hand and as Walter disappeared from her sight, tears streamed from her eyes.

Verse 6. Dark Angel Gabriel

Now left alone with It-666, Doctor Gabriel Purallee gave an unfathomable dark look to the young woman upon the hospital bed. Still crying silently, she started shivering under his stare. Her lips trembled and she tried to whisper something but couldn't. Gabriel approached and presented her with a pen and his notepad, exhibited the note that she had scrambled earlier and stated coldly,

-Clear communication is such a blessing. You can write what you want to express yourself but you can forget about asking any of us to kill you. Try to dry those tears. You do know I would rather have Bambi in my clinic instead of you, an individual with the mark of the Beast. This I made quite clear, and I am far from sorry for it and will not plea for your understanding either. If you have something to say, just write it down for me.

It-666 nodded, anxiety spreading upon her, wishing that Walter was here, the only man she had ever met who had shown her kindness. She understood that she would probably be a friendless being all her life very early on, let alone being a very despised one. Despite desperately hiding her powers, controlling them, she was such a freak of nature that she could only admit it to herself. Maybe she truly was what they all feared, just maybe, because she didn't want to, deep down, she just knew she didn't want to be It-666, the Beast. She seized the pen and wrote,

-I am sorry to be. Forgive me for being.

Gabriel ignored the content of the message in purpose to focus only on assessing the young creature, he had in front of him.

-Very neat indeed. Nice cursive writing. Are you left handed, Beast?

It realised that Gabriel was determined not to be her best friend.

She couldn't help shivering and her tears kept streaming silently. She wrote again, to answer him,

-Ambidextrous.

Purallee nodded before quizzing her,

-Walt seems to think you had the bad luck to be born on the wrong day, is that so? What is your date of birth? Time and place if you do happen to know them too, please. I thought I told you to cease crying.

She bit her lip and wiped her tears with the palm of her left hand before picking the pen up to reply,

-Six of June ninety six. London. Six sixteen in the morning.

Gabriel grinned at the paper and raising one of his brows mocked,

-Are you scared of writing your date of birth in numbers, Beast? Don't you think it would cut the chase, making it simpler and faster?

It-666 closed her eyes taking the full blow of his remark. She could feel her other type of tears coming slowly but surely to her eyes. If she didn't want him to see just how freaky she was, well this would not happen. She wrote down quickly,

-I am scared. I am a freak, I know I am. Sorry for these coming tears, don't be frightened, please don't.

She hid her face, lifting her left arm to cover her eyes as much as she could, and the blood tears pouring now from them. Gabriel read her note, removed her arm from her face firmly yet with care, and lifted her chin to inspect them closely. He asked in a softer more concerned tone of voice, trying to tease and ease the mind of the being in front of him,

-Well, well, what have we got here? Do you want to play peek a boo, Beast? I bet those hurt. Come, now, let's dry those. Do not be scared of me, I won't hurt you but I will examine you and assess you. I need to figure you out. Presently I have got to come to terms with seeing you being so sensitive, if I ever imagine an Antichrist you would definitely not fit my bill. I am pretty damn sure you would rather want me calling you Bambi than Beast too, am I not right?

She managed to smile shyly as she agreed with him by a positive blink of her eyes. Gabriel pursued, as he collected a little blood of her tears upon a small tool and dipped the instrument into a test tube,

-Here we have it, finally a smile. I have to say that given all the shit that must have happened to you, I find you a rather gentle thing, polite and well behaved. Of course I am not going to give into it. So 1996, makes you sweet sixteen on human terms, a teenage Antichrist, but like Walt said some mistakes must have been made somewhere, for if I read my holy books correctly, I was rather expecting the opposite sex to yours. As I have got my blood tear sample now let me wipe all the rest, and try to be less emotional Bambi.

He took some paper towels from a nearby dispenser, sat back upon the bed and carefully cleaned her pale face of tears. It was looking at him with confused green eyes. She had tried to read Doctor Gabriel Purallee thoughts since she had arrived at his clinic yet she was failing at it miserably. There was something about him unnerving her greatly however she was not in a state to be able to run away from him. He gave her a self assured smile and considered her shaved and damaged scalp before stating,

-So it looks like you haven't met a lot of sweetly caring hands dealing with you. Your state is appalling. A lot of babies born on the same day as you did, and maybe the same hour enjoy happy and normal lives, all over Earth, this is to dispel the Walterism that we both heard earlier. I do not believe in luck, bad or good whatsoever. Your date of birth on its own, is not a condemning feature, although it is significant when added to other facts. None of those children were marked like you have been by the Beast's number.

None of those children were made to inhabit a cage below a pentagram drawn with blood like you were. I am pretty sure that they don't shed blood tears either, like you do, probably because they are truly human. Now what is, how can I put it mildly so you don't cry blood again, condemning and rather damning, is your own admission of being a freak. So you are going to explain yourself upon it. Confide. What makes you think so? When did you start feeling like one?

It bit her lip and felt an overwhelming desire to tell all to the black man before her. She swallowed her breath, decided to surrender her own security, to give up her shrouded silence and secrecy, as she spoke unbeknown words, which she translated straight upon the pad for Gabriel's understanding.

-Where shall I start? I felt abnormal since the beginning.

The Doctor gave her a winning smile, stood up and went to fill a couple of metallic bowls with warm water. He put disposable gloves on, returned by the bed with one bowl and a small pile of antibacterial wipes as he told,

-Right, first I need to give you a good thorough clean if I am to stay alive by your side. You smell like hell, Bambi. Second, I will always rate and appreciate open honesty which brings about my third don't be scared of talking with your natural voice and language with me, and revealing your true self to me. Now, where shall we start: defining your own conception of freak, and what you do to qualify yourself as one within your mind would be a very good start. Specifying what you do mean by your beginning will not go amiss either.

It was totally baffled at the fact that Gabriel didn't stir hearing her true out of this world voice. When he started cleaning her, carefully, gently, with a face that betrayed no frown of disgust, she tried to say her first human words since a very very long time,

-Thank you.

She carried on by writing a translation of her thoughts,

-Thank you, for being calm around me, for listening and talking on the level you do. I do not know my proper and adequate definition. I fear very much it to be the one that they branded me with, hence my willingness to die. I don't want to be It-666. I have powers and skills I don't understand. I can hear and read minds around me. Your thoughts are the first ones that escape me. I can't hear them. I read Walter, your sister and little Micky sleeping within these walls who is having a bad dream, he is falling again and again upon a football pitch. I have total comprehension of all languages. I am scared of my own self and what I can do. May I express myself by telepathy with you, for it is faster? I do not mean to offend you, or intrude your mind.

Gabriel read the notes, took another wipe and rubbed it upon her bare back while he warned firmly,

-If you have control over your mind reading, Caroline, Micky and Walter's minds are a no go area. I am watching over them like an Angel. Abstain from telepathy too, with myself and others. Presently you just managed to express your thanks in a human way, this is welcomed, therefore try to express yourself that way from now on. If you don't know your own definition, do you want me and you, us, to find out? I have the means to do so, without mentioning your inability to walk away from examination with your badly dislocated hip. I rather think you are a trapped little Bambi, don't you?

It-666 smiled and nodded in agreement, making efforts to speak humanly once more,

-Yes, Angel Gabriel.

Verse 7. Be-a-St

Gabriel cleaning the bare filthy back of the young being with antiseptic, removing the dirty layer, noticed deep flogging marks all across it and told,

-Perhaps, it is time for you to tell me all about yourself It-666. Whose hands did you fall under? Who has been mistreating you in such a way? Have you been a misbehaving and very naughty Antichrist at such a young age?

It-666 could feel the smirk drawing upon the lips of the Doctor as he finished his last question. She looked down with sadness, at least Gabriel was making sport of her appalling state. She remembered every minute, every gruelling second of her trials and tribulations. It was not something she wanted to disclose. She could feel rage and a scream rising from deep within her. She had to contain herself. She wrapped her left arm around her body and cradled herself in a gentle soothing motion. However beneath her the bed started to shake badly. She wrapped her left leg across her right and sang something melodious in tongue for herself. This time the bed ceased moving. Her blood tears ran freely upon her face, as the Doctor who had stopped what he was doing to step back and witness what was going on, asked,

-What was that about? Beast, do you mind answering me? I am trying to get you into some sort of shape down here, if you poltergeist that bed across the room, I'd rather have a little warning beforehand. Did I upset you?

She held her hand out to him, and making considerable efforts spoke humanly to explain herself,

-I am sorry. I had to contain myself. It's not your fault. Your questions triggered the visions of everything done to me. I remember all of them. It makes me want to scream and rage but I can't let myself do that. It would be atrocious if I let go of the wrath within. I am not speaking about a bed flying against a wall, I am speaking of destruction. Gabriel, I cannot talk about my ordeals, I hurt too much inside. I contain and bottle up everything and desperately try to behave. Please forgive me. I was flogged and harmed because I refused to use my powers to do the evil bidding of the people that got hold of me. I tried to make them believe that I was a normal human and not a freak so they would get off my case. I succeeded in the end as they decided to let me rot and die and they went to quest for another being that could possibly be the Beast.

Gabriel was taken aback by her confession. He gave her tissues and turned around her bed in a worried fashion, before pestering, and admonishing,

-Destroying, damn! Did you ever do it, Beast? Did you ever let your wrath put on the big ugly display? How does that work? Can you control the extent of the damages or not? I am sorry but you have fallen into my hands: they are safe and secure. Now, I have just seen you controlling yourself. It was done by your cradling and the lullaby, wasn't it? Let me tell you something and warn you, It-666, I don't care if you hurt too much inside or outside for that matter. You and me know that you are far from being human, far from being a cute little Bambi. I need your full history and you will give it to me whether you like it or not. I will have you figured out in no time, and you will be dealt with appropriately. I am seeking precision and definition from you, and no shallow graves of your damn fucking past shall be left unturned. I want to know everything right to every single individual classified conveniently by you as 'they', who managed to put their hands on you, tried to use you and abused you, for they shall also be dealt with very strongly indeed. Talk, Beast, talk.

Shivering, the young It answered straight away, surrendering to his inquisition,

-I let my wrath out only once. I was five. The person looking after me was murdered in front of me. I liked her almost as if she was my mother. I never knew my parents or if I had some. All I knew was her. She was a nun named Theresa. She was very strict yet I felt her care went beyond just the one of my welfare. We lived secluded from everything in the Black Forest. The men who killed her, had come for me, to abduct me. As she died, she told me to run away. I didn't, I fought. When I saw her expiring, my wrath was unleashed and the men were destroyed before my eyes. I understood that I did that to them, to the four of them. I remember running far from the place of the murder, angry and lost, the Earth trembling beneath my feet until I bumped into someone, who contained me until my wrath was gone. He sang that song. He was not human. He stayed and soothed me until I was asleep at his feet. Whenever I feel my wrath grabbing hold of me, I repeat to myself what he said and sung for it calms and pacifies me. He gave me the control over myself. I lived in the woods in an almost feral state for three years, but for his intermittent presence. He warned me to always stay in the woods because it was where the little animals and beasts should live. However, one day, children came into my woods on a school trip. I was overjoyed to see people, looking just like me, young and carefree. I wanted to befriend them, join them, so tempted I was that I did so. They mocked me for being wild and feral, pushed me and treated me like a leper. I suppressed myself from talking from then on when I realised I could not talk like they did. The sounds coming from my mouth were inhuman. I came to the attention of their teacher, Johann Baum who dragged me out of my forest, and handed me to the authorities as a lost child. I was placed in a psychiatric hospital for observation. There, a nurse seeing my mark, saw me as an opportunity to make money and reported me to someone who smuggled me out of Germany to America. I was given to him, the one Walter calls P, and he put me in the cage, where Walter found me, my home for almost eight years. At first they tried to coerce me into showing my powers. I didn't but I was caught a few time using telekinesis by myself by a surveillance camera. So they employed harsher and harsher methods to impress upon me. Until I tried to play that I was thick and stupid and in my last torture, I lied atrociously writing that I saw another child with my mark at the hospital where they took me from, sending them on a wild goose chase, as so many years had passed, thinking that I would pass away before they came back to me empty handed. This is my story so far. Now, for the 'they', I can write a list of all the names, I heard while there. As for my destructive powers and my control of them, I will show you a sample once and for all. Do not ever ask this again from me for I refuse to hurt anyone and to use them. It will be focused, within the four walls of this room, anyone outside will be safe and I will make sure that I do not even wake up Micky from his sleep. I will just perform an earth tremor, it will be mild enough to not destroy any of your clinic equipment yet the furniture will move. It will just be for your understanding of me. You will have to hold that pillar in the middle of the room and remain by it to stay safe. Give me your authorisation and I will proceed to show you what I can do, your mind will have to amplify the sheer scale of what you will witness to perceive the true nature of my power. Then if you make sense of it all, please deal with me, Gabriel.

Doctor Purallee just knew that he was facing the real thing: It-666, the Beast. It was young, It has been abused and tortured, yet It was displaying incredible restraint, and a strong will to never hurt anyone. He was baffled by It. She was shattering all his preconceptions. If he was in front of her, the Beast, he had to be on his guard at all times. At all cost he had to remain fully distrusting of It. She would not get the better of him, he will get the better of It, and slay her if he had to...

Verse 8. Tremor

Gabriel gave It-666 his darkest look and stated sternly,

-You have just damned yourself in front of my eyes by your confession. First manslaughter and four dead at five years old, Beast and you are still wondering what you are. In psychology the adequate term is denial. You feel deep down that you are It, the Beast that all fear yet your young emotions are rejecting the fact as unacceptable, so you are desperately trying to find another definition that would fit and spare your feelings. Well I have no intention to spare you: I will make you come to terms with what you are, and the only definition befitting you. You are the Beast incarnated. If you fear you own self, my joy will even be greater for it. Tell me if I am wrong, do you have that intimate knowledge and sensation that you are It?

The young being looked upon him and nodded positively, her blood tears appearing again streaming down her livid face. She whispered in a very human way, apologising,

-I am sorry to be, Gabriel. Do I have to be? I surrender to you. Do whatever you see fit, I will not struggle.

Gabriel's lips quivered. Here it was again, the incredible doubt seizing him, and he couldn't help remembering Walter's strong admonishment, that he could only see someone who had been dealt an extremely bad hand. His heart sank. His voice rose again, this time with a considerate tone, as he asked,

-Show me what you proposed earlier, about your destructive powers. Let me make sure that all is secure in the hallway first. Then do it. I will tell you afterwards what I am going to do with you.

He went to the corridor, taking a pen, he carefully made notches by every furniture in there, upon the walls, marking their exact emplacement. He couldn't believe that the tremor would not spread beyond the walls of the emergency room. It defied his conception of quakes and radiating earth vibrations, but he could only admit that the Beast had defied all his preconceptions so far. For so young a being to have that kind of power and that level of control would be beyond beliefs. Deep down his own heart kept screaming at him, that It was not beyond understanding nor reason. Could he, Gabriel, give It-666 his understanding, like Walter seems to have done? He will have to figure It out in order to do so. He could never flip a coin in the air with blind hate on one side and reason on the other. Pure reason will always be his chosen path. He returned to the room, considering her. She was just a sad sight. She said softly, and very shyly,

-I will be very careful. I will keep you safe throughout. Make sure you stay by the pillar. Please do not be frightened, I vowed to never harm anyone. When you are ready tell me. When you have seen enough, raise your hand and I will stop.

Gabriel went to the pillar within the room and ordered,

-Show me you have got, damn Beast!

It-666 had no problem in tapping into her internal wrath and the ensuing tremor was powerful. Gabriel held the pillar, watching her attentively from his position. As she closed her left hand to a fist, he could feel the earth vibrations becoming weaker. As she slightly raised her fingers in turn within her fist apart from the middle one, different parts of the room were consecutively a little more affected by the tremor. The place where he stood remained at a lower vibration level than the rest of the room. The furniture shook, some lighter pieces moved. Gabriel noticed as It opened her eyes that they were no longer a human looking like green but now looked demonic and totally black. It sent shivers through his spine as his gaze met the Beast's one, yet the Beast lowered her gaze respectfully and bowed her head to him. She addressed him, speaking in tongue,

-Order and I will obey, Archangel Gabriel.

Gabriel raised his hand and the tremor ceased immediately. He looked around him and assessed the room. Everything was displaced but nothing was damaged. He went to check the corridor and could only admit that nothing had moved there. He returned to the emergency room to confront It-666, the Antichrist. The Beast did recognise him as the Archangel Gabriel, only a being from beyond could do so. Gabriel knew that she had given him clear signals throughout of her surrender. As he stepped in, he saw her being sick over the bowl rather than pleased with the great level of control she had demonstrated. As he stood by her, towering her, he realised her eyes had returned to their human colour. She just looked like a distraught teenager and sounded like a confused and kind being. She asked him, concerned, in a low whisper,

-I am it, the Beast, am I? Please do not fear me, after what you saw.

Gabriel took her left hand within his and confirmed,

-You are the Beast and I do not fear you. You surrendered yourself over to me. I will make sure that your heart that does not want to cause any harm to no one is fully respected. I will be your guardian and protect you from falling into the wrong hands ever again. You have my consideration for preferring being hurt rather than to hurt, despite having the powerful means to do so. I am taking you under my wings. I will teach you all about yourself. If you ever break your vow, I reserve the right to slay you and end your misery.

She smiled shyly to him, tears glowing at the corners of her green eyes,

-Thank you so much, Angel Gabriel.

He gave her his winning smile,

-You are welcome, Bambi. A vibrant heart always vibrates mine.

Verse 9. Of Rats and Men

Scrubbed clean, X-rayed all over, her right arm plastered, It-666 looked gratefully at Doctor Gabriel tending to her. Now that he had dealt with her dislocated hip, he had moved her from the emergency room to a private room at the back of the clinic, one with a self-contained laboratory and its own lavatory. As he placed her upon the hospital bed from the trolley carefully, he announced,

-No one will bother you here. This room is our quarantine area, usually reserved for our highly contagious, it is feared like the plague even by my nursing staff. I think it's a quite befitting space for you, don't you agree Beast?

She nodded smiling shyly. She didn't have the choice anyhow and would not be able to walk for a good month or two, Gabriel had said. She gazed around and saw the large three curtained windows with pleasure. Last morning she thought that she would never see sunlight ever again, that she would pass away silently and slowly in her cage, and this morning as she could perceive that the sun was about to rise, she was being looked after and given
a temporary room with a view. Could she truly hope for better days?

Doctor Purallee put the drips by her bed and told as he seized her left arm,

-Be a good girl, Bambi, it will hurt a little, but once the needle is in place and stays there, it will allow me to do tests and injections in a faster way. You are badly dehydrated and we need to get you out of the danger zone fast enough, if we want to avoid ordering a sending off box for your broken bones.

She smiled through it all and when all drips and needles were in place, Gabriel commented,

-I did hurt you a little more than I should have just now, and you did not react to pain. You kept smiling, Beast. Do you know how unnerving that is? If you did that during your ordeals and tortures, I know why you are in such a state presently. A defence mechanism to warn that you are receiving too much pain, is reacting, screaming and shouting. If you don't, a real torturer will not have his thrill and will increase his torture and the pain until you do. To act with physical insensitivity is not clever if done in purpose or to show strength, for it puts you in a greater risk to lose your life and incite others, the torturers to greater crimes. If someone hears pain, his heart should react, and restrain him to inflict more. It works like a sensitivity trigger. Now, more worryingly, can you feel pain?

It-666's nose dived and she looked down at her hand, which was already bruising around the needle in position. Pain was a subject she would rather not think about or dwell on. She had been on the receiving end of it for such a long time that she did develop some sort of insensitivity to it. She remained deadly silent.

Gabriel firmly seized her chin, forcing her to look back to him, and pursued,

-Let me help you, Bambi. I can clearly see that you want to avoid that question. This will only make me ask it again with more authority and try to understand your unease about it. Do you feel physical pain?

She blinked agreeing to give him his answer, and as he released her chin, she made considerable efforts to express herself humanly,

-I absorb pain. I used to feel it when I was younger, I don't any more. I worked a way to deal with it. I put it away in my wrath containment box, under my control. Physical pain doesn't affect me any longer. I do find it hard to talk about it. I have seen people without the heart trigger. It deeply unsettled me. Seeing people being truly unkind, cruel and revelling being so, motivated or not, this hurts me more on an emotional level.

Doctor Purallee nodded appreciatively at her answer, and diverted her attention onto another subject altogether,

-I noticed that you were a very sensitive little thing, Bambi, a very emotional being. It is not really compatible with an Antichrist's job description by all means. The insensitivity to pain, on the other hand, is quite a skill for one to acquire. A clever trait would have been to hide that it was the case so you don't end up so broken and damaged. Now, open your mouth wide and let me check why it is so difficult for you to speak.

She obliged him and let him scrutinised her mouth. Not before too long, he raised an inquisitive brow, and opened a wallet full of instruments upon the side table. He took tweezers and removed something from her mouth, smiling as he teased,

-This is not the problem, but that mustn't have been palatable. In a sweet sixteen year old mouth, which by the way has a perfectly undamaged dentition, tell-tale sign that sweets of any kind and your mouth have been foreign to each other since birth, I would not expect to find a rat hair. But then again, you are not a normal sixteen year old, aren't you, Beast? Remnant of your last meal, I suppose? As your cage was most probably not provided with cooking facilities, I guess that you ate your rats raw. How does that taste like, I wonder? How long have you been on a diet of rodents? How often did you eat them?

It-666 blushed in shame, took a piece of paper from the Doctor's notepad, rolled it into a ball in her left palm, and held it in front of him. The paper took fire, then slowly became a pile of ashes within her lifted hand. She confessed after her small demonstration,

-I control fire. I can combust things, by looking at them or holding them. I did sink my teeth into rats but they were cooked, until their skin was golden and crispy. I only ate when I was absolutely starving. I don't like killing for killing. I stunned the animals caught, and made their heartbeats stop just by stroking them to sleep. I have eaten like that since I was five.

Gabriel put the hair of the rat into a little dish upon the side table, then took the warm ashes from her left hand, and disposed of them in a nearby bin, looking unfazed. He gave her a reassuring smile, before stating,

-Survival, it's an instinct given to any creature. Take human history and you will have many examples of war besieged towns devoid of dogs, cats and a scarcity of rats at the end of it all. Although all the humans who survived with their exceptional circumstances regimes would hardly ever admit to them. You, eating rats is bothering me far less, than your ability to barbecue things by looking at them or holding them, and that other ability of yours to stun and stroke some animal to a deadly sleep. My question is simply this, are you able to do this type of thing to a human?

It-666 met the concerned gaze of Gabriel and if she wouldn't have been too damaged to be able to move, she would have thrown herself at his feet, begging him, to help her make sense of her abilities. As it was she simply nodded to him, and answered,

-I am able to. I can but I won't.

Gabriel stood up, took a very dark glance upon her, appraising her fully, and pursued coolly,

-Pray, how do you know that you can?

She sensed his unforgiving tone within his voice. She bit her lower lip, closed her eyes for a minute before whispering in tongue,

-For the combustion, this is how I killed the four men who murdered my carer. For the stunning, and the stroking to a deadly sleep, it is all part of a same ability, I use electric energy to different degrees. I never killed anyone after my first four men. However I experimented the use of electricity upon my torturers. I gave them the heart trigger, they missed. When I couldn't take any more pain, I played skipping the rope with their heartbeats. It went from making them missing a heartbeat, enough to give a concerning heartburn so they would end my torture session sooner rather than later, to giving them hypertension for a brief period until they stopped their harassments. I made their unease last for half an hour after they left me, to prevent them from returning to me as soon as they were well. I never overdid it. They are all in good health. But I learnt my electrical measuring with them and my rats.

Gabriel laughed heartedly, his look gazing at the ceiling with relief,

-Playing skipping the rope with heartbeats! Damn! And I thought I heard it all! I must say, I am not going to throw a stone at you for using your torturers as lab rats, Bambi. I am actually surprised that given your powers you didn't toy with them a little more, to get your own back.

It-666 smiled and softly told,

-I have no avenging thirst, Gabriel. Making sure they didn't know that I had very dangerous powers, implied either laying low or using them to destroy all who thought I had, and a carnage doing so. I prefer being destroyed than using my powers or being used and abused to do evil. Here I am all broken up for it, to preserve humanity from all I can do. And my vow not to harm anyone stands proud and tall, renewed for having seen only one man, Walter opening his arms to me, with genuine kindness, taking me away from my hell spot upon Earth. I can swallow any pain given, as for love and kindness I want to give it back tenfold. I read that Walter was not a happy man, he is hurting. I want to help him if I can. Repay him for the hope he gave me.

As she finished her sentence, a dishevelled Walter stepped into the room, with a half asleep, half awake worried look,

-Here you are! I didn't see you in the emergency room. I checked the clinic morgue, I thought you didn't make it. I had a bad dream, where Gab was putting you to sleep like an unwanted stray.

Gabriel smirked and moved to reveal his presence in the room, coming in front of Walter's sight, startling him a little doing so,

-What a befitting dream! Reassure yourself at once, I endeavoured to repair your newly found beast, all night. Bambi and I enjoyed a very nice conversation about rats and men just now.

Walter frowned his blond brows baffled, queried,

-Bambi? Conversation? Rats and men?

Gabriel winked at It-666, and went to open all the curtains to let the rising sunlight flow into the bedroom.

Verse 10. W-alter-ism: To Beast or not to Beast?

Walter went to wash his face in the hand sink in the room, trying to push away his sleep and tiredness, before facing Gabriel again. Drying his visage in a towel, he asked once more, requiring explanations,

-Bambi? Conversation? Rats and men?

It-666 smiled to him, overjoyed to see him. She proudly made every efforts to speak human to welcome Walter,

-Hi, Walt! I am still here. My choice, my answer to you, is life. I am called Bambi. I can speak a little, normally, or almost.

Gabriel realised that a deep connection had been made between the Beast and Walter. He could see the relief upon Walter's face at knowing that It-666 was still alive. And the glow upon It was undeniable, as her face lit up at Walter's arrival. He had no doubts that she saw him as her saviour. He decided to put his foot down and announced bluntly,

-Good morning, Walt. I don't want to be a killjoy but your newly delivered package happens to be the real thing: the Beast. It-666 is well quite something, very daunting and scary.

Walter dismissed him and went by It's bed taking her left hand within his and demanded,

-So you found out that she reads minds and can use telepathy, yeah, terrifying. What is the deal about being called Bambi, It? It's not a suitable name. It's a cartoon character, a lovely one, but no parents would give that name to their child.

It kept smiling to him, fully feeling his consideration, and explained,

-I like Bambi, Gabriel calls me like that. It's better than Beast or It-666.

Walter turned to Gabriel giving him his coldest look, admonished, asking further,

-And Gabriel took the piss out of you calling you so all night! How very thoughtful and kind of him! If you desire another name, we will find one for you, a nice one of your liking, a considerate, respectful, and pretty but normal one. Tell me what was the choice of demeaning name calling offered? Was it resumed to Beast and Bambi?

It-666 blinked a little baffled by Walter. She couldn't help thinking that he was somehow right, yet she had not seen it that way all the while. Maybe she was far too damaged to realise by herself when she was being demeaned because she had accepted disrespect as a common currency for so long. She remained profoundly silent.

Gabriel intervened and raising his voice, argued,

-The truth is her real name is the Beast. Bambi, although ironical and derisional is a far sweeter name, nickname or pet name if you wish, until a proper one is found. Let me tell you what I found out about her, which would terrify any living being. It goes well beyond telepathy and mind reading. She can make your heart stop beating by a simple stroke of her fingers. She can combust you by just looking at you. She can cause earthquakes and destroy at will. You have in front of you the Beast, It-666, the Antichrist.

It looked down, blood tears appearing at the corner of her eyes. Her lips quivered and she confessed,

-I am.

Walter stood up. He paced the room with a calm frustrated anger before releasing its full blow upon Gabriel,

-So all your conceptions have been force fed all night upon that traumatised being, is that it? Beast is your answer and so be it! Done with it. She can not be a supernatural being or anything else, because Gabriel Purallee knows better than anyone else upon this Earth. An Earth which I have walked upon for thirty-six years and for the time the Beast was supposedly alive, I never heard about such terrible earthquakes, fires, deaths done by such a creature.

He turned to It-666, and demanded,

-Did you kill anyone in the methods aforementioned?

It nodded positively, now fully crying of shame, replied,

-Four men.

The incarnated Angel Gabriel's heart sank, he came by her putting his hands reassuringly upon her shoulders, and added strongly,

-It accounts as manslaughter for the four of them. They murdered her carer. She was five and didn't know she had such powers. She has never killed since nor has any will to harm anyone.

Walter gave a winning smile, and pointed to Gabriel and then to It-666, stating strongly,

-Case argued and resolved. If upon your say we have a blank slate, and unless she behaves like a beast, she shall not be called one nor treated like one. The Beast is not. It, Bambi, you choose whatever you want to be. If you want to be the Beast that Gabriel is dreading then be it, make him chew upon his insults while you were still not one. If you want to be what your heart tells you to be, then follow your own stance and do not let anyone dictate to you about who or what you are. Your actions shall speak for themselves and reveal your true nature to all in the end. In my eyes you are no Beast at all until you behave like one. Do you understand me clearly, It? Your life is before you, and you define it.

She smiled through her tears, wiped them off, and held her arm out to him.

Walter sat upon the bed and gave her a hug, whispering,

-You chose to be. So I am going to look after you, after your life, as if you were my child.

Gabriel looked upon them, and felt utterly lost for words.

Verse 11. I had a Dream

Caroline stepped into the room, holding coffees, and announced herself,

-Morning Gabby. Walt, I just knew you would be here, somewhere, to check upon your unusual package. You kept tossing and turning in your bed. I guess you did not sleep very well. I brought you, guys, coffee. So what's the score?

Walter and Gabriel turned to her at once and told in the same solemn revealing voice,

-She is It-666.

Caroline looked at them amused and replied, handing their coffees,

-Nothing new here, that's her name.

Gabriel and Walt answered back, smiling and looking at each other, corrected,

-We mean that she is the real thing.

Caroline took the information in her stride, went to pick up a chair and sat by the bed. She scrutinised her brother's face and her ex-husband's one to gather any clues, eager for more details. Finally she had the courage to ask for explanations,

-Right, guys, I know it's early morning and that you both have your foggy brains on but please can you be clear on what the real thing is? Elaborate a little on what you both mean?

Gabriel was about to answer, but Walter prevailed upon him, raising his hand in a commanding fashion, stopping him, and declared,

-Let me do the talking, Gab, as you seem to be a little prejudiced upon the matter of It, I think it is better that I do so. Caro, Gabriel's opinion and mine about the nature of It-666 differ. Doctor Purallee having spent the night attending at the bedside of It, determined that she was indeed the Beast, the Antichrist. As for me, I keep an open mind about It, giving her the benefit of the doubt, she will be no Beast nor Antichrist to my eyes unless she behaves like one. Besides I do not subscribe into giving undue authority to any books, that have been copied and recopied endlessly by different hands, with so many different agendas, dictated by some great Angel, or not. For all I know, It-666 might be a supernatural being of some sort unknown to mankind yet. I need more proof and facts to be able to say that I have in front of me the Antichrist. First, I don't believe in any of that bullshit; second, I will not treat someone as a criminal if he is not proved guilty, or has not committed a definite crime. Presently, the girl in front of you, Caroline, has extreme powers and as I understand, deadly ones, but has also no will to harm or use them. You are entitled to your opinion, do not let me or Gab, influence you to form one. Let it be formed essentially by your own interaction with the girl.

Caroline saw her brother standing up, and going to the window drinking his coffee silently. He gazed outside, his face unfathomable. She couldn't help but wink at Walter, pressing his knee in a sudden affectionate move, and told,

-Well, I am reserving my judgement about It-666: not guilty until proved so. You were such a good lawyer, Walter. I guess, given the circumstances, you have just become the devil's advocate in Gab's eyes.

Walter shrugged his shoulders and pointing with his chin to the skeletal It, corrected before taking a sip of his coffee,

-Just advocate, Baby, for I don't see any devil in here, and the existence of God has still got to be proved.

The door slammed opened all of a sudden making Gabriel turn around with worry, and Caroline jumped upon her seat with fright. Little Micky ran into the room throwing himself into his father's arms,

-Daddy! I thought I heard you! I missed you. Are you still coming to my football game on Saturday?

Passing his coffee for Caroline to hold, Walter seized the eight year old boy lifting him from the ground, his face lighting up immediately,

-Here is my little ray of sunshine! So you missed me already, I saw you only this very last Sunday, Micky. Well I know the remedy to that, how about having pancakes for breakfast with your Ma and me in a nearby cafe, before taking you to school with my big partner in crime, Bud. Would you like that? And Saturday I will definitely be there cheering on my boy at the match, you can count on me.

The child smiled happily, and then said in a sad unexpected tone,

-Great! I am all for pancakes and you taking me to school but I am not sure about Saturday anymore, maybe you will be disappointed, maybe you will boo me.

Walter became serious and enquired,

-Come, Micky, what makes you say that? I will always encourage you, and never boo you.

Micky's brows furrowed and replied,

-Well, maybe not you, but maybe others will. I had a bad dream about the game. I kept falling and was no good at all and I thought I would never become a footballer.

Walter admonished the little boy tenderly,

-Now, listen little Mate, dreams are just meaningless when you do them while asleep. However, the ones that you do when you are awake, the ones you create and work upon to make them a reality are the ones that count. First, as my little boy, after any fall I expect you to rise again, get up and try over and over again and never give up those dreams for fear of falling or failing. Second, a fall in a dream will not stop you from becoming a footballer if it is what you want to be. You just have to work upon your real dream to be the best you can be at football. For example, did you practice this week since I last saw you? Practice has an effect and this is what you should focus on, for bad dreams are just that, bad dreams and have no effects.

Micky nodded, a very serious comprehending frown upon his young face,

-Well, that's mighty good to know but I am still going to be crap because I didn't play and practice all week. Homework and all, Pa. Ma doesn't want to run after a ball either.

Walter gave his son a comprehensive smile and told,

-Again, Micky, this is giving up before anything is being played out. Now that you highlighted your issues all we need to do is finding solutions. How about practising with me, every day until the match? I can pick you up after school and we can play football for an hour, if Mummy agrees, how would you like that?

Sure enough the little boy looked upon his mother with begging eyes, full of joyous expectation,

-Ma, please can I train with daddy until Saturday? I promise it would not have an impact on my homework and duties.

Caroline welcomed the offer of Walter and answered,

-Well, I will give into that. My only restriction is to have the training done in the garden and not in any random park so I can keep an eye on you, Micky and your timekeeping, for you to still have time for your homework and bath.

The child grinned happily, gave a high five to his father,
before noticing the poorly looking It-666. He considered her for a
good minute before saying sweetly acknowledging her,

-Hi, there. You look mighty unwell. I am sorry to jump about in
your room. I am Micky, what's your name?

The young girl smiled to the little boy, sorry to be so unsightly,
but remained silent to avoid scaring him with her strained
and raucous inhuman voice. Gabriel stepped towards the bed and
replied for It-666 to the child,

-She has no name, Micky. I nicknamed her Bambi, because your dad
found her in the woods and she can't stand upon her legs being too
weak. She cannot speak very well either. She suffered injuries and
ingested rat poisoning.

Micky nodded feeling sorry for the girl,

-Bambi, you mustn't worry too much because Uncle Gabriel is the
best doctor in the all States! He is mighty good to cure anyone, so
good that I never missed school for sickness. He is going to get you
ship-shape.

It-666 smiled widely. Walter turned to Gabriel teasing,

-Best in the all US: Gab, when did I miss the result of the X-factor
competition between doctors? What about Mummy, Micky, she is a
mighty good doctor too?

Caroline laughed and asked as she started taking his hand pulling
him,

-Come, Walt, let's go and eat something. We mustn't be late to take
Micky to school.

Gabriel put a few dollars in Walt's other hand and ordered,

-While you are at it, get me blueberries and maple syrup pancakes, and for Bambi, get her fruits of the forest pancakes with syrup. Also get her freshly squeezed orange juice. Her food and mine are on me.

Walter cocked his head to the side, and queried,

-Are you sure about feeding Bambi? I can take the tab on her. I would not want you having bad dreams about your ethics being sacrilegious.

Gabriel replied firmly,

-I am confident in my ethics, Walt, they do not lack practice either. But you scored a point, you made me dream that there was still hope for her. I had a dream that It was not what I feared. I will work upon that hope and upon her. You can count on me caring for her in good faith.

Walter nodded in approval and left the room with his family, a winning smile drawing upon his face, confiding out loud,

-Gab, I had the dream of hearing once more your sound good heart, I think I just did, Brother.

Verse 12. Across the Bridge

Gabriel closed the door of the room and turned to face the young It-666. She was crying silently. He sat upon her bed and wiped her tears with his thumbs, asking,

-Here, Bambi, why are you being emotional now?

It-666's big green eyes gazed at him and answered him by a question,

-Did Walter really mean to look after me like his own child? Am I allowed to dream of being part of a family like his?

Gabriel felt for the girl, a gripping sentiment invaded him about how lonely, downcast and loveless she had been during her all sixteen years. As the Beast and marked as the 'one', she had been denied everything. He tried to shake his growing sympathy for It-666 and standing up, replied in a firm tone,

-Walter meant what he said. He is determined to look after you and the way he has taken your side only proves it. Walter is a man of his word. The only time you can forget about trusting what he promises you is when he is drunk. Now, Walter's family is my family. He opened his arms to you and welcomed you. You don't have to dream of being part of our family, you are now part of it. Just make sure you do not deceive us. I will watch you very closely, Bambi, to be sure that you do not.

It-666 bit her lower lip and gave an emotional smile,

-I won't blow it, Gabriel. You are Walter's watcher, but he doesn't know you are his guardian Angel. He has no idea that you are an Archangel either. He is a firm atheist. Why don't you impose upon him? Does anyone know you are an incarnated Angel?

Gabriel told her sternly, his eyes glowing an ethereal golden as he did,

-No one knows and no one should. Only other Angels walking upon Earth have the knowledge of my identity. We keep humans in the dark of our presence among them. We do not interfere with free will, however we do guide those assigned to us. Walter was not always an atheist. He is questing and is still looking for answers. He did that all his life, studying and joining different religion, and leaving them still thirsty of something he cannot quench with any of the human's proposals of God or Gods worshipping. Yet he is closer to the truth than any human I have protected. I respect him far too much to impose upon him as an Angel. As for you, I respect you far too little to not impose upon you as an Angel. The question is: can you keep the secret of me being the Archangel Gabriel and of my ascendance over you, Beast?

She lowered her gaze under his intense scrutiny and replied,

-I will, Gabriel. I can keep a secret. I understand you about not giving me respect. Respect is something, I do not expect from anyone. My birth mark robbed it from me, like a luxury I shall never enjoy nor obtain. However I can feel my respect for every living being within me and can bestow it upon others, so I will respect you, Angel Gabriel and your authority over me.

Gabriel welcomed her answer, transforming himself before her eyes into his full angelic self. He held the left hand of the young emaciated being, assessing her feelings deep down doing so. His smile appeared slowly but surely, and he posed his other hand upon her forehead, addressing her in tongue,

-For such a creature as you, I am astounded to find such a considerate and good heart. Walter said you are no Beast until you behave like one, I will say the same to you. Even more, as an Archangel I can give you a new lease of life, take it or leave it. I have a proposal for you: Keep my secret, give me respect and behave following the goodness of your heart, and I will keep yours, give you respect, and will give you the love and affection you have never received.

Tears appeared at the corners of It-666's eyes in disbelief, hope suddenly rising within her, as her lips quivered her moved answer,

-Yes, please, oh please Gabriel. I accept your proposal.

The Angel gave her a kind and compassionate smile, reassuring her, as he put his hands to enclose her left marked foot,

-Quite the eager little beaver, hey, Bambi? Here, let us get rid of what robbed you of everything. I am making the mark of the Beast disappear from the bridge of your foot. From now on you will be able to walk your path without that terrible branding of your being. It is up to you to define yourself and be what you can be. Walter's words are instated as your new present reality and as your new lease of life. Your secret will be preserved by me and my family. If you ever break away from the terms of the proposal and be a Beast, your mark will reappear and brand you as the One again. I am presenting you with a bridge. I am expecting you to walk across it, and I will help you do so all the way. All you have to make sure of, is to never bring my wrath upon you, and for that you have to stay in the clear and far away, very far away from deception.

It-666 felt great warmth invading her via the bridge of her foot. Her tears were now streaming upon her cheeks, and her thanks streamed likewise endlessly flowing from her lips.

Verse 13. Hiding an Antichrist...

A couple of hours later, Walter and Caroline came back into the clinic's bedroom talking loudly and laughing. Doctor Purallee at his microscope, analysing the Beast's blood within the laboratory grew tense at their noise, stood up clenching his teeth, he muttered angrily to himself a very low,

-Fucking damn children!

Gabriel confronted the couple pointing at It-666 sleeping soundly upon the hospital bed and scolded,

-Silence, Bambi is finally resting. Both of you, in the laboratory, now. Behave yourselves, we have got the Beast upon our hands to look after for Christ's sake! Walt, put the breakfast in the microwave for later. Come and get briefed.

Caroline went within the laboratory without further a-do, while Walter gave a good inspecting glance at the room and the sleeping It-666. He noticed a bandage upon her left foot, her marked one. His brows rose full of intrigued curiosity and he followed his ex-wife quietly into the laboratory, as Gabriel held the door for him with his usual all-knowing smile. When Gabriel closed the door behind them, Walter couldn't contain his queries any longer, demanding in a low firm voice,

-So, Gabriel, I guess the new code name for the Beast is Bambi, as you seem definitely stuck on it. Now, I want to know what's the problem with her left foot, apart from her damning mark, for you to cover it up? And what's the deal with telling my son she had rat poisoning, I can tell you I had fun over breakfast trying to explain that one to my eight year old? How does someone get rat poisoning, daddy? I wished his damn uncle was there to clear that one up for us. As you are the best doctor in all of the US in Micky's standards, I struggled to keep that judgement he has of you intact as I tried to explain that diagnosis of yours. I managed to keep his delusion of you alive, but mine kind of went a little downhill in doing so. However, Gabriel, I am very eager to hear you talk all about It, It-666, Bambi, whatever Beast-Antichrist we have upon our hands. You spent the longest with her, all night, so spill the bean.

Gabriel grinned and answered as a matter fact,

-Yes, I do know more about It, than you could ever gather. Come, I just attempted to explain her appalling condition to Micky, the boy has never seen someone in such a state before. Besides, the rat thing was just weaving creatively upon real facts: the girl fed herself with rats for the past eleven years. I can also tell you that she wasn't overly keen on killing rats or anything for that matter, that a gluttony of rats never happened, for she has always let herself starve up until the instinctive survival point. And yes, I can't help calling her Bambi, now, but the irony is gone when I do so. And if you look at her kind eyes too big for her famished face, you'll find that it's her perfect pet name...

Caroline nodding in approval, added,

-The way you explained calling her Bambi to Micky made sense to me. We will find her a proper name of her own choosing soon enough, for the time being, I will go with Bambi. I don't fancy calling her Beast or Antichrist because she surely doesn't look like any of that...The poor thing ate rats to survive. If she is so sensitive about killing animals to feed herself, I can devise a vegetarian diet suitable for a growing teenager just for her.

Gabriel smiled and welcomed,

-I think Bambi will more than just appreciate it, Caro. She is so good natured, it's unbelievable after what she went through. She has the power to kick arse, all arses bothering her to damn nought, yet she won't. Hence her current state, she is willing to be destroyed to not be used against humanity for them.

Walter stroked his chin barely hiding an amused grin, as he teased,

-Gabriel, if I didn't know you better, I'd say you'd grown fond of the Antichrist. That's no mean feat! I accept your rat poisoning explanations about Bambi. Now, you haven't told us all and the reason for her bandaged left foot.

Gabriel waved his hand in the air in dismissal, and commanded,

-We have other cats to whip rather than to talk about It now. We have to ensure her protection. Caroline, you are going to take the 306 to a car dealer close to the state border, then drive with any bought random car in exchange until you reach the house of Uncle Raphael across the border, and give him Bud to look after for a few weeks. Leave the bought car there, stay at Raphael's overnight and come back tomorrow morning by train, not earlier, we will look after Micky for you.

If Caroline raised her eyebrows with concern at the orders, Walter voiced his full surprise and objection to them,

-My car to be sold, my dog to be given to lunatic Raph, absolutely not! Gab, what on Earth are you thinking?

Gabriel responded in an authoritative fashion which forbade any further argument,

-Someone who keeps getting in all sort of scrapes, brought the bloody Beast in my clinic, at three in the morning. He abducted her from a famous politician's compound, where he thought he was followed. I don't think he bothered checking any CCTV system in use in the aforementioned area or had any thought of disabling it. I also know that not only his white mother fucking arse is very recognisable, and although he cleverly wears leather gloves while hunting, his large Great Dane's paws have made very identifiable imprints and so his damn foreign French car that no one bloody drives any more. And I doubt very much, you swept clean your path and track to my clinic as usual, so, Walter, someone has to think of the give-away details so I don't end up with the bleeding Ku Klux Klan at my doors claiming the Antichrist! As a consequence, the dog will get anaesthetised, wrapped in the tartan blanket just like the one you brought the Beast in. Caroline takes the 'other' beast package to Uncle Raphael, exchanging suspiciously your obviously ominous car in the making. If you were followed, it should confuse a little the pursuers, and Raphael has got a lot of tricks up his sleeves to confuse them even more upon his received package which will send the trail far away from us. Trust me on loony uncle Wrath, he had his call and clear orders, the worst he can do is start talking to your damn dog for a month, and paint his coat to a believable other shade of Great Dane before giving it back to you, safe and sound. As you talk to your dog too, I don't think Raph can mess with his mind more than you do, Wreck-Man...

Walter shook his head in disbelief and surrendered, trying to sway for a compromise,

-The 306 is my first car, I love it. I improved it so much, with infra-red and so many more gadgets that I feel like Knight driving KITT. Can the 306 get a lick of paint too like the dog, and a month boarding at the car dealer instead? Pretty please, Gab?

Gabriel laughed,

-Jeez, man, you have a 'Knight Rider' syndrome in a fucking Peugeot 306, and you dare to call someone else a lunatic! Can you have anything damn normal around you, so you can lay low and blend with the crowd a little for at least six months? By the way your blond mop is getting trimmed short, and you will get dark brown hair for a while. Your flat is already up for renting. You're moving to my cabin until further notice.

Walter turned in the lab like a trapped wolf in a cage, and argued,

-Not again! I can hide anywhere else but your tree cabin in the forest. You don't even own a TV, man. Besides, I lived three damn long years at your place after my breakdown, it's more than enough. You're mothering and smothering. You even gave me a bleeding

curfew, to me, a fucking grown man! I had to hide beers and ciggies
from your eagle eyes. I'd rather be homed by my Caro for a while.
I'll get a damn haircut, grow a goatee and that is it. I stay blond, we
will limit the damages to painting my car and dog. Bloody hell!

Caroline couldn't help laughing as she told,

-Come, Walt, it wasn't that bad with Gabby. He got you back from
your brink. You know it was a very close shave for you to not end
up in a mental health clinic for good. Look upon the positives: you
are independent, you do talk and make sense again, you are an
excellent father, and you don't smoke any more. I think his
mothering and smothering did you a world of good. Shrugging off
his cabin in the forest, his home, his help is a tad ungrateful. But I
do agree with your refusal to change my blondie bear to brown,
only that, and I am definitely looking forward to that goatee of
yours.

Gabriel gave a tender smile to his sister, and admonished the
couple,

-Bloody blond he stays then, so your bear can amaze you with his
pertinently constant blondism, Sis. The fact is I have been over-
mothering you, back to sanity, Walter, because of my sister's love
for you, and for your young son. I have no doubts that Caro will
home you back for good in the very near future. But I cannot let
you go to live with them, straight away, because your delivered
package is special beyond beliefs and it would jeopardise the lives
of Caroline and Micky. It would not be because of It-666, herself,
but the people who want her, the ones aiming to use her and the
ones aiming to kill her. So, my secluded home is going to be yours
for the time being Walter, until we hide the trail of the Antichrist so
well, that we can raise her sixteen year old self like any normal
teenager. I am conscious that my ways of living are rather too
ascetic for your liking, and I shall not impose them upon you, nor
Bambi, when she is well enough to come to live at my place. Beside
I will need your help to extend my tree house to welcome her in two
months time. And you can bring your bloody damn TV if that's
what stops you from moving in, but no watching porn! I have no

problem with beer drinking as long as I don't have to put you to bed because you collapsed, or clean your patches of sickness from my sofa before I can sit on it, with peace of mind for my resting butt cheeks... So what do you say?

Walter hugged the black man impulsively and answered,

-Gosh, I wish I had shoulders as broad and as caring as yours, Brother. I owe you. I am sorry for sounding ungrateful. I will do as I am told as I am confident it will be for the best. But you don't have to shelter Bambi, I can rent a bigger place for me and her in a couple of months. I can take ownership of the problems I bring about. I can deal with raising an unusual teenager.

Gabriel pushed away from the hug and waved negatively his head, teased out loud,

-Jeez, as if I am going to let Wreck-Man look after a possible Antichrist unsupervised! You must be joking. Uncle Raphael and I can announce the bleeding apocalypse now if I ever let you do so! With no disrespect to you, I am deeply involved now and will look after Bambi with you, Walt. Although I am demanding, unrelenting and rough, psychology is my forte. The girl is extremely shy, sensitive and lived in a feral state before being caged. She is a thoroughly damaged little package, and if Caroline, you and me rather than just you provide her with parental guidance it would be invaluable and preferable for her. The lonely being need a family not a loner, and you are going to start back with heading that family forward, with me. Now, bring me Bud. The plan is going to fool any bastard on your trail. Caro, get the tartan blanket from the emergency room and ignore the chaos in there: Bambi just showed me how she could make the ground shake into an earthquake and control it so it affects only the area she has chosen to bring to upheaval. Let's all get moving, because if we think we have seen it all with our little Bambi, we are just kidding ourselves, for if extremists of the religious kind and irreligious sort knock upon our doors, we will have hell on Earth to deal with.

As Caroline left the laboratory, Gabriel added to Walter,

-Bambi's left foot is bandaged because I am using an abrasive to remove her condemning mark, to give her a chance of a normal life. She confided a great deal to me, Walt. She is fucking damned to death if we don't help her. And we are damned to death if we don't hide her properly. I know you are an unbeliever, and I won't force you to believe, but we are dealing with paranormal forces of the highest order with Bambi. She has to remain in our hands at all costs. If she doesn't, the so called apocalypse that many believe in will be upon us all. Up to the neck, Brother, I will dive in the mud to bring you to safe land. Get your dog. He will sleep his way to Raphael, sending the trail of the Antichrist far from us, keeping It, us and humanity safe.

Walter smirked, before leaving the lab,

-Talking about deep shit again, Gab! Maybe I should return you the favour of your psychological help you provided me in my time of need. If Bambi can cause an apocalypse, you need a damn shrink. But I'll be here, no worry mate, sinking deep into your sofa and my beers, ready to listen to your paranormal religious crap, and trying my very best to rationalise them back to you. And I won't let KKK put a hand on you, Brother, nor any extremists of any kind put a hand upon your freaking Bambi. In our mud until our family's safe landing, Gabriel.

Returning to his microscope, Gabriel Purallee swore to himself,

-Fucking damn children! Got fucking no ideas about the Antichrist, its conception and what it bloody involves to hide one. Just looking at those damned blood cells sends shivers throughout my angelic spine.

Verse 14. Solomon's Power

It-666 opened her eyes as soon as an excited Bud rushed into the room with his master, Walter, barely controlling him. The Great Dane put his large head upon the bed, licked endlessly the left hand of the girl, wagging his tail happily. Walter smiled apologetically and announced,

-Looks like you made a friend, Bambi. Bud has definitely adopted you.

Caroline came in the room, carrying the tartan blanket and Walter's camera, closing the door behind her. She asked her ex-husband eagerly,

-Have you seen the state of the emergency room, Walt? Bambi is a walking San Andreas fault! I am glad that she doesn't want to use her earthquake skills more often. It took me a while to tidy up.

Stepping outside the laboratory, Gabriel answered his sister, scolding as he saw the wide awake It-666,

-Trust you two to break the rest of Bambi! Caroline, may I remind you that the little one is a sensitive being and that any jokes about her being a walking earthquake maker are better avoided. Also Walter, may I remind you that your dog is in a clinical environment and should be restrained. It just licked all over the area of her hand where I had inserted my needles. Honestly!

Walter laughed it all out,

-I don't know what got over Bud, he usually responds to me, obediently, Gab. He was excited to see Bambi again, I guess. You will just have to sanitise her arm once more, that shouldn't strain you too much. You should chill out a little. The girl is not devoid of understanding. She will recognise harmless banter and jokes. You should thank your god, that we are not in a biblical time anymore, where all our towns with their advanced 'moeurs', freedoms and multiculturalism would have been looked erroneously upon as towns of sinners, like Sodom and Gomorrah, where our little earthquake maker on legs with eyes that combust things at will would mean the end of us all. Your namesake will not descend upon us and carry out god's dirty jobs of mass human massacre like in Sodom, any time soon. Chill, Gabriel, black humour is just that. If Bambi doesn't know about it, I will teach her, it can only enlighten her a little. What do you say, Bambi?

It-666 had blood tears appearing at the corner of her eyes and remained utterly silent. Gabriel shook his head in disbelief, saddened by Walter's words, and made a move toward her bed to comfort her. Only for the Great Dane to stand up confronting him, growling all of a sudden.

Caroline totally surprised, reacted by trying to calm the dog,

-Jeez, Bud, what's come over you? Don't you recognise Gabby any more?

The dog displayed his teeth, getting more upset by the minute. It-666 touched the Great Dane's head, stroked it, and told in her awkward human voice,

-Down in front of my Master, Bud.

The effect was immediate. The dog went to lay by Gabriel's feet, and exhibited his stomach in a totally subdued position in complete contrast of his earlier reaction.

Walter in complete shock at the whole scene, commented,

-Now, that's disturbing. Growling is out of character for Bud. And, you, Bambi, you cannot call Gabriel, your Master. What's going on?

Gabriel moved by the bed, held firmly the left hand of the girl, and with his other hand dried her blood tears, and gently reassured her before admonishing Walter,

-Here, Bambi. Calm yourself down. Take it easy. It's going to be okay. I will look after you. You are not the end of it all. I will make sure of it. It was just mindless banter from Walt. Now, Walter, I am going to tell you what is disturbing. It is that when I am warning you both, that our girl is a sensitive emotional being who has been hurt badly, as a well thinking adult, you chose to carry on ignoring that she has feelings. Once she has been educated by us, when she is less sore from all her tortures, she will then be able to go beyond her raw feelings and only then be ready to share whatever jokes and banter you'll throw at her. For the time being both of you, need to watch what you say in her presence, just ask yourself one simple little question before talking: am I being considerate or not? Did I make myself clear?

Caroline nodded sheepishly and apologised,

-I am sorry, Gab. I am sorry, Bambi. I didn't really mean what I said.

Walter, going to his dog and stroking him upon the ground, queried,

-Are the upset I caused within Bambi, and my dog's over reaction linked? I will be more considerate in the future, Gabriel. I need to understand something. You did witness that Bud obeyed her straight away but why did she call you her Master?

Doctor Purallee grinned a ready explanation at his lips, hiding the fact of the surrender of It-666 to his Archangelic self,

-Bambi is a deeply damaged little being on a psychological level. Having been treated as a beast since birth she identifies herself as one; not so much as the One, as it conflicts with her true caring nature and heart for the latter. To resume her psychological present state, she believes being a beast of some sort, but her mind went into denial overdrive in fear of being The Beast. She rejects so much the idea of being It-666, that she went on a self destructive path, letting herself be annihilated by others slowly but surely. Both of your jokes played on her fear of being the apocalyptic Beast, unknowingly upsetting her, and hurting her feelings thoroughly, hence provoking her most painful tears, the blood ones. Physical manifestations of some sort can occur as well when she reaches that distressed state. So do not get her emotional, and think that we have a powerful teenager going through a very difficult identity crisis to deal with. Her self esteem is at rock bottom. She thinks of herself as an animal rather than a human. Like a dog has a master, she is seeking one. As I tried to make sense of who and what she was all night, as I tended to all her physical needs, I impressed enough within her mind, unconsciously, to become her Master. With time, when she will get better and with thorough education, I am sure the disturbing 'Master' will subside to a more suited 'Guardian' and 'Teacher'. Now, let me ask, Bambi, what went on with the Bud thing? This was a tad unsettling. Can you explain this to us?

It-666 clutched tightly Gabriel's hand as she confessed, her eyes pleading for his comprehension,

-I do something to animals. I don't know what. They always come to me, are extremely well behaved and friendly to me but they also become overprotective of me. However, I talk to them directly or their minds and they obey. Maybe it is because I am truly a beast, and we speak the same language.

Gabriel welcomed her confession, stating,

-This skill doesn't make you a beast for some humans were bestowed with this peculiar gift, the most famous of all, King Solomon.

Walter went to one of the windows, opening it wide, and told full of circumspection,

-Right, saying 'Down' to my dog and him executing the order doesn't ring Solomon's mythical skill to me. Impress me, Bambi, call the little birds in here, and as you will fail, it will prevent Gab, going all biblical on us!

Doctor Purallee shook his head in disapproval, and ordered,

-Close that damn window, you, Muppet! I don't want any fucking birds shitting in my clinic.

Birds, large and small came flocking in, yet all perched upon the window sill, with some singing melodiously. Caroline clapped her hands like a child at the sight of the little robin, blue tit, wood pigeon, blackbird and collared dove mix. She expressed her emotions with a bright smile,

-Looks like Walt Disney's magic to me, Bambi!

Walter looked totally bemused, and nodding to the girl, he admitted,

-That's cutting my quack short! I am dumbfounded. You can let them go now, before one of them poops in his damn clinic, and before Gab gets his magical bat to show he is all out of patience with me!

Gabriel stood up with authority. All the birds went. He closed the window then ordered,

-Focus, children! Task at hand. I am going to anaesthetise the dog. We will wrap him up in the tartan blanket and off you go with it, Caroline, and follow your instructions to the letter. One more thing, not a word to Uncle Raphael, about It-666, being the potential Antichrist. She is just a living leftover of P's human sacrifices for him, a potential crucial witness to protect and should remain so. I coded her name as Bambi to him, refer to her as such always. Understood?

Caroline nodded her comprehension to his caution. She only knew too well the far reaching power of their uncle. It went beyond common laws.

Walter asked concerned,

-My dog will wake up, Gabriel, are you sure about it?

The Doctor already preparing the needle, answered in all honesty,

-There is a risk, Walt. I need to be a little heavy handed to make sure the dog is immobile upon reception, eight hours from now.

It-666 proposed out of the blue, surprising everyone,

-There is a safer way. I can make the dog sleep that long by affecting his heart and metabolism and he will wake up for sure as soon as Raphael lay him inside his home, and Caroline orders him to open his eyes.

Gabriel questioned her,

-Is it the stroking to sleep ability?

The girl nodded positively, adding reassuringly,

-But not of the deadly sort. The dog will be healthy as if nothing happened to him upon the wake up call.

Gabriel gave his acquiescence before Walter could argue, and explained to him briefly,

-Bambi uses natural interference instead of my chemical ones. The restoration of the living creature is more assured with her method than mine.

Walter saw his dog leaving his side to lay his head upon It-666's bed. She stroked his head gently and fondly. The Great Dane collapsed underneath the bed within a few seconds. Caroline helped her ex-husband wrapping Bud carefully in the blanket and headed to the car park of the clinic with him and Gabriel. The two men put the wrapped package upon the back seats of the 306. She took the wheel and drove off.

As she left, three cars pulled within the car park instantly. Nursing staff climbed down and shook Gabriel's hand as they entered the clinic. Doctor Purallee removed the sign officially closing his clinic and reopened it to the public. He and Walt stood hidden by an entrance window for a few more minutes until they saw a car leaving the car park hastily aiming to follow the 306.

Walter winked at Gabriel,

-You were right.

To which the Doctor replied,

-As always.

Verse 15. Opening Up

Walter kept looking at the car park, his mind riddled with worries. He scribbled a few notes upon a pad, as Doctor Purallee was already firing all sorts of orders to his staff, who were now coming into the clinic. Officially re-opened to the public, the first patients came forward within the hour. With satisfaction Gabriel went back to the observation window where Walter was still standing, and asked,

-What's the score, Brother, how many cars have left the car park within the hour of opening? There were seven cars this morning in all, including yours, mine and Caro's. That leaves four cars, one definitely suspicious which followed the 306's departure, so what is the result for the other three?

Walter showed his pad to Gabriel. It had the four cars number plates written up, a brief description of the cars, model and state, along with their times of departure. He confided his concern in a low voice,

-One car came back, Gab and the driver is within, having a burger, watching the clinic. If you flick through the pad, I have drawn the likenesses of three of the drivers, plus this new one. One of the cars left and when it returned it had a different driver. We are definitely being observed. I can't help being thoroughly worried for Caroline's safety.

Gabriel grinned and tapped Walt's shoulder reassuringly,

-Good work. Come, I have a lot more for you to do. Caroline will be fine. Before knowing you she was a pure tomboy who raced cars at illegal rallies, that was until I put my foot down coming back from university, and sending her to study in one. She will be able to outdo any pursuers even in your damn 306. Anyhow Uncle Raphael has sent his security guards along the way, expecting the Peugeot and it will be escorted without Caro nor the pursuers knowing it, ready to intervene at any given moment. Do you think I would let my sister run upon an errand if I didn't make sure she would not be safe first? I am not prepared to lose any of you anymore.

Walter sighed deeply, remembering the loss of his twin sister Wendy, betrothed to Gabriel. He followed the Doctor silently as he headed to his office. On the way, Purallee gave more orders, addressing himself to the clinic receptionist and a security guard standing by,

-Is the locksmith booked in before twelve, Liz? Are the press release and radio statements of the clinic re-opening done and dusted? Is Doctor Hamilton covering my minor appointments this week? Good Job! Arthur, sweep this car park regularly from now on, every fifteen minutes. It is only for doctors, nurses, and patients, for Christ's sake! It has come to my attention that people park in there to eat their breakfast regularly. Sort it out, man. Any car needs a reception desk ticket with a specific allocated time upon it, failing that, the car will be towed away. If this strict rule is not implemented with efficiency from immediate effect, Arthur, you will be escorted out. Get rid of the burger man taking the piss in my car park, now! Liz, get the skilled newbie to design and print lots of car park tickets to allocate to staff and patients, leaving the time blank for you to fill in. Send an e-mail to all staff with the rule being more stringently applied and asking for their immediate compliance. Last, order for a car park panel and warning sign to be made explaining the rule clearly and have them put it out in the parking by tomorrow. Thank you, Liz. I will check up on progress within the hour. No one is to disturb me until four pm, apart from you, Liz, by text only.

The red haired receptionist shook her head in agreement, raising her hand to an invisible cap in a military fashion, smiling,

-Yes, Sir.

Walter saw Arthur heading outside to monitor the car park with no further a-do. He blinked a few times to Gabriel,

-Jeez, man, are you running an army? Did you miss your calling somehow as tyrant, Gab?

Doctor Purallee opened the door of his office to Walter, his face totally unreadable, and closed it with a slight bang after them.

Walter stood in the middle of the office, looked around him and his eyes twinkled at the sight of the baseball bat by a bag with baseball gear upon it. He grinned worryingly and stated,

-Here is my old friend the bat! It loves patting my back every now and then...I guess, it is the time when I shut up, listen and become suddenly considerate.

Gabriel smirked and teased, before ordering,

-See, just its sight is enough to tame you. All is in the swing, and the delivery. Purely educational. Now, let's get on with your work. First, track down those cars and owners on the internet. Second, when you are done, I need you to develop your pictures of P's bunker in the photo lab of the clinic, by my office. Report to me when you have finished and try to have it all completed by one.

Walter nodded his agreement to the orders and confided,

-Yesterday, I was deeply worried to see you. I wanted only Caroline to deal with It-666. I am sorry I didn't call you on my return from that hunting trip. I guess I was concerned that your deeply religious morals would affect your treatment of the girl. I apologise to you, Gabriel. Once again, you took control of the entire situation, but let me tell you that I am grateful that you did so. I am now more than confident that Bambi is in the best hands to look after her. She is pretty special, in a bleeding damn-it sort of way, isn't she?

Gabriel tidying a desk by a window, removing files and papers from it, acknowledged,

-She is disturbingly out of this world, I must admit. But she is a sweet little thing. I accept your out of the blue apologies. Thank you for clearing the air between us. The thing is, what she is, or represents, means that looking after her will put us in great danger. Your initial fears about my reactions towards her were justified by my first outburst on seeing her mark. It took you, kneeling by Caroline, begging to see good hearts, to wake up mine and consider giving Bambi a chance. Tending to her all night, I can warn you that she does fit all conceptions about the coming Antichrist. To ask any human to go beyond that is out of the question, the girl will be slaughtered by the mob. However, heartbreakingly, Bambi is a good being. She has been letting herself fade away in silence to not embody humanity's fears. She can embody what we all fear, yet she won't. Free will power and its amazing glory and beauty have the capacity to baffle me constantly. She chose death for herself.

Gabriel stopped talking for a minute, installing a laptop upon the desk, before carrying on,

-Poor thing, really. And then, you, Walter, stepped in, right in the middle of her dreary harrowing slow motion suicide, her silent self sacrifice, you opened your arms to her and told her it didn't have to be that way. Let me tell you, Brother, that you are damn right, about the whole matter. You have my full support and protection. What we will be up against, Walt, has no description. But I will fight our corner with all my might, one that stands for hope, life and loving care, giving a chance to anyone.

He switched on the laptop, put a desk lamp by it, a mug full of pens, and a couple of notepads. Gabriel pulled the stool out from underneath the desk, and presenting it to Walter, announced,

-Here, this should do for the time being. I present you with your new temporary desk and office my dear private investigator. You should take a seat, now, before I brief you further.

Walter gave a quick worrying glance to the Doctor, sat at his new desk, and demanded,

-Just fire away, Gab. I am grounded at your cabin from now on, nothing can be worse than that. In the same time, I am warming up to the fact. You're a bloody control freak, but you have structure, and you think forward, to almost every single detail. And to be honest, I can't help feeling safe around you; just the way I did when I still had parents, before their accident.

Gabriel put his hand upon Walt's shoulder tapping it knowingly. He opened a small safe by the desk and pulled a file from it, which he presented to Walter, stating,

-I always expected that one day you will need this, Walter. Now give me all your forms of ID upon you, I will store them in my safe until further notice. I need you to hand me over your flat keys as well. I have arranged for all your belongings to be removed from your flat this afternoon and placed into storage. Tomorrow someone with your name, will be leaving the United States for Australia. He will assume your identity, Walter, for the time being, creating a trail which should give you safety, here. He works for the CIA and has a will to put P and any of his followers out of the big picture, like us. Brother, I have good contacts, mainly through Uncle Raphael. Like him, I am a Universal Secret Service Agent. You have been under my watch, pretty much since you left university as a troublesome human rights fighter soon to become a brilliantly fearsome lawyer, and ever since. You're under my protection and it goes beyond what you can imagine from a simply caring brother in law. Open the file, it is who you will assume to be from now on, until you can resume being yourself, the notoriously infamous for all the good reasons, Walter Workmaster.

Walter gave a quick glance at the file and its contents, providing him a complete new identity from passport to credit cards. His blond brows frowned, as his mind tried desperately to come to term with what Gabriel told him. He had suspected long ago that there was more to Gabriel Purallee than the efficient and thorough Doctor. But to have always been so close to him yet so far from his confidence after all those years of friendship, did annoy Walter most of all. He could not help asking bitterly,

-Whenever you Brother-ed me, from which year did you really mean it? Did you give me your friendship to keep an eye on me? Did you go out with my sister for your job or out of love? It doesn't overfill me with joy and glee to know that I am watched like a dangerous criminal by someone I considered to be my best mate. Let me tell you that I feel betrayed and right down hearted about it. After all this time, Gab, I am gutted and a bit disgusted.

Gabriel went to the side of the window by the desk, saddened. He adjusted the blind to let the light through, and remained there facing Walter. His jaws clenching, he confided,

-The fact that I am your Watcher, does not make me a lesser friend to you, Walter. I value our friendship and you. I was always there in your times of need. When you gave up on yourself and literally broke down, I didn't give up on you, I brought to you my entire support. I will always be there for you and offer you my protection. I was assigned to you, because you were a very important person in the making, more or less as a bodyguard rather than a spy upon your activities. Far from being thought of as a criminal, you are extremely valued in higher places, their expectations of you and your future realisation warranted their help to you, through me. More or less, I have been your servant, Walter, an expensive servant extraordinaire who would lay down his life for you. As for your sister, I wasn't supposed to fall in love whilst on my task, yet I did, helplessly as soon as I saw her. I thought I found my Paradise upon Earth. I am disconsolate since her death. I treasure the thought of her, everyday. I cherish her memory nowadays by devoting myself entirely to you, her twin, and your family, which incidentally is mine, and the only one I would ever have, now that Wendy is no more. Please forgive me, for I wasn't even allowed to tell you this much at any point in time.

Walter sighed. He still didn't know what to make of it all. Revelation upon revelation, he had a man servant, a bodyguard, a watcher in Gabriel, of which he never knew. The only thing he could say for sure, was that the presence of Gabriel had been a constant throughout his most difficult times. The man who removed the broken bottle from his hands when he was about to open his jugular with it and kill himself, six years ago, was Gab. The very same nursed him back to sanity for three long years, tirelessly, giving him his favourite nickname of Wreck-Man in the making. He looked upon his new given identification papers and demanded,

-How long have you been working upon making that cover up for me? I can't help noticing that all details are very thorough. The credit card is two years old, and the debit one, three, and almost due for renewal. I can also see through the respective bank statements that both were in use convincingly throughout that time. Another thing is striking me: my regular income is paid every month by your clinic. As you described yourself as my servant, I find it rather fetching that you should pay me...Is it a kind of Freudianic unsettled underlying-wish?

Gabriel grinned and answered,

-I never thought of that, but yes, maybe as your assumed character works for me, for the past three years as a part time ambulance crew and as my part time Personal Assistant, and will carry on doing so. Having you under me is most reassuring under our new given circumstances. That cover was created nine years ago, a month and a day after your wedding to Caroline, after your amazing success at the trial of Varoslav and his acquittal. It was maintained throughout the years, in order to give complete credibility when it would be required to be used fully. It was a protective measure created for a brilliant lawyer who could stir a lot of issues in his wake.

Walter smiled sadly and told,

-Well, I am no brilliant lawyer anymore. I am just the wreck of a man and as I have absolutely no clever purpose, I must be just a bleeding waste of your time, Gab, and a bitter disappointment to whoever your 'they', you are working for, are. I am baffled by it all, Gabriel and wished somehow that you focused on your fucking damn arse rather than mine for all those years. I don't know if I should be grateful or angry, right now. However because I am no good and because you spent your precious time serving me, I think a payback is overdue. Can I return the favour? Of course I am no member of a Universal Secret Agency, so my services and help would be largely downscaled to my brain, two arms and legs, if that's alright with you. You are a good man, Gabriel, if there was one, so I think I could repay your waste of time upon me, by working for you. You always looked after others, but who's been looking after you? Isn't it about time to concentrate on your own life and calling? Are you certain of not wanting to go beyond Wendy and have children and a family of your own? You helped me at her death, but you needed help too and you are still hurting thoroughly by her absence. Gabriel, may I help you in any way I can, to thank you for your time spent upon my downtrodden case?

Doctor Purallee went to a standing locker, opened it, and threw the key to Walter, who caught it in the air. He ordered in a teasing fashion,

-Bring your not good enough arse around here, my dear time waster! In here you will find some uniforms for you, and some different civilian clothes. You stay as you are for the time being for I am driving you to a hotel tonight in an obvious manner, where your alter ego will emerge from tomorrow to go to the airport. The swap will be smooth. You will effectively start working undercover for me tomorrow. I accept your willingness to help me, and welcome it, however as you can hardly help your own self, Wreck-Man, it is a great human mystery to me, how you will achieve your grateful payback help...However I am a believer of great mysteries, so I shall bestow you my faith and most needed patience. Now, by working for me, you will work for those Universal Powers at play, and may come directly into contact with them. There is one thing, I need you to understand: I want you to walk my line rather than theirs. I am using their help to hide Bambi and providing us safety. They understand that our girl is a victim, leftover of P's malefic practices, a human one, one still alive, which could testify against him. They do not know that she is It-666, the possible Antichrist, and they must never know. This fact stays between us, three, Caro, you and me, a secret not to be revealed to anyone. If we break our silence upon it, you can count Bambi as dead, and us too. Promise me your silence, Walter, by a blood vow.

Gabriel punctured his palm with a scalpel and handed it to Walter, who imitated his gesture. When both their hands were bleeding, they presented it to the other to be held in a silence vow. Walter realised that Gabriel was very much his own man, a commanding one, who was taking up the crusade of giving a chance to the teenage supernatural being in his care. He stood by him and seizing his bleeding palm tightly, promised,

-Gabriel, I am because you saved me. You have my silence regarding Bambi. I will walk your line, Brother, the one, you mentioned about love, care and giving a chance.

Verse 16. Humanly between Beast and Angel

Gabriel walked within the quarantine room, and saw the young It-666 bleeding thoroughly from everywhere. He grabbed her and swore, before demanding,

-What the hell? Bambi, what's going on?

He turned into his angelic self, all of a sudden, put both his hands upon her forehead, and calling upon his powers made her cease bleeding to death. The effect was immediate. Her pale face looked upon him, dazed, and she collapsed for a few long seconds. The Archangel shook his head in consternation. He clapped his hands, and the pool of blood surrounding the young It disappeared magically. The sharp sound of his clapping hands woke the fainting being up, and her aquamarine eyes opened to face the Angel. He grinned ironically, and whispered softly,

-It will never be that easy with me, Beast. You have surrendered to me, therefore I have the honour or dishonour of your killing. You cannot take your death away from me anymore, it does not belong to you. Now, tell me what's up? What made you do this?

It-666's gaze lowered to her hand and she confided in tongue,

-I can hear everyone within this building. I can hear the mind of everyone but yours. However, I heard your conversation with Walter. Your words stated clearly that I was putting you all, your family to a deadly risk, if I was not hidden safely. I do not want that. I do not want any of you at risk. I am making myself go, so all of you can remain safe. I am not worth the lives of Walter, Caroline and Micky. I do not want them hanging in the balance because of me. So I am jumping out of it.

Gabriel sighed deeply. Here again, the Angel could not help being

astounded by the creature before him. A truly caring and self
sacrificing Beast was beyond his conception yet he was witnessing it.
Or maybe the creature was deviously clever and playing hearts and
heads with others. One thing, he was sure of, was the fact that he
wanted to keep that being alive beside him, observe it and find out
more about It-666, and in consequences determine what creatures
hell could now spawn, that Angels would have to face and kill in the
future. He took her left hand and stroked the palm with his thumb,
gently, but told firmly,

-There is no balance. There is no measure. No one is worth more
than any other being. You do not have to die for anyone to be safe.
Remember, Walter's words, it does not have to be that way. He said
he will look after your life, do you want to show him now your
death? Beside I am protecting them, and will make sure they remain
safe while we help you, Bambi. And do not try to be cute with me,
for it will not work. I have you under my palm so you can rest
assure that the slaying of your Beast if It ever shows its face is a
sure thing. I reserve myself the right of your death, as an
Archangel, nothing will give me more pleasure. So you simply can't
remove the mat from under my feet by a mere suicide, it will not do.
It goes without saying that I will guard the right to your death from
anyone very jealously indeed. I can also assure you with certainty
that mine will remain safe during the process. So there is no need
for you to die yet, I will take care of that later.

The young being felt utterly sick, she bowed her head by the
bedside, and to her astonishment Gabriel presented her with a bowl
as soon as. She felt ashamed yet couldn't stop her sickness from
happening in front of the Angel. At the end, she was handed a
towel and a glass of water. She drank avidly then confided,

-Gabriel, do not make me sick. There is no security to be had
around me. Do not play with your family's lives for mine. I do not
want the pleasure of having me, my death, leading you astray, from
your angelic path, and from the other Angels. Like you said, the
hatred that surrounds me is beyond description. You, however great
and wise, do not know what you will face and what you will put
your family through by keeping me. I beg of you to slay me now, if

this is your secret desire. I can put my demonic face on to even give you more satisfaction upon killing me, so you can sleep tight tonight having killed the Antichrist. Go ahead kill me and please do not deceive me with false kindness. You warned me to stay far away from deception towards yourself and Walter to not face your Angelic Wrath. Let me reciprocate the warning. Please be honest with me, and with the other Angels about me. Don't use them to protect what they should worry about and kill. Stay safe, please Gabriel, don't walk alone, warn your kind about me, be true to them, get their advice and counsel to deal with me.

The Angel's grin faded, feeling deep down that It-666 was right. How could she ask him to be open and straightforward with other Angels? Was it another clever way for her to beg for her death? Was she really concerned by him, not to be laid astray from the Angelic and honest path, by attempting to reason with him? It made no sense for the Beast to do so, apart if she was no beast at all and a truly good being deep down. He decided to push her a little further, scaring her to find out, as he demanded, his eyes glaring with great anger,

-And how do you intend to show me your Beastly Wrath, pray? Can you really expect true kindness from anyone, let alone myself, my dear Antichrist? How dare you speak about truth and honesty, when you tried to hide yourself desperately from all? Let us be brutally honest then! Show me your true demonic face and I will get on with my Angelic duty whenever I see a Demon. The way I draw blood tends to be more painful than wrist slashing I am afraid. I deal with Beasts and Dragons in the Archangelic way of the like of Michael...

It-666 shivered and tried to transform herself before him, yet all she could manage was to have her demonic black eyes. She smiled piteously to herself and him. She was drained out of energy, of blood and will power. She was in no state to show a big satisfactory beast to the Angel for the slaying. A tear pricking in her eye, she tried to explain, apologising,

-Here, Gabriel, I can't do it, I can't transform myself further than my eyes. I guess I have no strength left. Please, just imagine me bad, ugly and all demonic, with all my terrifying potential being used, then just slay me. I won't put up a fight nor a struggle. I won't have you be untrue, dishonest and unsafe on my account. I won't have you stray from your Angelic path to keep me living. I won't have you and your family in danger for my sake. Please, Angel Gabriel, kill me now and not later. Just apologise to Walter on my behalf, say that you found me in my blood, like I intended and give him the note I wrote, upon my bedside.

The Archangel's wrath abated as he considered the young livid being before him. If he ever had a will to kill her, it was annihilated. His heart constricted. All he had in front of him was a really good creature, full of honesty, suicidal and self sacrificing. He seized the note and sat upon the bed, reading it.

'Dear Walter,

I am sorry to announce that I have changed my mind, and that I chose death.

Your help, generosity and kindness have meant to me more than any words can express.

The hope you brought me warmed my heart. But if my life means that yours and all your loved ones are dangerously at risk, then I would rather not be. I have lived through tortures which I do not wish upon anyone, especially not you, Gabriel, Caroline and little Micky. I am sparing you all by my parting.

Please forgive me.'

He folded the paper and put it in his lab coat pocket, when a beeping sound broke the silence within the room. Gabriel checked his smart phone and called out,

-The locksmith is here. Great, show him the direction of the quarantine room, Liz, and please bring me some strong coffee. I am starting to feel the effects of being up all night, Doctor Purallee has started to show up his grumpy side.

The receptionist laughed on the line and told him that she will get on it immediately. Gabriel smiled, and sighed facing It-666, as he turned himself back to his human form,

-Bambi, pull yourself together. No more demonic eyes, quick, I have someone coming in the room. Let us both tried to behave humanly. On this occasion, I must admit you did more than I did. But please do not kill yourself by kindness towards us, and do not incite me into doing it either. I do not wish you dead, but alive and well, little being. I have started working out a way for you to live safe and secure, along with my family although it is not going to be easy to achieve, it is possible. However I do not appreciate you dropping an ear upon my conversations, I guess it comes with all your package, that I will have to get used to and watch my words in the future. However I will take your concern seriously, I will be true and honest from now on, and warn the other Angels of your arrival upon Earth. But if their reactions or over reactions lead to your wanted death, being, I would not be able to feel anything else but extreme sadness. Let us hope that I can convince them of your good nature.

A knock upon the door cut him short. It-666's eyes turned green as Doctor Purallee opened the door to the locksmith and Liz.

Verse 17. Of Locks & Smiths

Liz presented the locksmith to the Doctor, handing him a coffee doing so,

-Doc meet George Gluck, specialist on digi-locks. He will install the one for this door in under an hour, then he will work on your office and our three laboratories' doors. By the end of the afternoon, he has promised to have all the jobs done and dusted. He understands that with our recent outbreak of meningitis, he will have to stay with us for 48 hours in observation, as a precaution, before he can head out of the clinic again. Now, the e-mails to the staff about parking have all been sent and cc-ed to you. The tickets are printing as I speak. And I love that newbie, Jessie, I don't care if she is a dropout with no experience. She is efficient, helpful and full of common sense. She is definitely a keeper, Gabriel. We could do with the likes of her in here, well, I definitely can. I have ordered your car park sign and it should be displayed by tomorrow morning, 10 am. I have the removal guy and the man who will be in charge of renting your friend's property coming in an hour to get the keys of the flat. Do I need to say anything further to them, than just handing them the keys? And here, Doc, strong, one sugar, as you like it. Just one more thing, I have room 101, cleared and without patient for two hours, between 2 and 4 pm if you ever need to rest a little this afternoon.

Gabriel smiled at the scruffy red headed receptionist, gave her the keys to Walt's flat and took a long sip of coffee before presenting his hand for the locksmith to shake,

-George, nice to meet you. Doctor Gabriel Purallee, director of the clinic. Thank you for coming on such short notice, and reassuring us about your efficient time keeping. Your first job, if well done, kept shorter will be the better, health wise. The patient, a young student, I am tending to here, is our last one with meningitis, hence the quarantine area. It's the danger zone if you like of my clinic at the moment, but if your work is done within the hour I am sure the risk would be minimal. You will be well looked after in any case, and let me reassure you again that the pay for your work and time spent here in observation, will more than compensate any inconveniences given. Now, Liz, I will review the trial period for Jessica. If within two months she can impress you that much, six are far too long to secure her with us for good. She can expect to be in my office for appraisal by the end of the week. As for the removal man, I need him to bring the TV appliances and DVD player to the clinic at the end of today along with all the DVD collection at the flat. For the landlord, specify that my friend is going to Australia for at least three months, and that this is the minimum term for any tenant taking the flat, and I forwarded to you earlier the email with how much we expect from the rent of that flat as a bare minimum. After spending a little time abroad, my brother in law expects a lump sum when he comes back to start him off again. Make sure this point comes across loud and clear to the landlord. Your coffee is perfect, Liz, as usual, and the nap room opening is most appreciated. Tell me, do you expect a raise for being at my beck and call, Liz?

The receptionist giggled away, and waved her hand in dismissal yet blushing,

-Purallee, as blunt as ever! Get me Jessie as a full timer on my reception desk, that's all I am after. Her background is not the most rosy, and a stable work and income can only do that girl a world of good. Money doesn't interest me as much as people, you should have realised that by now Doc with all your psychological credential. Well, and keeping you from barking at us all, around you, is a thorough pleasure of mine, that is the root of my efficiency. So no disruption up until 4 pm, that is understood and will be implemented. I will keep you informed by texts throughout the afternoon.

She walked away hastily back to her reception desk as Gabriel smirked.

The locksmith was already busy at the door, a little daunted to be in

the so called 'Danger' zone of the clinic and eager to be off to the
next safer door. The Doctor went to the microwave, put his
breakfast and the one of It-666 within it. He noticed her intense
gaze upon him and ventured,

-Reality catch-up, Bambi. Put your finger in it and you do
get literally swallowed, or the correct word might be, involved. I can
only recommend you trying your hardest to swim in it. Breakfast
will be ready in five. Now, let us check the damages you caused,
upon yourself.

As he reached the bed, he could see a faint yet worried smile upon
the young being. Sadly, he noticed that her pulse was considerably
down. Her skin had an ashen-grey colour tinge upon it presently, no
doubt due to her consequential loss of blood. She asked with a
naughtily pleased with herself smile,

-Am I in a bad way, Gabriel? Will I make it?

The locksmith dropped one of his tools upon the ceramic floor
tiles, caught listening worryingly. He apologised readily,

-I hope you do make it, girl. I do not want to be in the bad way you
are in. Pardon me saying but from down where I kneel, you do look
like freaking E.T.

Gabriel grinned wickedly, lifted his eyes to the sky in false
desperation, and deeply amused, replied,

-Please, George, concentrate upon the lock. The girl had brain
surgery, hence her shaved head. You cannot become the way she
look, as she has been anorexic for a long time, and her bad way was
self inflicted this morning, by a suicide attempt. I don't think
comparing my patient to E.T will help her recovery. As for you,
Bambi, it is too early to say anything. TLC is what you need right
now, good sleep and some food.

The microwave's alarm sounded and the Doctor went to it. The
locksmith paying attention back to the door, carried on talking,

-Well, I am sorry to hear that. Suicide, hmm, tough shit. You are young with a life before you, shame to ruin that. Anorexic, that's being harsh upon yourself, weight wise, right? We do care a bit too much on our appearances nowadays. Take my daughter, for example, pure teenager of twelve, she has hair all right, but the wrong kind in her mind. She is perfect to me and her mum. But there's this trend, call it fashion, call it whatever, and it will last, what, five years of stringent hell at most for its followers and whom they wish to demean, until it is replaced by a cooler one, as harsh for another group of people. Well, she burnt all her curls the other day in an attempt to have straight hair. She was being teased and bullied as the 'poodle' at her school. It makes me angry to know how cruel the young ones are with one another. But I do believe it is a reflection of their parents and who we are without a singular mind.

Gabriel furrowed his brows, interested, as he sat back upon the bed presenting her breakfast,

-Here, Bambi, eat, it's fruit of the forest pancake with maple syrup. It will do you a world of good. George, if you have a singular mind, how would you make sure that your daughter has one? And is it a good idea to show her not to follow society and others?

The young It took her pancake and smiled as she tucked in. This was the first proper food she'd had since nun Theresa's meals. She could see that Gabriel had relaxed since Liz's text and appearance. She wondered if the Angel had a little affection for his receptionist. Caught in reality, involved, this was the words of the Archangel Gabriel and his invite to her. She could see him taking a deep interest at the locksmith's stance. She blinked a few times puzzled, wondering if the presence of Angels upon Earth went beyond the care of a few humans to protect and watch. She had no doubts that the Universal Secret Services Agents, Gabriel alluded to Walter, were all Angels. She swallowed the blackberries with delight. It reminded her of the Black Forest. She could hear the conversation in the background as her mind drifted to the woods of her childhood.

George's voice seemed to go on and on, about survival camps where his daughter would learn to think upon her feet for herself...about Churchill and mavericks that corrected bad trends...about the hope and the future that he wanted his daughter to have...

Verse 18. Combination Free-One-Three

Sound asleep It-666 was dreaming. She was in the woods of her childhood, her Black Forest, walking and picking blackberries. She was alone, at peace, yet felt observed and looked after. She stepped by one hedge close to the road, she could see it between twigs, thorns and leaves, the black tarmac glistening under the rain, the white painted lines upon it and she could smell it, a mixture of petrol and diesel. This was the road to the human world, the path to it, the one forbidden to her. She wondered what it was like, what it would be like with her in it, and she ate her blackberries watching a random car pass by, like humans who ate popcorn in front of a big cinema screen. Sure enough, when she was caught wondering about humans and the world, she could hear him, his song, his soothing voice, his call and it worked like a magical charm upon her, she just had to go to him. She could have walked to him but she was eager to see him, she counted seven sunsets since his last appearance, so she ran to him instead. Like a deer, she made small work of jumping through little streams, hardly making any indents in the mud, fast and light, made no noise upon grass and fallen copper leaves. She was beside him within minutes. In the clearing she found him, sitting under an oak tree, upon a dead trunk. She sat by his feet, upon the grass, and silently waited until he spoke, however he didn't this time around, he carried on singing his lullaby, the one that calmed her down, his voice perspiring great sadness the more he sang, becoming more and more distant.

Walter had developed all the pictures taken at P's bunker and some were utterly unexpected, some he had not taken but were there... A little disturbed by it, he headed to the quarantine room as soon as the photos were dried enough to be handled. In the hallway, he noticed the room was not closed, with its door very slightly ajar, and great light seemed to pour out of it. He checked his watch, it was almost one o'clock. Early Fall's midday sun could still be blazing hot sometimes. Someone was singing a lovely strange tune, something slightly sorrowful, something in an unknown language within the room. As he stepped in, he saw Gabriel, surrounded by an amazing light, singing, sitting by the unconscious It-666's bed, stroking her forehead with a wet towel.

Walter stood there, gaping at the sight. Gabriel turned to him, eyes glazing bright and gold, asking in a commanding tone,

-Close the door, Walter. You are early, I expected you at one pm.

Walt did as he was told but when he faced Gabriel again, everything was back to normal. Baffled he wondered if he had been hallucinating. He had slept only for three hours that night and badly. It had been more or less a toss and turn affair rather than true sleep. Or maybe he was experiencing alcohol withdrawal symptoms, his very first ones, after all, this was now his seventh day without a single drop. Yet he had to ascertain the facts,

-Gabriel, have I just heard you sing in a most peculiar way?

The Doctor answered calmly and positively,

-You have.

Walter, a little unnerved, pursued,

-Were you glowing by any chance? I just saw you with golden nuggets for eyes.

Gabriel grinned widely and wickedly before teasing,

-No, my dear Walter. I dare say, that you dreamt awake. If my eyes had the colour of whiskey, you know what I will say to that. Why don't you pour yourself a glass of water and sit down for a while, just to get back your wit where it should be?

The man went to the hand sink and washed his face before drinking straight from the tap. He muttered to himself,

-Jeez, must be withdrawal hallucinations then. If staying in the clear gives me the same symptoms as if I am pissed out of my head, I might as well start drinking again.

Doctor Purallee rolled his eyes at him, and scolded,

-Reversed logic will get you nowhere. Be patient and give yourself credit. One week without alcohol, is a good first step, so don't backtrack at the first hurdle. Now, as you have to work in my clinic for a while, I would appreciate if you didn't treat it like your home. Drinking from the tap is frankly unhygienic, use a glass, if you don't want to be called the Germinator around here.

Walter smirked, and argued,

-Well, bad habits die hard. Name calling is no deterrent for me. Beside that one, linguistically gives the impression of germs great Schwarzy killer rather than germs proliferator, so I could live with that. But I'll try my best to be clinically minded in the future. Now, Gab, tell me, what the hell was that song's language?

Gabriel tried to avoid his inquisition by dismissing it,

-It's most probably something hellish. It-666 sang it to me during the night telling me it was calming her down, so I am singing it to her while she sleeps.

Walter rose his eyebrows full of circumspection, and praised,

-I am speechless, Gabriel, so you can listen to a foreign language, from hell or wherever It-666 really comes from, and if it is truly hellish it sounded rather pretty and sweet but also sad, and sing it like a native of the place themselves...It's unbelievably talented. You see myself, as a normal guy, I do not possess such a listening ability and imitative skill, even after hearing the same French nursery sing song a fair few times over the past six months from Cecile, Micky's French Au-pair girl, I just cannot sing 'Eel ate hay un petite naveere' like a native of the hexagon.

Purallee's eyes lit up with a pure sparkle of wickedness, as he answered totally unfazed, quoting in perfect French,

-You mean 'Il était un petit navire'. I can sing it for you flawlessly. Micky is close to singing it to the note perfect, too. It is just child's play. All you need to do is become a true listener, which requires understanding, comprehension and patience, and then you can be a parrot, which needs artistry, playful mastery and empathy, only then you can pirate your way anywhere, my dear Walt, like a Universal Secret Agent. Obviously, you do lack the skills, as the 'normal' guy, and please define to me normality when you are concerned and included within it, somehow normal and you do not make sense nor match together. However, Michael, your son, has great potential, at what, 8 and a bit. He loves that song, the darkness of it, the unbearable lightness of it upon the matter of the life to be eaten of that poor young sailor, and the miracle at the end of it. That's the comprehension part, and near any swimming pools, now, he sings that song like Cecile, just to give himself heart upon learning how to swim in the deep end of the pool... Life skills learning are still open in his young mind, while yours, Wreck-Man, have started to wilt, in a knowing all fashion, in which you can't teach old dogs new tricks.

Walter went by the bed and handing his pictures to Gabriel, could not help commenting, coughing slightly, with the corner of his lips twisting in a smirk,

-Thank you for your impressive listening skills and empathy, Gabriel. I needed to feel totally odd, inadequate, and like an old dog on its way out. By the way, It-666 is not looking very well. Is it me hallucinating, or has she taken a turn for the worse? She seems even paler than when I brought her here, if it were possible.

Gabriel nodded positively and pulled It-666's last note from his lab coat pocket to give it to Walter, who read it quietly. He gazed back at Gabriel for more explanations. The Doctor pointed to the bedside table with the assortment of medical instruments upon it and told,

-She used the scalpel. I managed to stop the bleeding, but her loss of blood was consequential and in her state, very dangerous. She has been drifting in and out of consciousness since the locksmith has left the room. The thing is her blood is so peculiar, so out of this world, that I cannot make her recover faster by a transfusion as I have no matching blood for her. We just have to sit, wait and pray that good rest, food, hydration, and the drops work their magic. I kept singing her soothing song, because if she was to pass away, I believe it is what would bring her peace of mind. Bambi had a slight fever too but it is under control, now. Walt, her being is in desperate need of TLC. Even if she pulls through, she will remain suicidal for a very long while. I will require your help for that matter. I fear that the control freak that I am, might be a tad too insensitive for her adolescent mind. You can warn me when I am a bit too demanding and you always tease me when I am full on. Please keep being honest with me, and call me Tyrant Gab when I am, so my empathy levels are always kept in check and alive.

His phone rang before Walter could give him an answer,

-Hi, Sis, is everything okay?

Gabriel put his phone on loud speaker, knowing that Walter was also eager to hear news about Caroline.

-Fine, I am at the car dealer. Got your message. I have a proposal from the dealer. As Walt is going to Australia for at least three months, he said that he could rent the car for that long instead of keeping it parked doing nothing, so that our cost could turn into gain instead. I think it is a brilliant idea, especially since Walt was looking for an income when he will come back, however, I know he does love his 306 like a baby, and the proposal does not guarantee that accidents will not happen. What do you think Gabby, your call?

Purallee looked at Walter, asking him silently his answer to the proposal. When he saw Walt's thumb going up, he replied,

-That's a W thumbs up, Caro, a winner. Go for it. How's the package?

Caroline answered,

-Alive and asleep. What's next a rent or a buy?

-A rent, Sis, just deliver to Raphael. Get the dealer to pick up the rental at uncle Raphy, that's it. Did you check the tail of the car, what's the damage?

-There's definitely a long scratch there. I tried to smooth it at the dealer, but it remains to no avail, it is there. The left back light popped in, like it used to oddly enough, like the good old times. I will deliver the package safely and inform you upon its arrival. I am going to miss Walt's departure, so give him all my love, thoughts and kisses and tell him to not worry about me too much whilst away. Big kiss, Bro.

-I will. Looking forward to your call. Big kiss, Caro.

As Gabriel turned back to Walter, ending the call, he confirmed,

-So she has been followed all the way through and could not shake them off her trailing tail. Persistent buggers, and they are observing her outside the dealer. But she spotted uncle Raphael's security men around, that was the left light mention, so we do not need to worry about her, she will be well looked after. Now, it reminds me that we need to put a code in for this room's new lock.

He and Walter went to stand by the door, and applied the agreed code in, with Walter commenting upon it,

-So the code is just for me, you and Caro, only for the three of us?

Gabriel translated the code as an answer to the question,

-Yes, it is. The three of us, makes the three in the combination, It-666, makes the one, and the other three, which are us, stand for freedom.

As he finished his sentence It-666 opened her eyes upon the room waking up from a dream, saying out loud,

-Mavericks!

Verse 19. PI's P's Pictures Perfect to a pi.

As It-666 woke up, she realised the worried eyes of Walter
Workmaster upon her, and the concerned smile drawing on Doctor
Purallee's lips. Gabriel sat back upon her bed and holding her wrist
checked her pulse, saying in a kind teasing tone,

-Back with us, Bambi, and mumbling already something to startle
us, what about mavericks? Bad dream? Now, your pulse is getting
there, picking up, to its beastly erratic way again. I dare say it sounds
better than it's almost inaudible state like it has been in the past
couple of hours. It tells me my Beast is alive and kicking...But I
rather you abstain on the kicking even if you have accumulated
reason to do so throughout your sixteen less than tender years.

Walter couldn't help his amused smile as he realised that he was
picking up all the little clues and signs from Gabriel, when he really
liked someone. He knew that to be a very rare occurrence. But this
was happening right now in front of his eyes. The usually
cool Doctor had been singing by the bedside of his patient, that
alone was a clear tale tell sign that Gabriel's heart somehow was
touched and that the ice surrounding it was melting. Walt
commented out loud,

-'Your' Beast? Well, after de-branding her as the One with
something abrasive upon her foot, it makes you, Gabriel, very much
the Samuel Maverick of her dreams. If we follow the controversy, I
do not think it was done by lack of interest, or care, on the
contrary...

The Doctor cut him short on his trail, starting considering the
pictures within his hands,

-Look who's talking? The maverick per excellence, you almost made
a job of it. Actually, thinking of it, let us correct that, you made a

life of being a maverick, full on, with no days off. Now, I remember the locksmith working on the door talking about mavericks and him, mentioning Churchill was one, when Bambi was drifting slowly to deep unconscious sleep. So I think this explains her dream pretty well. Let us focus on your work, PI. There is a lot of photos, more than I expected.

Walter grinned and looked about with unnerved confusion,

-I don't mind so much being a maverick if Winston was one. Gabriel, I didn't take all the pictures. Some are there, which, I didn't do. Do you remember, when I told you it didn't cross my mind to do some of It-666 in situ, and if it did I would not have done so? Well there are a fair few of them, exactly as I saw her for the first time, when I pulled her up from her shit-hole.

Purallee nodded at Workmaster's declaration, looking appreciatively at all the photographs, taking particular attention to the ones in question by Walter. Gabriel turned to It-666, with an inquisitive brow raised, and asked her directly, scolding,

-Bambi, is there anything you need to share upon the matter? I will not have you confusing Walter without warning. The man is already fucking damn confuse as it is, without adding some paranormal shit into the mix.

The young being smiled shyly, full of guilt, and explained in her raucous human voice,

-I wanted to help you, both, mavericks, in your framing of P. I understood you were trying to stop him, because of his trail of human sacrifices, done to the evil forces. I am deeply saddened and grieved that it inflicted the loss of Wendy upon you, which wounded you both to your core. Gabriel, I felt your tremendous pain, yesterday, when you took pictures of my appalling state, crying out that she was your life to be. I responded to your wish of in-situ pictures there and then, created them using Walter's vision of me as he found me, as I could not move away fast enough from your over pouring pain. I swallowed it. This is one result of it. There is more to come. I digest pain. The outcome is not always beneficial, but wants to be, and desperately, tries to be...

She coughed as her voice disappeared at her last words. Gabriel dropped all the photos upon the floor, seized by deep worry upon her confession. If the young Beast had truly swallowed and digested his Angelic wrath and pain there would certainly be other matters at hand to deal with rather than a few pics in the very near future. He asked in a shaken tone,

-Can you control the outcome, Beast?

But the young It-666 had no more human voice to answer him. She tried but no sounds could come out. She lifted her left hand, mimicking writing moves asking silently for a writing pad.

The incarnated Angel trying to recover handed her his pad and pen. He ordered Walter, hastily,

-Dehydration. Water, Walt, please, or better, the orange juice. Bambi is in great need of vitamins of all sorts.

Workmaster went to pour a large glass of orange juice, and having noticed Gabriel's unrest and worry, teased,

-Are you sure about giving vitamins to the so called Beast? Are you not a tad worried than she will turn all apocalyptic upon us, especially since she swallows pain, digests it and, well, pours it out again in an half hazardous manner? I wonder what could come out beneficially from the suppressed pain of an introverted man like you, Gab... A time tomb maybe, a full on apocalypse most probably?

Gabriel warned Walter strongly,

-Shut up, right now, before I fetch my bat to make you do so! I am sure about giving vitamins to Bambi, because we are here to give the girl a chance, and myself, I am becoming a maverick doing so. But she asked me to be straight with my Universal contacts about her

ID. She heard us, Walt. This brought about her suicide attempt. Suicide or not, she said we didn't know what we are dealing with by protecting her, and that I should require the help of the other Universal Agents in an honest manner regarding her. Personally I think it is another way to beg for her death, which she is still seeking. It is just suicide again. However, I can only admit that I am out of my customary depth with her. Beyond the crimes of P, we have found more than we bargained for. My pain and wrath would be ready to use the supernatural powers of that Being in order to bring P down and make him finally pay for the death of Wendy. But I cannot forget that if It-666 has restrained herself for so long, suffered so much to not be used and wants her own death, it is only for very good, valid, and apocalyptic, here is the dreaded word, reasons.

As he finished his sentence, the young Being pushed the pad back to his hands with her written answer. Walter gave her the glass of orange juice which she drank avidly. Gabriel read silently her note and passed it to Walt who read it out loud,

-'Controlling the outcomes is still very much a learning process for me. When I feel in my guts, it is going to be bad, I tried to retain them. If I can't, I make the walls around me bleed slowly, when I am completely alone. My shit-hole smelled like death because of it.'

Then Walter commented upon it,

-Gabriel, this is Amityville kind of tricks. I won't go ballistic on that if you do not. I have seen plenty of horror movies to have my heart well hung up for It-666, aka our sweet sixteen Bambi. What do you say? Can we, mavericks give her a chance? Or do we really need to answer her suicide call with the big Universal Agents cavalry?

The Doctor stood up, as Walter picked up the pictures upon the ground, and replied,

-Bleeding walls do not worry me as much as what happens when her trying to retain, control or learn to control does not occur. I promised Bambi to get help to deal with her. I can only think of

one Ange...mmh, one Agent, maverick enough, to consider It-666
like we did. But it is no given. Once his opinion is formed upon
Bambi, the girl will either live through it all or die without prayer.

Workmaster looked worryingly at Gabriel, and probed,

-You are not thinking of your uncle, Gab? You must be kidding.
Raphael knows everything inside out about laws and makes a point
of doing everything disregarding them. He is the daddy of all
mobsters. I have memories of him, making sure I would spend a
night in jail when I lost it back in the days in one of his nightclubs,
against a guy that nearly raped Caro. I also remember coming out
of jail to the news that the man was found drowned that very
morning, that me being behind bars that very night, cleared me as
the first suspect. You can't wave my suspicion that your universally
good and powerful uncle avenged his niece, somehow, maybe with
his bouncers, at some point in the very early hours that day...

Gabriel grinned widely, wickedly,

-Such ingratitude towards a man that got you out of jail as many
times as he put you in one! You are your own worst enemy Walter,
or your temper is. Whenever Raph sent you behind bars, it was for
your own safety and protection. What you have to understand is
that he truly believes that his own words are the Law, which makes
him oblivious of any States or Country laws, he happens to step in
or upon. He is a very controversial Universal Agent, but also a most
effective and influential one. If it was not for him or me, your
protection from the Universal powers would have disappeared when
you broke down six years ago, warranting you a place in a mental
institute. I am afraid to say that you are falling very much under
Uncle Raphael's wings and maverick jurisdiction. Nothing is picture
perfect, Walt. What goes around comes around. Can you give me
the complete value of pi or an approximation, from the top of your
head? Well, Uncle Raphael is unsettling enough to declaim the value
of pi to the in-cult, to great effect. Thereafter they tend to listen to
him, like he holds the entire Earth within his hands, the full circle
of life. Well, he doesn't but he knows the schemes more than
anyone else and learnt how to play with them better than all of us.

Yes, I do want and wish Uncle Raphael on board in regards to It-666. Welcome or not, I intend to seek his advice.

Walter turned to the young girl and warned her,

-Well, Beast, if you haven't seen a beast of a man, you are about to meet one in your near future.

Verse 20. Uncle Raphael: Who's the Daddy?

Caroline checked the mirror of the car: she had not lost any of her followers. She was quite happy about it for she could now make a big display out of delivering the package to her uncle. A few more turns and she was there. It was dusk when she pulled in the car park of the 'AA Club', one of many nightclubs of her infamous uncle. The place renown throughout many States as a gangster hangout, had already his red neon sign lit up. She smiled remembering the grand opening of that club, ten years ago and the bickering over its name between her then fiancée, Walter and her uncle. Walter as usual was getting on his high horse about propriety, and how deviously ironic it was to call a nightclub, a heaven for alcohol, an AA Club, to which Raphael retorted that he was a fan of black humour, but that AA, didn't stand for Alcoholics Anonymous but for Angelic Anonymous, or the double A Club, in short. Her uncle had the last word over Walter, like he usually had with anyone.

Somehow she was dreading the meeting, and the lying to her uncle part, wondering if she would ever be able to pull it off and get away with it. She stopped the engine of the car, and saw six men dressed in black suits, black shirts and matching red ties, coming out of the building, and heading towards her car in an orderly fashion. Her lips twisted in a slight smirk, as she thought seeing them, that this was her welcome comity to her uncle's bespoke Mob-land. Another man, tall and extremely fit, dressed in a bright white suit, red shirt and white tie appeared at the entrance, and made his way to her car. Caroline had no doubt that this was one henchman that had passed a few grades at her uncle's services. He opened the door for her and gallantly presented his hand to her in an affected manner,

-Mademoiselle Caroline, if you would follow me, your uncle is most anxious to see you. I believe you made a safe journey. Our security team was impressed by your driving skills. You made the package look so precious that two other cars joined the first in your pursuit.

Mastering the art of the wild goose chase, the make-believe, the cat and his mouse playfulness could only come directly from Raphael. He always speaks very highly of you.

Caroline stood out of the car, pointed to the wrapped body of Bud in the back seats, eager to get on with her job, and for any flattery to cease,

-Sorry, although I do vaguely remember you, I didn't catch your name. I would hate to make my uncle wait. The package is a little on the heavy side and needs to be handled with the utmost care, as to stay wrapped at all times, to only be revealed to Raphael's eyes.

As she finished her sentence, one after the other, eight cars pulled in the car park. She recognised immediately with some anxiety that, one car, the first to arrive, was her follower since her clinic departure this morning. The henchman smiled reassuringly to her, and opened the back seat's door for his men to pick up the package, exhibiting to Caroline that all was under control,

-Let's make this a very official delivery. Guys, you heard the cautionary advice of Mademoiselle Caroline, 'du doigté, mes enfants'. Do not be alarmed by your followers, they can only be observers. They cannot attempt anything towards you nor the package here. The contingency security arrived at the same time, ready for any actions, within our five cars. My name is Azryel Mortimer, head of security at the double A, at your service.

Caroline gaped watching the twenty black suited men with red ties, stepping out of the five black Audi, soliciting an amused grin from the henchman, who continued,

-Your uncle would never spare any expenses when it regards his niece's security. I can also assure you that those guards are the best bouncers to be found this side of the Atlantic. I thought you would never be that easily impressed Mademoiselle. Maybe 'accoutumance' to the lower standards of your ex-husband made you forget about the higher ones of your family.

Caroline saw red and snapped, thinking she had definitely stepped into Raphael's territory, full of men with opinions bought to match his,

-Mortimer, this was one comment too many. I am definitely not impressed, any more. Bring me to my uncle and your complete silence on the way would be most welcome and appreciated.

The henchman dusted his own shoulders with ostentation and raising an amused brow, replied full of arrogant politeness,

-As you wish Mademoiselle. Only here, your desires are met like orders. Pray, follow me.

Caroline could not remember one time she was as infuriated with someone, or maybe just Walter, many times with Walter. As she walked behind the man, taking a quick glance that the wrapped package was right behind her, she asked him, in a derogatory fashion,

-Do you happen to be French, Mortimer?

The henchman half turned to face her, with a wicked smile upon his lips, scolded,

-What on earth made you say that? Prejudice doesn't suit a pretty face, nor any face for that matter. My grandmother was French, and she babysat me quite often. Now, if you pardon my French, I rather shut up than talking to someone who can exhibit racist tendencies. 'Le silence est d'or, la parole est d'argent'.

She saw the man walking faster, depriving her of a chance to apologise. She mumbled for herself, half pestering,

-I am no racist, for Christ's sake, I am black like you, man.

One bouncer behind her, replied to her in a philosophical manner while carrying his load of the wrapped Bud with others,

-Racism is as widely spread as the colour of the rainbow,
unfortunately, it reaches any skin tones you can imagine. It is
actually a prejudice to believe that a white man would be more racist
than you on account to his skin colour. Like the rest of us, the poor
bugger didn't get to choose his/her parents and his/her receiving
culture at birth. Now righteousness, love, fraternity and open mind
is a culture of the heart available to all to transcend and go beyond
their disparities and differences. The question anyone should ask
themselves is if they did create boundaries in the landscape of their
hearts, like humans created boundaries all over Earth, making it
a dis-figuration, a war-zone doing so. For in reality there are no
boundaries. You can cross a river, a sea, an ocean, a mountain range,
a desert, and find your perfect home beyond them. For all you know
Mademoiselle Caroline, the ancestral genes of his grandmother
might be linked to yours, with all due respect. Have you ever read
Cavalli-Sforza? I highly recommend it. It is a sword through the
dragon of racism.

After crossing a bar, a dance floor, 'the Club', a more intimate bar, a
more cosy and plush dance floor, and the VIP zone, they finally
arrived to the penthouse part of the Club, her uncle's headquarters.
Azryel knocked upon the door, in an odd rhythmic fashion.
Caroline   thought for herself that she should have paid attention
as a girl scout and learn her Morse code, as weirdly enough, it was
still very much in use by some. The door opened by itself and she
followed Mortimer within a long mirrored corridor. This reflective
hallway was surely a new addition to the place, as she could not
recall it whatsoever. Did her uncle develop a solar ego   since she
last saw him, like Louis the fourteenth, the Sun King of 17th
century France, she wondered, or was it always there, within him,
latent? At the end of the hallway, an arched double door stood,
much higher than the one at the entrance of the penthouse.
Caroline had not noticed that the hallway was bigger at one end
from the other, but it was, she stood confused for a good minute
looking back and forth. Until the philosophical bouncer put her out
of her misery, in order to be able to move forward with the
package,

-Visual trick. The mastery is in the mirrors positioning. Your uncle designed it. Don't try to understand it, it will drive you insane.

Caroline was a little annoyed by all the cleverness around her, and felt somehow that she had to show off that she had been to university, that she was a doctor, that she was an intelligent woman, and that she could comprehend things,

-Very clever indeed, this was inspired by la 'Gallerie des glaces' of Versailles, I presume. Trust my uncle to make himself feel like a king.

Azryel coughed in his hand with exaggeration at her comment, and went by the side of the door, he waved onto the mirror and a panel within it opened, exhibiting a small ivory piano keyboard.

The philosopher chuckled and corrected Caroline,

-Presumption. Ten per cent was inspired by it, the mirrors. The other ninety are to be found in 'Willy Wonka and the Chocolate Factory' like the visual trick in a hallway and more. Now, what would you presume it tells about your uncle?

She sighed deeply, that her attempt at trying to be clever with historical references was simply being outdone by Roald Dahl and literally clever literary ones. What could it say about her uncle, that was a good question, or was it? Because, she realised that all she would end up doing would only turn out to be presumptions. Mortimer brought her back from her thoughts playing a tune upon the miniature piano, the entrance code to the black leather doors. She recognised the tune from the kid's movie and clapped her hands with delight that she knew a little something and told pathetically,

-Rachmaninoff!

Azryel turned back to her with a mocking expression upon his face, and with a graceful gesture, invited her in,

-After you, Mademoiselle. One advice: forget about presumptions, assumptions, and prejudices in front of your uncle, it will only bring you more trouble than you wish to have. He will not leave your case until you are fully free of them. That is if you wish your son to remain under your education and parentage. You will have to show him a better behaviour than you showed to us. Don't get me wrong, it is a friendly warning.

Caroline blinked a few times, a knot forming in her throat. Visiting her uncle could mean that her son could be taken away from her, because she could be judged as an unsuitable mother. She shivered uncontrollably as she stepped forward into his den. She was about to lie to that man and hoping it would be okay when just a few sentences got her into trouble and disregard by his clever bouncers. Who was she kidding? Guts, where were her guts when she needed them?

-Come on in my dearest child, and welcome back to my world. I missed you so dearly that although you expect me to home you only for the night, I made sure that I could extend your visit a little. Come and give me a kiss.

The voice came from an alcove right at the back of the open plan impressive room with amazing views of the city lights nestled down the hill. She walked towards it, and felt somehow a little reassured that all the bouncers followed her footsteps, still carrying the wrapped Bud.

At the entrance of the alcove, she froze, taking in the view of Uncle Raphael, upon a large black leather cushion, in a lotus position, eyes closed, hands resting upon his knees with fingers lifted and folded in awkward ways. He looked so young, so healthy, so in tune with his body and spirit, and yet so frightening all at once, like a living human mystery. Who could believe the man was seventy-six years old, when he could stretch his body into unbelievably hard yoga postures, when his face showed hardly any wrinkles, when his full set of bright white teeth could give you his gloriously wicked smile at any time? Dressed in loose black linen trousers, and a burgundy red cotton T-shirt, with his feet bare, his toned muscles, his salt and pepper hair tidied in dread locks that reached his waist, and most of all, his rare complexion, he was still very much a looker for any woman alive. His vert-de-gris eyes opened all of a sudden and he asked,

-Is it a dare to stare or a stare to dare, that you are uncomfortably enjoying, my child? I will not have you making miles to remain boringly silent at my sight and sides. Speak.

Caroline tried to recall her wits about her, and finally told,

-Actually it is a bit of both, uncle, but there is more anxiety to it than enjoyment. As Gabriel must have told you, we are in great need of your help. I delivered my package, safely, thanks to your intervention, and in a big displaying fashion. Now, all I wish for is for you to deliver your help to Gabriel's requests, and for me, now that my message was transmitted to return to my humble home and tend to my son as if nothing had happened to our lives.

The bouncers deposited the wrapped Bud at their feet, with care and stood by it waiting for their orders. The henchman stood forward, and came by Uncle Raphael, whispering a few words by his ear. Seeing that, Caroline nervously shivered. Her unrest was noticed by her uncle who stood up in a swift move, and strolled towards her, stopping right in front of her scrutinising her face. She bowed her gaze down. Raphael lifted her chin up and forced her to look into his unusual eyes, making a negative and disappointed noise with his tongue against his palate, not unlike showing his disapproval to a small toddler,

-Caroline, you are breaking my heart, my child. I thought I taught you infinitely better. You drove well, too well. You talk shit so much that all my men are eager to leave the room and wipe their feet off your security. To make demands my dear niece, true humbleness of heart is a must. I have just been told by my chief of security that I have a wolf in my sheepfold, and it saddens me to the core. I trust my sensitive Azryel like death, he never fails to show up in time, he never fails to be unforgiving, he never lies or attempts to.

Could it be more unnerving? She thought. Caroline trembled all over and took his hand off from her chin. She apologised meekly, and looked for an escape, just a good long moment on her own so she could regain her composure,

-Toilet! Very desperate, I am afraid. The long drive, I have been sitting upon it literally.

Her uncle stood aside full of irony and contempt, and asked the philosophical bouncer and another one,

-My dear Asha, would you trouble yourself to show my niece the commodities. Haurvatat, arrange for some nibbles and light food to be brought in before the little bird fake a fainting spell upon us, before we have finished with her interrogation. Now, let us look at the package. The poor old dog needs to wake up at some point.

Caroline ran to Bud before her uncle could reach him. She removed the blanket carefully and stroked the Great Dane as her uncle knelt by her, she ordered quickly and secretively to the dog,

-Wake up, Bud, wake up, good boy.

The Great Dane's eyes flicked open, and he started to move. Within a few seconds, he was up and wagging his tail to Caroline, licking her face clean of any make-up. Raphael stood up, a winning smile upon his face. He tapped the dog's head and put one of his hand underneath the dog's sternum and stroked him there extremely slowly. He nodded, before asking Caroline casually,

-I didn't know Gabriel had worked out a powerful anaesthetic that could wear out upon order? I am very interested in his secret recipe that can lower the heart rate of a living creature to hibernation point. My dear, dear child, your are so staying with me until you spill the beans. Uncle Raphael is pining for information upon what is really going on, right now, so don't let me use pins upon you, Doll, to reveal anything, for it would have a direct effect upon Gabriel, Walter and... also, in my benevolence, your beautiful body instead of your son's one. Call it voodoo, vodou, or the original vodun, I find it most effective upon any subjects. Now, you can run to the loo before the session starts, for it is not for the faint-hearted. Or, you can reveal all to Daddy Raphael, and be forgiven for your willingness to lie to me. Trust me when I say this, my Love, with the choice upon your hands, Gabriel will forgive you to give in to me, for if you don't, he will hurt so badly through and through that he will manage to beg you to tell all by telepathy. What is it to be?

Caroline stood up only to collapse before him, with a faintness that was very much real.

Verse 21. Tell me all about It?

Raphael worryingly knelt by his collapsed niece, checking her pulse, and demanded,

-Azryel, come, Caroline is properly out of it. She is not faking it. Feel her pulse and then check the Great Dane, the last thing she touched, and tell me if you notice something odd, as I do. Asha, you followed her car almost since the start, did my niece stop for the commodities on her long journey? Did she eat something on the way? She is extremely weak right now.

As Azryel obeyed and took the wrist of the fainted woman within his long fingered hands, the philosophical bouncer, Asha, replied,

-Her only halt was at the car dealer, Raphael.

The incarnated Archangel Raphael lifted his niece within his arms and took her to a large cream leather sofa within his impressive room. He deposited her carefully upon it, and turned to his henchman waiting for the confirmation of his suspicion. Azryel was now by the dog, his hands stroking the length of his body silently, insisting upon the sternum, heart and lungs of the animal. He nodded for himself, stood up and announced talking in the angelic tongue,

-Someone powerful knows how to play with life. I can feel the energies used upon the dog. There are deadly, yet controlled to harmless levels, nothing that cannot be undone by the learn-ed. Raphael, you were meant to originally wake that dog up. However, I can feel an order given to your niece to do it. The human had not our strength to handle that type of energy, hence her collapse. I believe someone tried to send you a warning, one of an unusual nature.

Azryel came by the sofa and continued,

-I can undo it. Caroline in her state of weakness will sleep otherwise until tomorrow morning and wake up with the sun as if nothing happened.

Uncle Raphael's eyes glowered with great anger and told in a dangerously cool voice, as he fetched the mobile phone from the jeans pocket of his niece,

-I have no appreciation for any kind of warnings, friendly or not, especially one which affects a member of my family. Let me have a word or two with that damn Angel Gabriel before I damn him, before we wake up his sister. He will know how I feel about him playing with life and death.

Azryel corrected him, and advised,

-There are no angelic powers over that dog. It is not Gabriel who played with life. It's something beyond my capacity to determine. All I know is that it is not human. I feel it extremely dangerous, infinitely aware, and kind without measure.

Raphael pointed to his unconscious niece and almost shouted, full of growing wrath towards the unknown new powerful player who dared to warn him, Archangel Raphael. What was the warning about? He will have to find out and the answer was with Gabriel, he was sure of it.

-Kind! Do you call that kind?

Azryel shrugged his shoulders and held Caroline's hand within his. His long fingers glowed with sparks of blue electricity that he sent to her body waking her up doing so, slowly but surely, he replied,

-I call that very kind. Instead of Sleeping Beauty, Raphael, you could have a cadaver, right now upon your sofa. It has the power to kill all yet it doesn't. I have the same power, and I unkindly obey to my orders, without exceptions, all in 'good' time...

More upset by Azryel' s answer, Raphael put the phone to his ear, calling out Gabriel. It was not long before a warm voice picked up the call,

-Hi, Sis, how are you, babe? Did the delivery go well? How is Uncle Raph?

-Hello, Gabriel, how do you do? I can tell you how is uncle Raphael as you have him on the line, right now, he is very angry, and utterly upset with your Archangelic arse. The delivery went awesomely well. However our little bird, Caroline, collapsed putting her hands upon it, or soon afterwards. Inexplicable or is it?

A very concerned Gabriel replied in tongue like his uncle,

-How is she? Caro has done a twenty four hours shift at the clinic, yesterday. She had roughly three hour's worth of sleep in all.

Raphael grinned and scolded,

-Now, there is more than lack of sleep to the whole affair, Gabriel. Azryel is waking our Sleeping Beauty up. For the Angel of Death to recognise dangerously deadly powers similar to his all over my niece and your precious package do not enthuse me whatsoever. He also spoke about a warning. I do not think you know how well I do appreciate to be warned, in any form... It is something I will have to show you physically I am afraid, just to make sure the experience makes you feel how displeased I am, more palpable. Unless you come clean and tell me what you are hiding.

He suddenly heard Gabriel talking to someone else in a very annoyed fashion, within the room he was at his clinic, in tongue,

-For crying out loud, Bambi, did you try to warn my uncle?! Are you asking to be killed, again? Bloody fucking suicidal Being! What did you do to Caro? Did you harm her?

Straining his ear, Raphael listened carefully to a weak answer given to his nephew in tongue,

-I did warn him. I have never ceased to ask for my death, Gabriel and will never cease to do so unless I can be controlled to do only good. Caroline is safe, I gave her only the most needed rest and sleep she needed after having worked and strive so hard, just a deep beauty sleep. I would never harm anyone. Raphael needed to be aware of my existence sooner rather than later.

Then Gabriel finally answered him, his voice shaking slightly,

-Walter found a Being, marked as the Beast in P's bunker. Uncle, she is powerful enough to be the dreaded Antichrist. But you have to assess It-666 as I did. If I could, I would beg for her life. She is a good Being, uncle, desperately good. The Beast has repeatedly asked to be slayed and I cannot bring myself to do it. Her warning is an open invitation for you to claim her life.

Raphael shook his head in disbelief and calmly announced,

-Thank you for sharing what I just got myself into by helping you hide It-666. It is most appreciated yet so delayed that you owe me and will be held to repay. If there was no warning would you have told me?

Gabriel confessed,

-Yes, eventually, I would have, only because I was pushed by It to do so.

Raphael's brows rose, as he asked concerned,

-Does the Being has some convincing power over you, Archangel Gabriel?

-To some extent yes, uncle. She swayed me into being open, straight and truthful about her existence to other Angelic Beings.

-Right. Your creature intrigued me enough to make a move. Expect me tomorrow. Do not worry about Caroline. She is exhausted, but Azryel is tending to her. I will make sure she has something to eat, a good rest and bring her back to you, personally. By the way, how is Walt?

Gabriel responded, in a relieved manner,

-Thank you, Raphael, for your time. Walt is good, in the clear and fond of It. He wants to give a chance to her sixteen years old self, bring her up as his own daughter...

Raphael spat at him,

-Does the bloody man have any inkling that he is asking to raise the Antichrist?

Gabriel grinned and replied laughing heartily,

-Yes, he is fully acquainted with the matter and does not give a shit. I don't either and I am ready to give him a hand. This could only be very damn interesting...

Raphael cut him short into his sentence, and hung up,

-Or very damn apocalyptic! See you both, fools, and your Antichrist tomorrow.

Uncle Raphael turned to his niece who looked at him slightly bewildered to have heard him talked in such a strange language. He smiled kindly to her and explained,

-A coded tongue between your brother, me and my men. So I have heard that you were a little overworked Caroline. What a shame! But I am sure your starving self could not refuse a three course meal with all the trimmings to your dotting uncle? Your brother filled me in upon the Beast. So you can relax and give me a little more details over dinner. An intriguing package from Walter that your brother's clinic is harbouring right now. I am eager to see it, It-666. Well, to answer your solicitation from earlier, I can provide my help to your brother, most certainly, but for you, both, but also Walter and your son, now, being acquainted with the Antichrist, I am afraid any return to normality, to a normal humble life, is absolutely gone to dust. Gab and Walt seemed to embrace the fact. Have you had time to adjust to it, Caro? And do you think your son will?

Caroline tried to sit up and was helped by Azryel. She looked at him a little annoyed by his intervention. He gave her an amused apologetic smile and told,

-Unfortunately for you and me, I happened to be the first-aid person in the house. You just passed out upon us. I will lay my helping hands off you, presently, most happily. Asha, would you help her to the rest room. Mademoiselle Caroline, all you need now is food and thorough rest.

The Philosopher offered his arm to her. Caroline stood up and took it gratefully. She looked back and apologised to the henchman,

-Thank you, Mortimer. I am sorry for offending you. I think we got off on the wrong track. I wish to wipe the slate clean and start all over again.

Azryel grinned wickedly as he answered in a cool polite manner,

-You would be astounded by the number of humans who begged the very same of me. Unfortunately, it is just wishful thinking. I do not give second chances Mademoiselle Caroline. You did not see eye to eye with me and I absolutely do not with you. Thank you for your apology, this is welcomed. You can keep your thanks however, if it was not my duty and job, I would not look after you.

Caroline couldn't help shivering and walked away silently by Asha. She wondered if she was such a bad person. She never felt at such a loss with anyone. What was up with that henchman? When they left the main room, the bouncer turned to her and showed her the rest room in another large hallway. As if he knew what she was feeling and thinking, he told her in a friendly tone,

-The less you think about Azryel Mortimer, the better you will feel Miss Caroline. His profession doesn't allow him to grow a heart. He does not do forgiveness, never did, never will. He is at odds with all, not just you.

When she returned in the main room, she saw her uncle and his henchman in deep discussion, in their coded language upon a huge balcony. One bouncer was standing protecting the double glass door to the balcony, his arms folded. She sat quietly upon the sofa, as Asha brought to her a crystal carafe of water and matching water tumbler. The fact that she did not have to lie any more and could be open to her uncle somehow had lifted a huge weight of her shoulders. She was still very concerned about her behaviour. To have them think that she was a possible racist, shamed her more than anything. Deep down she knew it was far from being the case, and call it tiredness, silent tears started rolling upon her cheeks, unchecked. Asha without a word gave her his red handkerchief before heading to the balcony. The bouncer stood aside to let him pass and closed carefully the double doors behind him.

Caroline holding the silk tissue was astounded that in this day and age, some could still have that dainty piece of clothing. A lovely frankincense perfume came from it as she wiped her tears. She noticed black capitals letters entwined and embroidered within it, 'AA'. She wondered if it stood for Asha something, his surname possibly starting with A, or the name of the club and if all bouncers were provided with that delicate item in their pocket, if it was only the utmost quaint detail to their uniform, or for the odd lady's tears they might meet upon their jobs. She smiled finally thinking that her uncle presided over a very well educated and distinguished to a T Mob-Bouncing-Land. She saw Asha talking to her uncle and his henchman then Azryel gave her an unfathomable long look, before addressing himself back to Asha, who came back to the room almost immediately.

He presented her his arm again, and invited her to follow him,

-I have been told to show you to your room. You will be able to retrieve yourself a little in there. The dinner will be ready in an hour and a half. You can have a good shower in the meantime, but Azryel recommended me to run the Jacuzzi instead for you, on sea mode, with Dead sea salt, lavender and rosemary essence to restore your tired muscles. Forty-five minutes to one hour minimum in it, will manage to relax your strained mind from all the events of today and yesterday, he said. He has no doubt that with a good hearty meal, you will manage to sleep like a baby tonight, especially if you tell all to your uncle without reservation, as it will bring you peace of mind too.

Caroline got up and taking the arm most willingly confided,

-I must admit that what he says sounds good and that for once I might just do as I am told. That was kind of him now, wasn't it? I am sure he cannot be that unforgiving.

Asha gave a sad smile, as he replied,

-And you would be wrong, Miss Caroline. Azryel has an acute knowledge of bodies. When he helped you from your fainting spell, he assessed yours. He knows exactly how to make them, and how to restore them in a very frightening manner. However even if his cold advice is always devoid of kindness and feelings, sound it remains and to do as he says always goes a long way, especially if we don't want to see him cross our paths.

Caroline stepped in the luxury en-suite allocated to her, as Asha went to the bathroom to prepare the Jacuzzi. She was more than happy that she did not end up as a voodoo pin doll, that her brother gave the crucial bit of information about It-666 to her uncle, and that the bouncer Asha was tending to her welfare rather than the unsettling Azryel Mortimer. She picked up his conversation, and stood at the entrance of the bathroom watching his every move,

-You sound grim, Asha, when you talk about your chief of security. Do you fear him?

The bouncer turned on the Jacuzzi's waving system muffling his answer by its noise,

-I sound grim, because it is grim, Miss Caroline. He 'earned' to be called the 'Grim Reaper', and yes, I do fear him, like anyone should.

Caroline blinked a few times with disbelief at the strongly built bouncer, thinking that if she had that amount of muscles upon her she would fear no one on Earth. She could see him measuring carefully the Dead sea salt, the various herbal essences before pouring them in the warm water of the Jacuzzi. He explained his actions to her to give her an inkling of the expertise of Azryel,

-Your perfect bath at this moment in time is a science, Miss Caroline, courtesy of the 'Grim Reaper'. You are recovering still. One drop of lavender in excess and you will sleep at the dinner table to the disappointment of your uncle, who is eager to know more about It. One drop of rosemary missing, and it might not revive your mind to the perfect level to be probed to remember every little detail by Raphael. The salts are to revive your circulation and muscles, so that you will not collapse again in front of us during your coming interrogation. This is the extent of his kindness. I will leave you to it, and will knock upon your door at dinner time. In the walking closet, you will find a huge array of clothing at your size. However, your uncle expects you to dress casually for dinner, in what makes you the most comfortable.

Before Asha left the bathroom, he opened a jar of dried red rose petals and threw a couple of handfuls in the water of the Jacuzzi. Caroline asked him quizzically, totally thrown out of countenance by the secret recipe to make her talk,

-And what are those for? Is it another loosening tongue device?

The bouncer smiled kindly and whispered winking to her in a friendly fashion,

-My input. It just smells nice and heavenly. But if you do practice meditation, you will find them useful to relieve the stress that has been imposed upon you. I am all for looking upon any heart chakra, your Anahata. It is a beautiful Sanskrit word which even Walter

Workmaster, still your husband at heart, would love the meaning of.

Caroline repeated it as if tasting the unusual word, and queried,

-Anahata. What does it mean? And thank you for everything Asha. You are a very good man.

Asha told before closing the door of the room,

-Unhurt, un-struck, unbeaten. Walter would want you to follow your heart at all times.

Caroline stood for a second, completely dazed, repeating the Sanskrit word like a mantra before stepping out of her clothes and into the welcoming warm scented water of the Jacuzzi. She closed her eyes listening to her heart beats, growing more peaceful after every minute passing.

Verse 22. Eat It All.

Dressed with understated elegance, in a baby blue wrapped dress floating below her hips to her knees gracefully, Caroline felt much better and more relaxed as she followed the security guard Asha back to the main room to have dinner with her uncle.

She saw Raphael trying to order the Great Dane of Walter about to no avail. When ordered to sit the dog would lay on the ground, and if laid upon the ground already he would stand up right away. Azryel Mortimer, seated upon the leather cream sofa nonchalantly, couldn't contain his ironic laugh at Raphael's fruitless attempts. However as soon as he spotted Caroline, his smile disappeared, his face becoming deadly serious, he stood up politely and warned Raphael of her presence within the room.

Her uncle turned to her with a sigh full of desperation,

-Walter's dog is a beautiful one, but also the most useless and stupid, I must say. How long will I have to look after it? It needs complete retraining! But I can afford it.

The Great Dane rushed to Caroline, wagging his tail at her. She put her hand upon his head and made him follow her without any struggle. As she stood before her uncle, she corrected him by a simple demonstration. As she snapped her fingers together, the dog sat by her, in an almost statuesque position, and explained,

-The dog is fully trained. But Bud was trained by Walter. Which means he will only answer to him, as the traditional orders do not apply to him in the usual fashion. You have a month to work those out Uncle Raphael, but I would be very disappointed if a spell in your dominion means that our Bud becomes an ordinary dog.

Azryel asked all of a sudden, kneeling by the dog, his wicked smile back upon his face,

-Frustrating Workmaster, as always! Which training method did he employ?

Caroline answered him, worried by his peaked interest,

-Purely and simply Pavlovian.

Azryel tried a few words, falsely at random, watching carefully the effects upon the Great Dane, and stated,

-Classical conditioning, Raphael. Good old Walter just messed up with the words and substituted the real orders he wants by gestures. If you let me keep that dog overnight, I will know his control pattern and reflexes and we will know how to order him about the Workmaster' s way. I would not spoil his amusing frustrating work upon his dog, I respect it. I haven't laugh as much for a while.

Raphael looked at Caroline with desperation, commenting,

-Right, your Walter, even not present has managed to make me look like a fool in my own home for a good half an hour. You couldn't marry someone normal, could you? Azryel, as long as you understand twisted human behaviours along with animal' s ones, I will gladly let you take charge of that bloody dog. By the way, I do like that breed, and if you do fancy training unusual guard dogs that look the part, Azryel, I would welcome about five to eight puppies of those, either blue, grey or glistening black.

Azryel stood up raising his eyebrows deeply amused,

-Yeah, right, half an hour of Raphael with a damn dog and I end up with the tall order of eight puppies to raise into guard dogs. I put that into the account of 'Walter Workmaster' s hearts laundry', cleaning who he can reach in mysterious ways, like a single 'Bud', making softies as he goes along without knowing.

Uncle Raphael gave a side glance and a wink at Asha, enjoined his niece to a lovely carefully laid table in the middle of the room, and replied to his henchman,

-Well, something is sprouting in your chest, most definitely, Azryel. I did not order. I proposed to your own will. And from seeing Walter's dog, you, as well, are ready to raise eight guard dogs out of a possible minimum of five... Your own choice went for the highest number of puppies... Hmmm... As long as I do not end up with hell dogs at the end of your training, I would love to see this. Dinner is there. Let's eat.

Caroline sat next to her uncle while Asha was on her left and Azryel sat opposite her, at the square table of four. She smirked at the candelabra giving a romantic and intimate look upon the lovely table. She realised that they were the only ones left in the room, and that all doors were closed. Asha dished out the first course from a porcelain soupiére, into the soup bowls carefully. It smelt delicious. Caroline was famished and looked at all the men with anticipation for the polite go-ahead, we can all eat signal. Her uncle scrutinised her with a condescending smile and asked softly,

-Do you still pray before a meal, my child?

Caroline looked upon them all with frustration. She just wanted to dig in, in peace, and only answer the rumbling call of her stomach. She waved her head negatively to her uncle, and explained, in her simplest terms,

-I have no faith, Uncle, just love to give, like Walter.

Raphael sighed deeply, and replied,

-That is a good enough answer, child, you are welcome to my food. Start eating as long as you are thankful for it.

Caroline beamed to him her most genuine smile, before diving her silver spoon in the fragrant paprika, blue point crab and sweetcorn broth,

-Most thankful, uncle, I am starving beyond belief. Yet, Walter took
Micky and me to the pancake place by the clinic before school this
morning. I guess it was the car chase and skipping lunch that
knotted my belly in such a way. Come to my home, and I will return
the favour, with my humble cooking.

Azryel broke a loaf of bread and distributing it, told as a matter of
fact,

-I hate misapplied use of words. 'Humble' does not describe you,
Mademoiselle Caroline, as much as 'humbled' or more accurately, a
rich brat descent to a rag rat. 'Bon Appétit'.

As she took the morsel of bread presented by him, her gaze
lowered painfully, unable to sustain his dark green one. However her
voice rose, almost strong and joyful,

-Thank you, Mortimer. Your Jacuzzi-bath-spa recipe did me a world
of good. However, I doubt it will turn me around and make all my
words good and useful. The wonderful thing about rats and rags is
that when you reach that low there is no more fear of falling further
down. The only way left is up.

Raphael smiled and advised,

-Interesting point. I can see that Azryel has managed to get on your
tits, Babe. He has that effect somehow with everyone. But I'd rather
you made sure that your words are good enough and useful to us.
As unfortunately, my henchman can show you how a rat can
fall further down, by removing any rags it holds onto. He can show
any rats a bad time with great pleasure, from a gutter trip to a river
drowning trip, to a stripping rags, flesh and muscles trip. Palatable to
none but his taste! Do you really want to cater for his taste-buds
tonight?

Caroline looked with dismay at her uncle, struck by his clear
warning. If she was not so starving, and not shitting herself with
fear, she would have stood up and thrown the massive soup
container upon Azryel' s lap or face, whichever would hurt more.

But she tried to remain as impassive as she could and dipped the bread into her soup with shaky fingers, as she finally answered,

-I intend to remain in one piece for my son and Walt, thank you very much, uncle. I will talk. Do not worry about that, without any pin cushion torture or drowning one, for that matter. I just wonder how both of you can sleep at night?

Raphael grinned wickedly and replied amused,

-I don't. I sleep during the day.

Caroline gave him her most irresistible yet unwilling smile and shook her head in disapproval. Her querying eyes remained transfixed by the deep seriousness of the henchman's dark gaze, as he crushed a large crab claw apart within one of his hands, making a chilling noise doing so, as he dared to smile back to her with his answer,

-I can never sleep. Done far too much to ever be allowed to do so.

An unnerved Caroline ate a chunk out of her dipped bread, then with her mouth full in a very impolite manner, commented,

-That's very disturbing. You do realise that don't you, Mortimer? No human can survive without sleep for very long without going insane. That would explain a lot.

Azryel ate the crab meat straight from the claw, with his hands, licking his long fingers regularly, in an unconcerned and annoying fashion, his intense gaze maintaining the one of Caroline,

-That I am inhuman and insane, those are facts, and not to dwell on. Friendly warning, number two.

Caroline said across the table, and handed her crab claw to him,

-Blast! Stop licking your fucking fingers. Get some meat out of my food, so I can stop looking at you with ravenous eyes, mad henchman. I beg you, please. And just for the record, I am well past beyond warnings. I already love a mad man. And I truly hope you lot can help my rat of a husband, my Walt, and my big Bro.

The three men laughed out loud, and Azryel took the claw, broke it in one go within his palm and spread carefully the meat upon a little white plate which he handed back to Caroline. He told in a soft encouraging fashion,

-Well. At least we just had a few truthful words from you, Mademoiselle. Carry on, please, we are most eager to know about It-666.

Caroline's eyebrows sagged with great sadness and told,

-I never saw such a withdrawn, hurt and tortured living being. I threw up when I saw her appalling state. Walt said he cried when he first saw her. Her stench was unbelievable.

Raphael nodded and asked,

-What was the first reaction of Gabriel?

She blinked a few times and recalled herself back to the unwrapping of It-666. She answered,

-Gabriel has never been big on the emotion all his life, but he had tears in his eyes, uncle, and he remained speechless. When Walter stepped back in the room, Gabriel's eyes turned to him for an answer, an explanation to what he was seeing, yet he stayed silent.

She turned her spoon in the soup, thoughtfully, a few times before adding,

-Have you seen pictures of survivors of the holocaust, the grim naked, skeletal humans, shadow of themselves yet still alive, although barely? If you can picture that, you will picture Bambi as we saw her.

Raphael grinned,

-Bambi. I heard Gabriel talking to a so called 'Bambi' over the phone. Is this how he has dubbed the Beast?

Azryel gave his wicked smile, commenting,

-Sweet! He always had a good sense of humour.

While Asha frowned his eyebrows, and told as a matter of fact,

-If one recalls the beginning of 'Bambi', and the birth of a special prince emphasis of it, it actually gives me a little chill down my spine, knowing it is the Antichrist's nick name.

Raphael strained his memory a little and blinking a few times after a short while whispered,

-I see... Very clever. Very chilling and scary, indeed, yet so ironically cute, I must applaud my nephew upon that one. Between us, here is the approved code name for the Beast, Bambi. She does answer to it too. Am I right?

Finishing her soup, Caroline replied,

-She does. She prefers it to Beast or It-666. It came about because of Walt bringing odd things to the clinic, from a deer ran over by his drink driving to a politician with his arse pelleted like Swiss cheese. Gabby said he would prefer those two alternatives to the Antichrist. The deer option sank into Bambi as a joke. I liked the way Gabby explained her name to Micky, because she was found in the woods by her dad, because she could not walk and because of her big eyes too big for her starved being.

Azryel finishing his own bowl of soup repeated,

-She cannot walk?

Caroline nodded and pushing her bowl away answered,

-Hip dislocation. The girl has been tortured regularly for eight years, I understood, put away afterwards, in her cage, in her shit hole, under a pentagram, probably made of human blood, and she was not even fed.

Azryel stood up and picking up the empty soup bowls from the table, put them upon a nearby trolley. He stated coldly,

-The girl is still alive therefore she ate.

Caroline sighed deeply, and revealed,

-Yes, she did. Gabriel assessed the girl all night and found out she survived upon a diet of rats.

Raphael smirked,

-Nice! Fancy being an Antichrist, guys?

Asha laughed and took the next course from another trolley by him, displaying the dishes upon the table. Lamb chops, pork ribs, and barbecue chicken wings grilled to perfection, made Caroline's mouth watered instantly. She could not care less for the delicious roasted red pepper stuffed with turmeric pilau rice. She tucked into the meat greedily without a word. As her teeth worked their way around ribs after ribs, gnawing cartilages noisily, she realised that Azryel was looking at her very intensely. She grew uncomfortable under his stare, acknowledging, that with the voracity that she displayed, her ladylike manners had totally disappeared only to be replaced by her carnivorous rapacious self. Azryel finally broke his silence, spelling out what bothered him, as he put a few lamb chops upon his plate,

-If one educated woman can display such bestiality eating cooked meat, one can wonder how the Beast actually ate her rats. First she had to kill them, which would involve, hunting, luring, and the 'coup de grace'. Second comes the butchery part of it, if there was any. Did she ritualise her killing and eating habits? Survival instincts do not die with education. A man can turn into a cannibal in particular circumstances. Our cute so called Bambi has learnt to kill with her own hands from a very young age. Whatever attempts Gabriel and Walter will try into civilising her Being will only result in making her instincts hide until they rise again at the first urge.

Caroline shivered at his comments, feeling that they might all be very right indeed, yet she was eager to contradict him, not only because her appalling eating manners had provoked his dark reflections, but also because she knew a little about the subject,

-The girl hates killing anything. If you could see how she is just skin and bones, you would realise on your own that she doesn't eat extremely often even with the capacity to do so. She did let herself starve, up until she has to eat to survive and only then she would make one kill. It-666 does not have to hunt, nor lure an animal to her cage. She controls animals. They come to her. You should have seen Bud's reaction to her. Gabriel said she has the same power that King Solomon possessed. My sceptical Walt put her to the test by opening a window and daring her to call in the birds from outside. She did. It was unbelievable. She didn't utter a sound, yet the birds came flocking upon the window sill. So when she wanted to finally eat, a rat would come to her silent calling and she would stroke it until it slept and then she would make its little heart stop beating. She also can combust things by looking at them or touching them. She cooked their flesh within her hands. As I said, and Gabriel told me, she despises killing and hurting, given the choice, now that it is possible, with us, she wants to be a vegetarian and I will be in charge of developing an adequate veg diet for a growing teenager like her. You spoke about circumstances, given the possibility of being civilised, Bambi is embracing it with all her heart, that is if anyone will let her live long enough to do so.

Raphael commented,

-That is quite an apology on her behalf that you just made Caroline. She has definitely make an impression upon you all. She impressed me by making you pass away in front of my eyes, using the very same sleeping to death skill you described. She can time it, she can use a medium to carry it further, in this instance, she used the dog, she can lower it to a harmless level, like the big deep diving sleep, she gave you and Bud. Now, Azryel, what did you make of that?

The henchman smiled and told laconically,

-Most instructive and fascinating. However, let's not dive the little bird too deep upon the subject.

Raphael nodded in agreement, as well as Asha. Caroline felt at a total loss into what was said and hinted upon. She tried to argue with what her uncle had implied,

-I fainted because I was starving, tired beyond belief, scared that my son would be taken away from me, and terrified at your marked will to torture me to speak, and in doing so, using me as a 'medium', the voodoo doll, as you called it, to hurt my big Bro, and my Walt. This my dear uncle was too much for me, it had nothing to do with Bambi!

Raphael whistled amused and shook his head in a disapproving fashion,

-Spitting fire at my table, my child, this is asking for trouble. I would not mind asking Azryel to correct your table manners, or just you for that matter.

Caroline pushed her plate in front of her, and looked in desperation to the three men. Then, with almost begging eyes, she pleaded her case directly to Azryel Mortimer, and Raphael,

-I only said the truth as I lived it at my door. You can't frighten people the way that you do without consequences. I am a weak fucking woman and I fucking fainted. And if I had my normal day, my normal night, a smaller shift, less adrenaline, fear and anxiety, a little more food earlier, I would have been my stronger self who would have shown you my two fingers in a rude fashion. Correct me if you will for being honest but what would be the purpose? Teaching me to lie, and be nice when I feel that I am being stepped on, and trampled upon regardless of any feelings I may harbour. You can't possibly put the constant threat of torture upon my mind, and expect me to say great, I am very happy about that my dear uncle, let's get on with it! You must be joking. That's wrong! Honestly, how do you want me not to speak my mind about it at some point.

She giggled pitifully and tears prickled in the corners of her eyes. Azryel stood up, started clearing the table, and told in an appeasing and reassuring fashion,

-I will not touch your body in a torturing way even if ordered to, Mademoiselle Caroline. I can hear Workmaster through you. You made your point and your case, vividly clear and it is a valid one. However, and my only correction, is this, your uncle was right about It-666 affecting you through the dog. You are right and told the truth, and I quote you to show your own limitation, 'As you lived at your door'. I know what he said to be so for having assessed both you and the dog. But we also do know the fact is certain for the Beast, herself admitted to it to Gabriel, over the phone, she wanted to give you a nice rest after all your hard work, with no true harm in mind. If the dog had to be told to wake up, in order to make Gabriel's plan work, for you, it was much gentler, by sun rise tomorrow after a good night sleep, you would have woken up by yourself. It was very safely done, with your welfare in mind.

Caroline looked upon him with slight confusion. Maybe the henchman had kindness after all, she dared to think. His comments were picked up by Raphael, who closed his hand into a fist and hammered the table once and soundly, and demanded,

-Azryel, I order and you obey without discussion. How good would you be otherwise?

The henchman carrying on taking the empty dishes, shrugged his shoulders and replied with a huge grin upon his face,

-I think it would make me very good, very good indeed, to all, but probably not to you.

Asha couldn't help smiling back and told with utter disbelief,

-What got into you, Az? You are a born torturer.

Azryel filled the glass of all with more red wine before confessing,

-All I know is someone was born to kill and doesn't. All I know is
that Gabriel has a civilised Beast under his roof, who has gently put
someone to sleep soundly just to ask us to kill her. All I know is that
I will be asked to do the task if it has to be done, like any torturing
around this house, or any punitive killing. And all I want to do is if I
am a born torturer, is to try the ways of the Beast, and see if they
truly work, to experiment them upon me the harshest one there is
around, if I can be...

Raphael sighed deeply, and finished his sentence,

-With a heart. You will end up with the same conscious turmoil,
begging for your own death.

Asha stood up all of a sudden, stating, while dishing out the dessert
to everyone,

-There is the order. And Death has to be. Azryel, willing or not you
have to cut it, otherwise we as a whole, will have to do it.

Caroline blinked a few times feeling utterly lost in translation. She
was actually scared to comprehend what they said. It raised so many
questions to her tired mind. She wanted to argue, fight, fend and at
the same time put her head on a pillow and forget all she heard that
evening. Thinking of Walter kneeling by her, his head on her lap
crying and begging, like he had the previous night, she whispered at
first but then her voice grew stronger as she spoke,

-Walter cried out to see good hearts, last night. I feel like doing the
same right now. Forgive me if I am wrong. Why do we make the
choice for someone? Why do we think or assume they should do
this or that? Why do we remove their freedom of choice? Why do

we pressure them? This morning, my Walt said something that touched me, deep down. He asked me to make my own judgement upon the Beast. My very own judgement. He was the first to meet her, and had a good opinion of her by then. Gabriel had spent the night tending to her, and had a very thorough and opinionated view on her. For me, it would have been easy to dismiss my own judgement and rely on them, in the belief and faith that they knew best. He asked me to rely on my own observations and interactions with her, and not theirs. Like him I do not believe someone is born bad or good from the start, but that everyone has the potential to be either given the chance and upon the circumstances. One has the choice to lead his/her own life as he/she chooses. Azryel is no born torturer and the Beast is called so only by us and is in fact a very lost, downcast, and beaten up supernatural being. Like Walter, I plead to give someone the opportunity and the chance to express who they truly are or who they want to be. And like him, I would plead for not beating anyone to a pulp at any random point.

Raphael tapped his fingers in an annoyed fashion upon the table, and told in a commanding tone,

-My dear child, it is well past your bedtime. Eat your pudding and no more talking. Then off to bed. I will not have you spreading the seeds of Workmaster' s sedition at my table, in the presence of my most useful men.

Caroline gazed alternatively at Asha and Azryel. One was totally impassive while the other looked intensely and smiled kindly at her. She picked up her dessert spoon and dived it into the banana split ice cream. She shook her head and whispered as if for herself, but to her uncle,

-You do know how to make someone feel like a wayward child. I guess I am definitely not fitting into your world anymore. Anyhow I feel like it. I went astray, and will remain so.

Raphael grinned and replied harshly,

-That is what you get for going with a Stray.

Asha commented in a soothing fashion,

-Following the way of the heart is not going astray, Caroline. Workmaster is a good man, in comparison, this house is the one harbouring the dogs, the guard dogs, the pack with laws that goes beyond your understanding.

Azryel and Raphael looked at each other laughing. Her uncle quizzed,

-House of dogs, Asha?

The bouncer nodded with a wicked grin silently and positively.

Uncle Wrath's henchman Azryel took a flask from his jacket, poured alcohol upon his ice cream and taking a silver zippo set it on fire. He passed his silver flask and lighter to Raphael,

-Here, old Wolf, fancy trying the Workmaster's way? Drown in alcohol, set the place on fire and melting the ice doing so. All roads lead to Rome. You might enjoy it before you know it.

Caroline saw her uncle smiling irresistibly and imitating Azryel, pouring generously the amber liquid over his banana split and setting it alight. Then her uncle passed her the flask, encouraging her,

-A little rum, Caroline, 'flambéed' banana, chocolate and vanilla, are a marriage made in heaven. Whatever I say I do like your Walter. He has a way of pleading which stirs us all the time. Now, pray tell me why did he cry last night asking to see good hearts? What did upset him?

Caroline took the silver flask and noticed the carved pirate emblem upon it, the skull upon the crossed bones. The zippo had the same design upon it. She gazed at Azryel's belongings and then to him. It reflected so much his dark personality yet also his quaint refinement and maybe his few pleasures in his harsh life, a little strong alcohol and most certainly smoking. She shook her head to refocus herself to her uncle's questions, and replied as she did pour some rum over her ice cream boat,

-Walter was upset by Gabriel's reaction when he saw the mark of the Beast. When he first saw Bambi, Gabby was moved and ready to help her. When he saw her left foot, with the three sixes embedded in it, he removed all his consideration at once and shouted. Walt pleaded like only he can do, for the poor wretched thing, something about symbols of significance, religious or not, which removes sympathy to one being, almost a comparison to the yellow David star and the treatment of the Jewish during WW2. He sank to his knee by me, and cried upon my lap, begging to see people using their hearts. His plea worked upon Gabriel who decided then to look after It-666, overnight but on his own. Gabby sent me for being tired and Walt for being all worked up to bed. By morning, although Gabriel had no doubts the girl was the true Beast, he was also very caring towards her, considerate about her sensitivity, and patronising her the way he does when he actually likes someone.

Before she could light up her ice cream the zippo was removed from her hand, by Azryel who did it for her and passed it to Asha as he commented,

-Patronising, that is what all of us guard dogs do best. Now, eat it all and off to bed.

She stared at him but smiled and did as she was told. She was exhausted and the rum sent her straight on her way to bed. As soon as her head reached the luxurious pillows in her guest bedroom she fell fast asleep.

Verse 23. The Angelic Anonymous Apostasy.

Caroline turned and tossed upon the large bed, her sleep troubled. One toss too many and she fell heavily on the floor. Her eyes opened upon the room, panicked, not recognising her surroundings at first. She could hardly breathe, there was a scent, a heady perfume suffocating her. She stood up, feeling lost and tried to catch her breath desperately, yet she felt faint so faint. She needed air, and slowly recalling that she was in her suite at her Uncle Raphael's penthouse, she decided to go to the main room and to head to the balcony there.

A quick glance at the rococo bronze clock by her bed indicated to her that it was very late. It was three thirteen in the morning. She had slept for a good four hours at least. She didn't want to wake up anyone, and tried to make no noise as she left her suite. Tiptoeing in the grand hallway, Caroline did not light it up to prevent the security to pounce upon her. She opened the door to the main room, carefully and slowly, yet eager to open the one of the balcony in her mind, and gaining access to the fresh cool air of the night.

What she saw stopped her in her tracks, and she stood there gaping at the scene before her. She wondered if she was purely and simply dreaming awake. In front of her, in the middle of a circle of twelve angels sitting in lotus positions stood her uncle, glowing tremendously, and he bestowed four golden wings. He was admonishing them in a soft yet authoritative tone, and Caroline could recognise the language she had heard him talk to her brother over the phone early on that very evening. She could distinguish Asha in the circle of the twelve, glowing too with intensity, a little more than the others. Then she saw that Azryel was by her uncle, kneeling by him, within the circle, his head cast down. He had raven black wings neatly folded, and the hand of her uncle was laid upon his forehead as if Azryel was giving his body to support her uncle, almost like if he was a statuesque piece of furniture.

She had not been there for more than a minute, when Azryel rose his head, opened glowing green eyes that pierced right through her and spread his black wings. He was aware of her presence and his gestures had warn all the others and her uncle who spread his four wings as well in response and looked at her in an unfathomable manner. Caroline realised that she had just witnessed far too much, that she was holding her breath, that she was struck by awe and felt that she was not allowed to move.

Her uncle finally spoke a few words in his strange language,

-Death, deal with my niece.

She saw Azryel standing up as a result and coming towards her, his glowing green eyes transfixed upon her. She felt great fear rising within her, her breath failing, her stomach knotting itself in a sharp pang and the inability to run away. When he stood before her, she gulped and dared to look at him straight in the eyes. He was fearsome, handsome as hell and a black winged angel. She closed her eyes remembering he was doing the dirty work for Raphael, and unable to breathe, she felt her faintness reaching all her limbs.

Azryel stroked her cheek gently in a painfully slow manner and stated,

-Looking for fresh air in the wrong place, little human. Open your mouth now, Caroline, and take a deep breath. Hold my hand and follow me.

Caroline closed her eyes for a second, 'yes', this was a confirmation, she was a human and she was among angels, she was not dreaming. She tried to breathe but it caused a sharp pain in her breast and she leaned upon the door frame to gather support. She explained in a whisper,

-Asthma. I need some air. Long time without any crisis, I have no Ventolin.

Azryel turned to the room and told in his angelic tongue to
Raphael,

-Your niece is in distress right now: asthma attack, her first one
since a while, five years to be exact. She came here to reach for the
balcony not knowing there is one in her suite, just to be able to
breathe some fresh air. I can feel something triggered the crisis in
her bedroom. I am going to sort it out. Do you want me to clear
her memory from our sight before I cure her and put her back to
sleep?

Raphael sighed deeply, and answered,

-I do not want my Caroline to be brain washed. She will have to
cope with the fact of our existence. If she accepted the existence
of the Beast then she will have to accept the world as it is, with all
his paranormal highs and abysses. We will not tiptoe around Walter
either. I want him fully aware of us and secure at the earliest
opportunity. After all they are in charge of the incarnated
Archangel Michael, they are his human parents. Azryel, I leave you
in charge of the revelations to be done upon them. As
for subservient, I do not think we can bring those two to heel, so
do not even care to try. Beside I love them as they are.

Azryel gave him a bright smile and scooped Caroline within his
strong arms as if she was as light as a feather. He disappeared with
her briskly down the hallway back to her allocated suite. As the
black winged angel stepped in, he could smell the heady scent of
rosemary in the air. It was overwhelmingly strong. He passed the
bedroom and went to the drawing room of the suite where a little
cosy balcony was. He opened the French doors to it quickly and
deposited carefully Raphael's niece upon a swinging black iron cast
sofa, covered with cream leather cushions. He apologised to
Caroline briefly, before putting one of his hands upon her chest,

-Please, forgive me the intrusion.

Caroline saw blue sparkles of electricity going from his long fingers to her constricted breast. The effect was immediate, as she felt the tension going away. Slowly she could breathe again, with the pain of it decreasing. She smiled and whispered, still awed to be facing an Angel,

-You are forgiven, readily forgiven. Thank you.

Azryel stood up and ordered,

-Concentrate on making your breathing paced at a peaceful rate. Think of something or someone you love, visualise. I will be back soon. Something in your bedroom or bathroom is causing the nauseating and suffocating smell that triggered your asthma attack. I will sort it out and aerate your bedroom for a while before letting you back in.

He went and Caroline pulled her knees up upon the swinging sofa and started to swing it gently. She talked to herself as she used to do as a little girl, just to comfort herself a little,

-Curiouser and curiouser. I certainly do feel like I fell inside a clothed white rabbit's hole, an unusual rabbit, a commanding one, one that carries wings. Oh, damn, oh damn, oh damn... What's the fuck is this? I have absolutely no idea. Concentrate on peaceful breathing.

Caroline closed her eyes and started to drift her mind to the happy places and moments of her memory. Her happy thought number one, was little Micky laughing and giggling upon his dad's shoulders, as Walter ran across a field pretending to be Seabiscuit. It's a mother's day Sunday afternoon she will always remember, under a glorious sun. Happy thought number two was her amazing wedding proposal. Walter told her that elephants could fly. That she just had to believe in it or watch 'Dumbo' over and over again. It was a joke between them. He invited her to come to France, for a human rights conference in Paris he was attending for a week. They stayed in a remote location, in a dinky hotel of Normandy, near Balleroy. Somehow one evening he took her to the ground of the castle, upon a huge grass field, where a hot air balloon in the shape of a circus elephant was waiting for them. She thought she was celebrating a step forward for human rights with him, all along, as they drank the 'Veuve Clicquot' Champagne, that night flying under the stars. But as le Mont St Michel was in view, as well as the sun about to rise upon a pink and lavender dawn, Walter made his declaration of marriage to her. She accepted overwhelmed, and vowed that her first child would be named Michael or Michaela, as she knew she was with child earlier that week, but she had kept that fact away from Walter all along.

Her happy trailing thoughts were stopped when Azryel stepped back upon the balcony. He grabbed her hand to assess her and told with a pleased smiled,

-Good. You are much calmer. Workmaster worked his magic. You thought of him. He is an endearing man.

Caroline noticed that his appearance was human again, yet she could still see an emerald green intense glow within his eyes. She pinched herself with some strength and did the same to Azryel upon his forearm. He did not appear to react to pain but smirked and quizzed her amused,

-And the aim of the operation is?

She blushed confused as she stuttered,

-Ass-assessing that I am awake and not dreaming. Did I see what I saw? Are you lot bloody angels?

Azryel's grin grew wider and he nodded positively to her, before answering and correcting her firmly,

 -You are awake and you did not dream us. As for the bloody qualifying adjective, I am the only one who deserves it, none of the others do.

Caroline confessed,

-I am sorry, I didn't mean to be that derogatory. I felt that I stumbled upon something I shouldn't have. I couldn't do anything else but stare at you all in stunned shock.

Azryel turned his back to her, nonchalantly leaned upon the black iron railing of the balcony, gazing at no precise point in the horizon, and explained,

-I know. I could feel you. I am attuned to humans in such a way that none can move, breathe or think without me knowing all, from their mind right down to their metabolism. We were having a meeting and it concerned the existence of the Beast.

Caroline recalled Asha warning her that Azryel knew everything about bodies, how to make them and how to keep them alive. She sighed deeply, and shifted uncomfortably upon the swing. She tried to rock the swing gently to reassure herself a little, her mind struggling to make out what kind of angel Azryel was. She always assumed, well within her imagination, that angels were looking like cherubs, cute babies with pink flushed cheeks, and pretty little white wings flapping above the human they were in guard, invisible to all. She couldn't have been further away from the truth. She remembered how unsettling the presence of her uncle, Azryel and Asha had been all evening. Well, she thought if she felt out of her depth then, she truly had no conceptions of how far and deep out of her depths she truly was. She whispered all of a sudden giving words to her growing puzzled thoughts,

-I feared you, all, from almost the start. Are angels to be feared? As for you, Asha, strong and peaceful Asha, your own kind, fears you. I gathered you were a killer and a torturer, so how can you be an angel?

Azryel turned back to face her and considered her as she fidgeted, fright growing irresistibly within her, as she was concerned to have dared a little too much by her questions. He remained impassive, took a silver box from the pocket of his jacket, one embossed with the skull and cross bones, opened it and asked politely,

-Do you mind me smoking, Mademoiselle?

She blinked at him a few times, cradling her folded legs against her and answered, bemused,

-I don't know why you do ask for my permission. I fear deep down that you can crush me at any point in time without my consideration. Am I right or wrong?

Azryel lit up a long and slim Havana cigarillo, gave her his wicked smile and replied coolly as he leaned back against the railing of the balcony, gazing at her with intensity,

-You would be right. However, all come in good time. So am I to take your fear of me as granting me your full permission to be uncaring in your presence human?

Caroline gasped at him, and considered him as he smoked his cigarillo, pursed his lips in a 'O' and blew out a perfect 'O' of smoke towards her, in a mocking fashion. She couldn't help smiling and coughing at the same time, offended,

-Bloody hell! You enjoy scaring the living shit out of people do you? This should not be allowed!

Azryel came to her, tapped gently upon her back and told,

-Calm down and breathe, little woman. I am sorry. Freaking out humans a tad is one of my rare pleasures.

Caroline stared at him as he left her side to lean against the railing and smoked away from her, most peacefully. With his help, she had managed to catch her breath again. Frustratingly he knew exactly how to make someone feel bad and how to make them feel well, and it was frightening. She commented with no hidden irony,

-A tad, is an understatement. You didn't answer my questions. Am I allowed to ask them? Surely, being the niece of Raphael should make me off limits to you?

Taking the cigarillo of his lips, shaking the ashes from it,
and extinguishing the incandescent ones fallen upon the ground
with his brown leather Richelieu shoe, Azryel stated as an answer,

-No one is off limits for me, Caroline. I am the Death Angel. I
bring all lives to an end at their requested times. And you should
relax with me a little, because you are not yet due to be picked up. I
deal with my own kind just as well and this is why Asha and all the
others, even your own uncle, fear me. However among angels, we
form strong allegiance, bonds, and partnerships. I bowed to
Raphael, submitted to him my powers, and only accept his orders
and advice.

Caroline unfolded her legs and putting them upon the ground,
asked in a whisper, digesting the information given to her,

-T'was the kneeling by my uncle, wasn't it? I saw that. Somehow, it
makes sense of my all evening with you guys, well angels... My uncle
is a very bossy one.

Azryel smiled widely and kindly. He took a puff of his cigarillo and
admitted,

-You can say that. Raphael is an Archangel and so is your brother
Gabriel, and so is your son, Michael. We, Angels, incarnate upon
Earth, at regular intervals, and form brotherhood circles,
generations after generations to look after humans. Raphael has
been the leader of a very specific circle of angels since biblical time.
We are Angels of Actions. We interfere with the human world,
allowed or not, asked or not. The end of World War two was down
to us, Us, in the background, pulling unseen strings.

Caroline put her hands upon her lap and looked upon him in
bewilderment,

-Gabby is one of you! That would explain a lot about his
authoritative righteous ways. Gosh! And my little Micky! Shit, was
your friendly warning, a little about that? Do I have to cater for an

angelic child in special ways, and if I do not, will Raphael take him away from me?

Azryel put his cigarillo upon the railing, in an impeccable balanced position and knelt by her and held both her hands upon her knees, looking at her reassuringly straight into her eyes,

-You are a good woman, Caroline, never doubt that fact. You would never have been given Michael if you were not, and the same goes for Walter. Raphael always goes a long way to find his human families to have his angelic soldiers. He never leaves them entirely alone either. He appointed Gabriel to look after your husband. He appointed you and Walter to carry his line. You will give a little sister to Michael, in the near future, a little girl, like you have been yourself, a special one, like you are, which among angels are known as the carrier of the angelic line. And that very special little girl, will carry back your very uncle among the humans, and living beings for another century, just like you carried Michael, just like your mother carried Gabriel... It is an endless circle of life, or almost.

Caroline gazed in amazement. Her mouth muttered silent words and she could only see Azryel standing back up, and taking his cigarillo back upon his lips, as he carried on talking in a sad and angry tone of voice,

-Some Angels and carriers did lose their lives in the process. It's a risky business. Angels of Action fight evil, and demons. We do not always come out on top with the upper hand. The current political climate is an evil breeding pool. So much so that your uncle has to work now underground. However Raphael is a force in himself, challenging the order of the day, always. As I am Death, I granted him the eternal return, and for his angelic followers the loophole to do so, but at their own risks. If one of them lose their fight, my duty is to take them to the other worlds. I hate my work because I gave myself to Raphael and belong to him and his fights.

Caroline pulled her legs back against her, feeling a little insecure, and swore,

-Blimey! I wish I was not so asthmatic right now, I would ask for a cigarillo and join you in a seen it all, cynical smoke. I am speaking to Death at what, four in the morning, about Angels, Archangels, demons and carriers. Let alone seeing an Antichrist yesterday, at about the same time, and I can only swear like my Walt, in his usual way, 'that's a fucked up bloody mess, baby, but don't worry, we will work it out, eventually.'

Azryel smiled at her comment, presented her with his silver flask, and proposed,

-Here, have a little rum, a little alcohol, well controlled, it makes the medicine go down. It is almost a Workmaster' s way of dealing and coping yet mine has seen so much, that it has become indulgent.

Caroline took the flask and pushed herself aside on the swing, making a place available. She tapped gently over the cushion and invited,

-Come, sit and be friendly, damn Angel of Death. I think you need a little help. I know someone who is the master of coping and that's Gabriel. Did you ever talk to Gabby, I mean in a seeking help way?

Azryel laughed loudly and replied,

-What is making you think that I require help, pray? What is making you think that anyone would give just an inch of care about my welfare? I take the life of all, away, one by one. I cannot be a friend, never. Do you think that the psychological mastery of Gabriel could ever solve any of my dilemmas?

He shook his head and turned to face the starry night, and the rolling landscape below the balcony, shrugging his shoulders as if he had heard the most inane and preposterous thing in all his eternal life.

Caroline drank a large amount of rum silently and finally answered,

-I like sedition and the Workmaster' s way. It re-establishes the slates, gives back the chances. Who did spell it out for you that you will forever be alone and without a friendly soul to give a shit about you? mmh? Tell me, Death Angel, as you are so full of knowledge and information? Is the world such a fucked up place to be in when you have to pick up the Angels you fight by, and bring them to some unknown place?

Azryel gazed back at her and commented,

-That's enough rum for you, Mademoiselle.

She shook her head, clasping the bottle to her chest and smiled wickedly,

-Tata! You can fight me to the death if you will! I am gonna drink it all! If you sit by my side and stop being stuffy nose Death, I may hand you back the flask to share a sip. Do you know that the Beast found friends in me, Gab and Walt?

Azryel cocked his eyebrows interested and sat stiffly by her side, as still as a statue. He threw his cigarillo down and squashed it, under his foot. He asked with a gentle, shy smile,

-Can I have my flask back, human?

Caroline handed it without a struggle and whispered,

-You can. I was teasing you, Death. I think what I am trying to say is that Walt and I are open minded, and so is Gabby, given time and facts. I am offering you my friendship, and don't frown upon it because I am a little drunk, because it will remain there on offer tomorrow and the day after. And I know for a fact that if I talk to Walt and Gab, that their doors will open just as well, to you.

Azryel stood up again as soon as he had the flask in his hands and put it back in his jacket pocket and admonished,

-First, my name is Azryel and not Death, only your uncle

is authorised to call me that, as I am his servant. Second, befriending the like of me and the Beast is not a good idea, and not to be undertaken. Third, I would make an appalling friend. Presently, your breathing is restored, your bedroom aerated thoroughly, and you are drunk enough to sleep like a baby. So it is bed time again for you, Mademoiselle.

Caroline pouted but accepted his helping hand to stand up and followed him. However she argued gently,

-How would you know you would be appalling at something you never tried? I am sorry if I offended you, Azryel by calling you Death. Thanks for looking after me and explaining things to me, it is appreciated. Walt and I give chances to people but I guess it is not your thing, or am I being presumptuous and all assuming insultingly again? And if I am, I apologise.

Azryel pointed her to the bed as he went to close the window. When he turned back she was already within the bed underneath the covers. He approached, turned the light off for her, and whispered,

-Thank you for your kindness and your offer. I am afraid because of who I am, I have to decline it. Sleep tight. By the way, I do give chances but never second chances. All your apologies are accepted, but you can keep your gratefulness, I was ordered to tend to you and tell you the truth by Raphael.

Caroline sighed sadly understanding. Somehow she felt very small at that moment and like a knot forming in her throat. She was thankful for the darkness surrounding her, as she could feel tears prickling in her eyes. As Azryel turned away, transforming himself back into his angelic form and headed for the door, she called him back, her voice very low and begging,

-Please, don't go yet. I am sorry to have blown it with you, Azryel. I will warn Walter so he does behave better than I did towards you. Would you accept his friendship? Would you give it a try? Or even just consider it and think about it, please?

The Death Angel standing by the door, without a glance back, put his hand upon the door knob and replied with a little sarcasm,

-The idea of me in need of a friend and help got stuck into your brain, somehow human. Why won't you quit it at once? I have more important duties to attend to than brat-sitting all night long.

The retained tears slowly ran upon her cheeks as Caroline took on the full blow of his comment. She looked upon the dark ceiling and tried to focus on appropriate words to say. Her mind was a little fogged by the rum, yet she dared to utter,

-Maybe I have got it upside down, maybe, you do not need a friend but that someone out there needs you as a friend. You compared yourself to the Beast, yet she is so fragile, so sensitive and emotional, she doesn't stand any comparison with yourself. You have spent years and years upon Earth, while she has just spent sixteen and she already wants her own death. She begged for it to Walter and Gabriel. Azryel, this is right up your street, this is what you do bring dutifully. What will you do when you do see her poor self? Will you answer her plea and take her kind soul away?

The Angel turned around this time, switch the light back on upon the bedside table, and knelt by the bed, putting his hands upon his laps, his back straight, his black wings spread open, his glowing green eyes staring at Caroline's face. He frowned at the sight of her tears and presented her with a red handkerchief, silently.

Caroline shook her head in negation and refused to take it,

-Don't you worry now, about the effect your words have on people. I am not your friend so you can remain as uncaring as you are about my feelings, you can even get even with me whilst you're at it. Besides, it only hurts because it's just plain home truth, I thought I was past the brat stage, but I guess I was just kidding myself and being complacent. Surely, you must have seen an overdose of tears by now to protect you from being affected by them, mine won't fill your vase to the brim and make it overflow. So don't let my bratty self ruin your precious angelic time any longer. All I need to sleep better and what I am just begging of you, is to reassure my mind upon Bambi, if you can, or tell me the truth, if you can't.

Azryel' s eyes lowered and he looked upon his own hands. He confessed in a sad low voice,

-I am deeply affected by tears. I always have and I always will be. Please, do accept my apologies, human. I wish I could reassure you upon the Beast's fate, but I cannot. It has not yet been decided. Gabriel is a very respected and powerful Archangel among us. The very fact that he has decided to look after her Being, and help Walter do so, is challenging us directly to consider her. We could all have reacted like he did when he first saw her mark, or like he did afterwards when hearing your husband's plea. I felt her great kindness through you and the dog, and I pushed for the latter option. Although Raphael was reluctant at the dinner table, when I suggested trying the Workmaster' s way, he consented to it. He imitated my moves, put fire upon his plate, showing his agreement to the proposal. During the meeting, he supported my opinion as his own. So all I can say is that Bambi will be given a chance, however slim it may be with us Angels, she will be offered one.

Caroline found her smile back. She knew that something went on beyond her understanding during the dinner. It was all in a blend of cryptic moves and words, between Asha, Azryel and her uncle, and things had then been decided. She wiped her tears away with the back of her hands. Maybe she did help them into forming their decisions by what she said to them about the young Beast. So the Death Angel had already interceded in Bambi's favour. She felt like hugging him yet she restrained herself and quizzed him further,

-Thank you so much, for what you have suggested to my uncle and managed to accomplish doing so. She is so young, yet so sad, and pathetically suicidal. You are the Angel of Death, what will you say to her Being that wants out, when she will beg you for her removal?

Azryel' s gaze lifted back upon her and he gave Caroline his most wicked and all knowing grin, before replying,

-Like I say to everyone, all in 'good' time. Do you remember Asha saying that there is the order? When it comes, one goes. I am merely a servant of the order. Beside the girl gave herself to Gabriel, which means Gabriel will fight for the right to slay her, and well, he doesn't want to slay her and I respect him too much to fight him. However if the order comes I will have to do it, and upset Gabriel, which I am not looking forward to.

Caroline blinked at him a few times, and threw a pillow right in his face angrily,

-How can you say that my Bro did something with a sixteen year old girl? You haven't bloody seen the poor thing, have you? Skin, bones and so brittle that one would be afraid to break her, well apart for her torturers that is, who brought her to that state. And Gabby is no killer Angel, is he? Is he?

The Death Angel stood up and laughed heartily. He sat upon the bed giving her back the pillow as he explained,

-I fear having said too much and not enough to the lay human. Your so called 'Bambi' is a Being that knows our angelic language and rules. When I said that she gave herself to Gabriel I did not imply that she had sex with him whatsoever. I gave myself to your uncle, and well, my arse is as tight as it will ever be and remain. It is physical but not in a human sense. How can I explain this in simple terms? Let us take my example, I have extreme powers, not unlike the ones of the Beast, devastatingly dangerous. I could be well arrogant and all powerful about it and squash whoever for my pure pleasure. Yet I don't, for my own sanity and to keep my morals in check at all times, I submitted myself and my powers to the almost complete supreme control of a superior Archangel, Raphael. I humbled myself right down, do his will and fight his fights. I think if I didn't have Raphael around, I would be as suicidal as your Beast. Now, I felt an adverse reaction upon the dog towards Gabriel which she tamed right down, and the dog subsequently submitted to him, am I not right? This is my clue that she has given herself to him.

Caroline nodded and recalled that moment,

-Disturbingly, Walt and I heard her ordering Bud to go down in front of her Master. Walt quizzed Gab about it but he smartly dismissed it, saying the Beast felt like one, not so much as the One, as like an animal, and that like a dog, she was seeking a master, and that having tended to her all night, he impressed upon her enough for him to be one in her young mind. Holy fuck! But Gabriel would not slay her, surely, he can't.

Azryel stood up and paced the room with a winning smile upon his face. He had just been given the most crucial piece of information, the confirmation of his suspicion. He looked gleefully at Caroline, revealing,

-Calling someone Master among Beings is the fact that we surrender our life and will to him. It means thorough obedience. It means if we misbehave, and step out of line, he has the right to dispose of us, and it goes from punishments to a sure death delivered by his hands. The young Beast has surrendered her extreme powers to Gabriel. It is good news. It means she can be worked upon. However it also means Gabriel will have to surrender to one of us, to further the strength and security of his hold upon her Being, but Gabriel is very proud and so aloof like the humans he looks after. Yet he will need that support. The slaying of a surrendered Being has occurred, but rarely. Caroline, thank you for this bit of information, my Master, your uncle, will be more than happy to hear it. I have to leave you now and return to him. Sleep tight, we will work upon Bambi, as a whole. It can only mean increased chances for her unless she is deceptive.

He turned her light off and almost ran out of the room, yet he stopped at the entrance as he opened the door. He whispered,

-As I obviously got my own back with you. I was wondering if your friendship door will still remain open for the two days you said. I might consider it and think about it. Although I don't admit that I need help, I love helping others. Your uncle could tell you that I am dutiful and loyal, as a servant.

Caroline smiled in the darkness of the room and replied,

-You make yourself sound like a good dog. The door is open, and I am not going back upon my words on that one. I will try my best to be a good friendly bitch, if you give friendship a go, Az, with no prejudices, assumptions and presumptions: Gosh that sounds like a tall order for a human. But as I want sweet dreams I will wish those to disappear across the world. Wouldn't it be swell?

Azryel agreed with her,

-Yes, it would Mademoiselle. Good night. We will depart tomorrow morning at eleven. Asha will knock upon your door to wake you up at nine. You will be expected for breakfast at your uncle's table at ten.

He closed the door carefully behind him. Left alone, Caroline sank her head upon the pillow and closed her eyes, her mind a little more peaceful. Despite wanting to dwell upon all that was said since she had stepped in her uncle's AA Club, earlier that evening, she slumbered to a deep sleep almost immediately.

The Death Angel walked back to the angelic meeting, his traditional wicked grin upon his face. As soon as he stepped within the room, all the Angels fell silent and gazed upon him anxiously. He enjoyed the disruption he had caused for a minute, as they broke the circle in order to let him go into its centre and to Raphael.

Asha asked him, his eyes glowing with true concern and irony,

-Although dealt with, did you let the human live for another day?

Azryel looked at the tips of his fingers, checking his nails, arching his eyebrows doing so, in an unnerving fashion. Claws appeared upon his hands, and his green eyes turned to Asha with a little anger. He replied coolly, slowly making his way to the lotus sited angel,

-The human will sleep peacefully tonight like all the others, I ever dealt with. However she will carry on dreaming for another night, day and a little longer. It could have been otherwise, and not of my own making. I noticed that you have been harmful to her, unknowingly Asha. From comfortable, you have managed to make the human so uncomfortable as to trigger a physical ailment upon her which she did not suffer from for years, by your very own clumsiness, in the very place where she should have been secure. I had to correct the effects of your actions. Can you not follow a recipe to the point perfect? Can you not add your harmful good thoughts and deeds upon my orders? Or if you have to add them, can you be careful administrating them so they do live up to their intended effects and not their complete utter opposite? Do you want me to teach you that life is a matter of precision to not become a matter of death?

He grasped Asha' s chin within his clawed hand, forcing the Angel to look upon him, as he raised his other hand, and held it up high, ready to strike. Azryel encouraged coldly,

-Answer me. Your reply will influence your punishment. Do you know what happens to Angels failing to be beneficial? Do you want to physically know what happens to careless Angels?

Asha gasped at him, fright grasping hold of him and asked full of sorrow,

-I would not hurt a human for the world, especially not that one. What did I do wrong, please tell me, so I do not repeat it again? Please, teach me life and precision...

Azryel withdrew his claws at once and dropping the chin of Asha, dismissed,

-I know that you would not hurt willingly. I will fill you in and correct you privately later upon that one, Angel. We cannot lose any of us upon silly mistakes especially since we have an Antichrist to deal with now, and I do mean a fair few things by that.

Raphael cocking his brows with deep interest, demanded,

-Explanations are in order, Death. Did you gather more
information?

Azryel went by him and knelt, bowing his head down, folding his
black wings neatly upon his back, he smiled while tentatively
looking up to the Archangel,

-The little bird has been very forthcoming.

Raphael shifted uncomfortably and quizzed most worried about the
happy smile upon his Death Angel,

-And no torture was involved, was it? Your smile always worries me
about the humans you have dealt with, and we are talking about my
niece...

Azryel blinked innocently his eyes to him, and
answered sardonically,

-The very one, you have frightened all night long about me doing
just that. Concerned, now, are you? In fact for all I did, for the first
time in my eternal life, I have been offered terms of friendship by a
human. If that is worth anything, it nonetheless touched me a tad.

All the angels stared upon him as one, some daring to have the
ghost of a smile upon their lips. They looked upon each other as if
something incredible had just been said or happened. Raphael laid
his hand upon the forehead of Death and asked further smiling
blissfully,

-Oh, a miracle, indeed, at your doorsteps. Did you accept the
human offer of friendship?

The Angels looked up upon the Death Angel with their
expectations and hearts rising sky high, thinking at once that there
was hope for everyone. However, Azryel shook his head negatively

very slowly, making eye contact with the twelve of them in turn, and watched the hopes written upon their faces sinking gradually into despair. His voice lowered and took a bitter purposeful tone,

-I declined. But I realised I had no offer of friendships during my eternal life, not even from my own kind, the one I fight by. It makes you humble, and the human proposal was said to remain open for a couple of days, for my consideration. So I will consider the human proposal, as no other kindness has ever been made to me, apart the one taking me into servitude.

Raphael surprised lifted the chin forcefully of the Death Angel and cried out loud, almost shouting with great anger,

-What's been itching you, Azryel?

Death replied standing up and spreading his black wings before him,

-Sedition. I can do what I want whenever I want. I can be whoever I can achieve to be. Workmaster's words: 'to Be-a-St or not to Be-a-St?'. I find those very applicable to my case. I may go on a vacation of a lifetime and leave those poor human sodding souls alone for a very long while.

Raphael shrugged his shoulders and pushed him forcefully upon his knees before him, admonished,

-Well, you simply can't. You are Death. If you do not serve the order, we would have to.

Azryel stood back up and pushing the hold of Raphael off him, challenged,

-Then do so, and take the full grinding grunt of it! I have been sacrificing my soul and integrity for you all for an eternity. Take upon my work with the order and obey to it, spread it among you all, and realise the toll of it. You will soon behold your full reward within your grasp for your compliance, the hatred of others and the hatred of your own self. Live with it and kneel to the order without sedition nor friendship forever afterwards. See how long you can cope and like it...

Azryel sunk upon his knees by himself all of a sudden, dreading the loss of his servitude to the Archangel and cried upon the thigh of Raphael. Asha stood up and came to kneel by Azryel. He put his arm across the black winged shoulders and tapped them gently, before lifting his eyes in a silent plea to Raphael. His gesture was imitated by all the angels within the room, who knelt like the Death Angel by Raphael, one after the other.

The Archangel sighed deeply,

-It's about time for us to show bloody Death a little consideration, for his work, well his sacrifice for us, all, Angels.

He stroked Azryel's forehead gently, repeatedly but asked firmly,

-You simply cannot be off duty. If you are, the ones, kneeling by you, will be in charge of it. You do know what it would mean to me and my soldiers... I think their silent plea ask as much for my forgiveness of you speaking up, for once in such an eternity; as for you to keep sacrificing yourself for them. What is it to be?

The Death Angel looked up, and whispered as a single tear of blood appeared at the corner of his green eyes,

-It is going to be my sacrifice. I can hardly bear the death of any of yours. It is like the slow death of my heart. I would prefer my life to disappear rather than any of theirs, at any time.

Raphael wiped away his blood tear with his thumb briskly and admonished,

-We are soldiers and sensitive is hardly our thing, Azryel. We are blood brothers, friendship is beyond words for us, it runs deeper. You just had the example, of our one for all and all for one mantra, at this instant. You have embodied that mantra for us since biblical times, we do rather look up to you, rather than down. You are very much part of us and not a black sheep by all means. Now, I've dealt with you for an eternity and, you, giving a damn about your own self is very much out of character. So confide and tell us what is going on?

Death stood up and asked,

-What do we do in front of a challenge, do we obliterate it or embrace it?

Asha laughed and enjoined all the other angels to reform the circle,

-You are a Master in both areas so please tell us what should be our preferred choice?

Azryel slapped him hard across his face and scolded,

-Lesson number one, never ask someone to do the decision for you, even if you believe them to be more informed than you. Follow your own heart. Take ownership of your actions. Do not blame upon anyone the fact that you pulled a trigger and that you became a murderer. So what would be your own choice obliteration or embracing? Respond, soldier.

Asha looked upon him upset with heated eyes, and answered, trying to gather his wits about him,

-It would depend upon the challenge, Az. The choice cannot be done without assessing the challenge thoroughly.

Azryel gave him a winning smile and teased, before carrying on strongly,

-If only we could get the truth from your mouth faster, Ash, you would be perfect. Our present challenge is the appearance of the Beast upon our earthly landscape. Just the mention of the creature curdles our angelic blood to react at once with all guns blazing without questions. However, the Being needs thorough assessment.

There are a fair few factors that come into the picture in regards to her and those need our entire consideration. We may have a much larger problem upon our hands than we think, and going in there with intentions of obliteration, might not be rewarded with the desired effect. This is a warning to you all. I need you, soldiers, to be cautious, careful, and observant in the vicinity of that young Being but also crafty. She is never to be underestimated, at any point in time. On the other hand, we may well have a challenge with ready and peaceful solutions but also a powerful Being that could be trained to fight our corner. Trust is not to be granted to the girl unless she earns it, and then again caution at all times is to be applied to her case.

The Archangel Raphael nodded, a serious look upon his face as he demanded,

-Az, we do like being straightforward, open and honest upon our actions rather than crafty and subtle. Now which factors do we have to consider? You seemed to describe the challenge as one coin, with two different possible sides, changing our luck, and game. Somehow, head or tail, and what it could entail worries me deeply. You appear to have gathered enough information to envisage both aspects. Please, go through those in details.

The Death Angel replied in his commanding tone,

-Let me enumerate those factors to you, all. They are based upon assessments of Caroline, the dog, observations, listening carefully, and getting clues after clues. First, our Beast has lived upon Earth for sixteen years without giving us trouble or making us aware of her existence. She has let herself be tortured for half of it. And when I say let, it is a carefully chosen word as she has the power to obliterate all at once. Question for you to reflect on, why would she do that? I have similar powers, and I can tell you that I would not show that kind of restraint upon any human torturers, they would have to plea mercy under my toes, before I would reciprocate like for like and then drag them to hell without a sign of mercy in my eyes. Now, here comes some of the listening part, Raphael heard it too, over the phone to Gabriel, the Beast spoke, and gave a possible answer and a clue. A, she would not harm anyone. B, she spoke in tongue like all angels to Gabriel. Elaboration on A: I felt her kindness through the dog and Caroline. The way she dealt with them, shows great care, great concern to make sure both would be alive and well, but also a precision which indicates she knows what she is doing to the point of perfection. The care coin for us to assess can go two ways for the Beast: Is she a truly caring Being? Or is she an extremely cautious and careful one? Elaboration on point B: She knows our language, perfectly well, and I doubt that one night spent under the scrutiny of Gabriel would have sufficed in that kind of proficiency. I think the Beast has met an Angel during her childhood, that he took her on and taught her a great deal about our ways. It would also explain her great restraint for such a powerful Being, her dislike of killing, and her will to put her own body through pain and starvation through long period of time. This could also explain the origin of her kindness if the Beast has been tamed by one of us, early on. Are you all following me so far? Have you got any questions before I pursue upon the factors?

Asha asked rising his brows intrigued,

-What kind of Angel would take on the Antichrist? How can we be sure this did happen in her childhood?

Raphael joined the circle of Angels, sat among them in a lotus position, leaving Azryel standing alone in the middle of the circle, and added his questions,

-I would like to know who rather than what kind. It is intriguing but the Beast was definitely fluent and she did sound tame to me, very considerate and thoughtful in the manner she addressed my nephew. But what touched me was the way she said, that she would never cease to ask for her own death unless she could be controlled to do only good. He told me that her warning that she was alive, through Caroline's collapse was her clear invitation for me to just kill her.

Azryel felt uncomfortable standing on his own, and knelt in the middle of the circle, looking desperately at Raphael, before he answered, his voice remaining strong, secure and steady,

-Asha, as Raphael mentioned the kind is less important than who. Our own Gabriel took her under his wings. As for the Beast sounding tamed, this is because she truly is. She surrendered herself to Archangel Gabriel. She has been heard calling him Master, by Caroline and Workmaster. Walt quizzed Gab about it, who told that the young girl felt like an animal, seeking, needing a Master and that having tended to her, he impressed upon her enough to be one in her mind. Presently this is a very important factor. If an Angel of the like of Gabriel protects the Beast, soldiers, you just simply cannot go in front of his nose killing his pet project. Crossing that Archangel is something not recommended nor to be undertaken without great caution and knowing entirely what you are doing from A to Z. As it is rarely the case, it calls upon us for subtlety and craftsmanship. An allegiance between those two formidable Beings is something extremely daunting. This is more, much more than our initial challenge. It calls not only for the assessment of the young Antichrist but also for a pro eminent and powerful member of our kind to be checked but also made to bow, to one of us in order to secure him and prevent him to be lead astray by the dark powers under his wings. Knowing Gabriel, if we can manage to make him accept a supreme hand over him, it would have to be to someone more powerful than him, and there are only so few that could qualify. To be honest, I don't fancy the shoes of the Angel that will have to do it. But I can only see one among us suitable for the task.

He glared at Raphael who pestered, out loud,

-Don't look at me like that! I am not doing it! Bloody hell! Am I to become the Master of all the dangerous ones upon Earth? Looking after you, Death is already more than enough upon my plate. Why don't you rise to the challenge yourself? You are guarded, because you have me as a backup. Also, as the Beast has similar powers to yours, you can more than any of us advise appropriately Gabriel on how to deal with her. You have an eternity of practice under your belt which qualifies you as the best guide and Master for the task at hand. If it is the will of the girl to be controlled to do good, I know you are intolerant enough to not let her do otherwise, and Gabriel has a similar attitude to yours, usually. It is compounded guardianship that we can offer her Being, and doing so we will promote our own security and the one of Earth. I like that, it sounds like a peaceful deal that we can offer our two, and if they refuse, then we are going to have fireworks. Presently, every one of you needs to be aware that our Beast is influential, however young she is. She has touched the hearts of the few she has met, and will have an affect upon you. The way she has drawn people in so far and one Archangel, was through her kindness. I suspect she is using this as a weapon and that will need thorough investigating. Azryel, you sniff the truth out of anyone and never took any prisoner upon the matter of their honesty. Find that fox, and if we truly have a hound, be the iron fist in the velvet glove and bring her to heel.

The Death Angel stood back up, spread his wings open and asked Raphael, slightly shaken by what was said,

-You are certain about making me be the Master of Gabriel? That would put him on my hit list if he fails Us. I would despise myself for being responsible for his last 'supposed to be' eternal breath. Am I to consider what you said as an order?

Raphael joined him back in the middle of the circle, and teased him in a firm manner, admonishing,

-Always seeing the gloom and doom, Death. There is an option for you, the only one I would accept upon my... here is the big word that will make you comply, 'Order'. You just have to be the best Master one can be, so that our Gabriel never fails, so that he remains his eternal Archangelic self. If this was not an incentive enough, I have another one added to the first and only option: your head will be on my hit list if you fail to keep my nephew alive and walking our line. Here is your tall task, transform your dread and ours into hope. Can you work and do that for me?

Azryel knelt by him and bowed his head,

-I am at your service. I will do it, for you and all of us.

The Archangel Raphael nodded with a winning smile and clapped his hands, in an authoritative manner,

-This concludes our meeting. All of you get some rest. We are flying at eleven tomorrow morning to meet with our new apocalyptic arrival. Maybe she will turn out to be our best enemy or our worst friend? Who knows?

Verse 24. Helios, Heli-cop-ters, Hell & I.

The knock on the door came punctually at nine. Caroline felt rested despite her strange night. An hour later as she finished preparing herself, she could hear Bud barking outside. She headed to her drawing room balcony worried about him. But when she stood there holding the black railing, leaning dangerously forward, she saw the dog running playfully to and forth from Azryel, in the grassy field beyond the parking lot. She smiled reassured and noticed that the Great Dane had the planned colour change. He was a glistening blueish-black as he fetched the stick thrown by the incarnated Angel.

Lost in the contemplation of the deadly henchman, she didn't hear the second knock upon her door, and was surprised when Asha stood at the entrance of the small balcony, coughing mildly to announce his presence. Her small fearful jump was perceived by the bouncer who smiled kindly,

-Only me, Mademoiselle Caroline, nothing to worry about. I am here to inform you that breakfast is served.

She noticed a bruise upon his left cheek, below his kind eyes, and couldn't help asking,

-Was there a brawl at the Club during the night?

A shadow of sadness fell briefly upon the Philosopher's face as he dismissed,

-Clumsiness from my part, Mademoiselle.

Caroline sat upon the swing sofa for an instant, a dizzying flashback of her past, coming to her memory at his words. She recalled herself saying those same words to explain bruises upon her to

Gabriel, a night, six years ago, which she could never forget, the night Walter broke down, the night that followed the day of the death of his twin sister. She remembered his cry, his complete distress, as he threw everything around him, breaking any object that could fall under his hands. There was absolutely no aim in his destruction of their home. It was as if he could not see anything or anyone, he looked utterly lost, she had tried at first to calm him down but he was not responding to her, as if he couldn't hear her whatsoever. When she couldn't move fast enough from a falling cupboard, she realised she was powerless to reason him but was also in danger and her little two year old Micky too. She called her brother to the rescue, and hid underneath a table with her son, holding him tightly, protecting him with her own body, from any flying projectiles of that living room. At one terrifying moment, Micky started to sob loudly, giving their hiding place up. She heard Walter calling her son, and her son ready to leave her arms to respond to the call of his dad. When Walter, lifted the tablecloth, she felt in her heart it would all be over, for her and her little one, so scared she was, so terrified as she had been for the past hours. However, Walt knelt at the sight of his wife and his son, his head shaking in disbelief, a glimmer of understanding passing through his eyes, tears rolling heavily upon his face and he apologised. 'Don't be scared, babies, daddy was only passing by. I am so sorry, so sorry. I won't scare you no more, no more. I am going to see Wendy in Neverland. She can't grow old with us any more so I don't want too either. I am so sorry my babies.' Walter stood up and left the room, Caroline was too scared to follow him, and cried out to god for the first and last time in her life, to prevent Walt from killing himself. She heard the shatter of glass, she crawled out from underneath the table warily, Micky clinging to her. She saw Walt re-emerge from the kitchen with a broken bottle of wine, leaking everywhere its Burgundy, which he held by the neck. He walked past her and all her begging had no effects. He was lost again in his mind. Seemingly not hearing nor seeing his surrounding, he sat upon the sofa, slashed both his wrists and was about to do his neck, when Gabriel arrived upon the scene, and removed the bottle from his shaky hands. She remembered collapsing upon herself cradling Micky to and fro, and crying endlessly as her brother took care of the entire situation.

Caroline was recalled from her painful memory by Asha who asked concerned at her livid face,

-What's the matter, Mademoiselle? Are you unwell?

She stood up, and brushed her unhappy thoughts away by teasing him,

-The excuse for your bruise, makes you sound like a wife protecting her husband. You didn't fall upon a doorknob or open a cupboard a little too close to your face, in a moment of inattention, did you? The French have a familiar slang expression for that, which literally and ironically means kissing the cupboard.

Asha smirked and couldn't help smiling looking towards the field where Azryel was still playing with the dog. The human had gotten a little close to some truth unknowingly. He presented his arm to her and told,

-Breakfast will get cold. Your uncle is waiting. Let's make a move.

Caroline followed him, yet his dismissal had her complete curiosity as she pursued,

-The brush off is not working upon me, Asha. I saw how your eyes went straight to the Death Angel. Did he do that to you?

The bouncer explained finding ready excuses,

-My clumsiness brought his wrath upon me. I am responsible for the asthma attack you had yesterday. Carelessly, I dropped the bottle of essence of rosemary in the bathroom. It was laid flat on the edge of the shelf, and drop by drop it released all of it's content, which fell slowly upon one of the bathroom cupboard's lights. We are lucky to not have had a fire last night, because of it. However it worked like a powerful oil burner, spreading the heady scent all over your room. It triggered your respiratory distress. Literally, I was told off, and I feel lucky to have gotten away from that one by a couple of slaps from him to be honest.

She squeezed his arm in sympathy and swore,

-Jeez, you, Angels do take any little mistakes like if it was the end of the world.

Asha scolded her gently as they reached the main room, where her uncle was growing impatient,

-Carelessness can be unbelievably costly. Azryel doesn't tolerate it from any Angels. He had to pick up so many souls because of it, that he is utterly sick by it.

Raphael hearing the last words of his bouncer, told as he presented a chair to Caroline for her to sit,

-At long last, I was getting rather restless. Carelessness and clumsiness always gives my Death Angel very twitching palms, and if the consequences of it are dreary, he will withdraw into his deadly silence and cry his blood tears for a while. Only a fortnight ago, a British mother of three didn't extinguish her cigarette correctly, slept in front of her television, and unknowingly set ablaze her entire household. Her three children burnt to death in atrocious circumstances. She survived only a few hours after the blaze, damaged beyond recognition, and died upon a hospital bed with the full awareness that she had killed her children by her moment of inattention, and ultimately herself. We couldn't get Az to talk to us, without having him shedding his blood tears for a good couple of hours.

As she took her seat, Caroline, tried to be cheerful, yet was very interested by what was said and commented slightly amazed,

-Good morning, Uncle Raphael. Well, well, what do we live for? Another morning and I get up, knowing that you are an Archangel, that my brother is one and that my little son is one also. And the topic of conversation seems to be upon one of your deadly Angels. Yesterday, I was thinking, what is it with you, and your extremely clever bouncers? Did you want them to go all Shakespearean in a brawl, smashing someone's face, reciting some good stance, like to be or not to be to the poor punter? Today, I woke up having been enlightened upon a fair few things and Gosh, did it finally put yesterday into perspective. Do all Angels cry blood tears, because I have witnessed Bambi doing so? Gab explained her tears to us, me and my Walt, as her most painful ones, the ones that touched her deep down. He said it could be accompanied with other physical manifestation. Do you have them to?

Raphael sat opposite her at the table,

-Where is my damned Death Angel when we need him? This is a bit of information about the Beast that would not have fallen onto deaf ears. He would have worked out something from it.

Startling everyone in the main room, Azryel warned of his presence, his wicked grin upon his face, his green eyes shining strangely. He was standing and smoking nonchalantly at the open door of the balcony one of his cigarillo. The dog sitting still like a statue by him. He exhibited his half smoked cigar to Raphael, and revealed,

-I have been here long enough to hear all, from my twitching palms to Bambi's blood tears.

Raphael gazed at him and scolded his henchman,

-Why don't you use the main entrances like everyone? You always sneak upon us, from anywhere. Do you realise it is a little scary?

Azryel staying at the entrance to finish his cigar laughed sarcastically and explained falsely apologetic, then addressed himself to Caroline,

-Coming unannounced is one of my specialities. No doors, windows, walls, physical barriers can stop me from coming to the unwary. And I am fully aware of how unsettling that is, Master. I lived with that fact for an eternity. This is part of my job description. Human, can you elaborate upon the other physical manifestations that went along the blood tears of the Beast?

Caroline nodded negatively and answered,

-Only Gabriel would know. I noticed Bud being upset when Bambi was, at that moment, and I think Gab implied it was one effect of her pain, somehow related to it.

Raphael sighed, and invited Death to take a seat by his side,

-Well, come, get civilised again, Az, join us. You have been away for hours with that dog.

Asha asked Azryel as he stepped finally within the room,

-Tea or coffee? Pancakes, omelette, French or full English Breakfast?

The Death Angel came to Asha, lifted his face up and scrutinised it silently, before saying in a soothing fashion, as he stroked his left cheek, blue flashes of electricity passing from his fingers to the tumefied skin, repairing it,

-Always kind and forgiving, Ash. It is good to know that you understand where I come from. Take care of yourself, watch your every step, Angel, you are one soldier I would despise to take away from the fight. I will have a double espresso, full English without beans. Thank you.

Then he went to Caroline, took her hand in a gallant fashion, kissing her knuckles gently, and keeping her hand within his long fingers, assessing her doing so, told,

-Good morning, human. I can feel that you are better, and recovered. Avoid milk for a little while in your coffees and teas. I am sorry that Ash's bruise and explanation for it, caused painful memories to you. I erased it, so you can look at him without flashbacks. Past is past, as a carrier, your duty is to move on and carry the future. I am still considering your friendship proposal.

He took his seat by Raphael, while Caroline gazed intensely at him, realising that nothing escaped the Death Angel. Her uncle gave a knowing wink to Asha and started the conversation,

-Strong coffee for me too, Ash, and a ham and cheese croissant will do me fine. So, Caroline, tell me, what made you propose your friendship to my Death Angel? Was it pity? For you see, he has been on about it, as none of us, for good reasons, ever did so. What would you like for breakfast, child?

She felt the deep wickedness of her uncle at that moment, and rather put upon the spot. Her eyes met the scrutiny of Azryel's ones, as she replied strongly,

-I will have your smile at breakfast, uncle, if you are pleased with yourself to never have proposed friendship to someone clearly devoted to you and your fights. Do you consider this angel more as an object and weapon rather than a subject and soldier? Does your mind strip him of a soul? And how could you do so when you have witnessed his blood tears upon the fate of a poor human family? So many questions, which I am really interested to hear your answers. I am rested, uncle, you will not find me weak before you this morning. Pity, there was some maybe in my offer, but I sensed someone good, more than good hiding in a fearsome cold cloak, and I would not be surprised that the cloak that he cannot shrug off has been imposed upon him. I am glad that he went on to you about that friendship deal. To be honest, I am ashamed to hear that none of you lot, angels, and I would love to know what are the qualifications, and definition of one, so called 'Angel', to never have considered friendship to be given unconditionally to one fighting by you for eternity.

Azryel smiled most happily and commented,

-Workmaster's little bird is definitely awake, alive and singing his tune. I usually do not inspire pity. Raphael, were your questions to her, designed to break any hope I could have about her human proposal?

Raphael looked upon him, his face saddened, and confessed,

-They were, Az. Dished out shame by a human at breakfast is rare. After our meeting and your subsequent scolding of Ash, you disappeared all morning, Death, preferring the company of a dog to mine. I would not and can't have you stirred beyond belief by words.

Asha corrected him, putting his breakfast before Raphael,

-Not words, promises, bonds that link one heart to another, a vow of care, friendship is all about caring, and feelings. You care how I feel, and I care how you feel. It is simple and beautiful. Denying it to one of us is atrocious. The mere fact that Death is a feeling Being should have granted him our consideration of friendship at some point in time, and the human is right about that. I know I wouldn't be corrected so much by Az if he didn't give a fuck about me making it fight after fight. My friendship is granted to him even if he dismisses it. Mademoiselle Caroline, what would you have for breakfast after your Uncle Raphael's smile, because I can assure you that it is definitely gone and replaced by serious concern?

Caroline blinked surprised and asked,

-Strong coffee, Asha, no milk. I will have the omelette, thank you. I am sorry to have stirred things up, but Gabby always says that anything that can be stirred needed to be addressed anyway at some point.

Raphael grinned annoyingly, telling her off, and then looked at Azryel earnestly,

-Thanks for stirring Death, my darling, like he was not already hard to deal with at any point in time. Well, I won't be put upon by a human. If you can offer him your friendship and it got a consideration stamp upon it, myself and all of my angels can do likewise, if it isn't too late for consideration, that is. And I truly hope that is the case, Az?

The Death Angel gave him a genuine kind and eager smile, as he replied,

-It is not too late, Master, it is never too late, coming from you. It will be considered just as well. Ash, yours is accepted.

Raphael dived his knife and fork inside his croissant upset, and vented,

-To be considered, like a mere human, Az, Jeez, thanks. You aren't a tad bitter, are you? Can I ever make it up?

Azryel laughed and replied deeply amused,

-First, I would not qualify your niece as a mere human. Second, as you are both questionable, I need a little reflection upon the offers. Third, well spotted, I wouldn't stroll the countryside like I did for hours if I wasn't very bitter and needed time to mull over what was imposed during the night upon my plate. As for you making it up to me, I am too humble to require it. The eternal support you provided me with, dispenses you of it, in my heart.

Asha after having served everyone, sat with a winning smile, and tucked in his own full English Breakfast without beans. After a few second, he mentioned out loud,

-That is giving me the honour of being Azryel' s very first friend.

Raphael said to him exasperated,

-That's because you collected enough black, blue, and green bruises from him without complaints for an eternity, Ash. What glimmering trophy could you behold, pray? Death knows nothing about being friendly. That makes you his Guinea pig, his laboratory rat, as he will experiment his first steps of trying to be a friend upon you. Yeah, you should be overjoyed.

Caroline gaped in shock, yet couldn't help smiling. She was

wondering what could good-hearted Asha be doing sitting at the table of her sarcastic uncle and his caustic henchman. The Death Angel commented wryly,

-Don't spoil it for him, Raph. He is the best friend I could ever wish for, calm, kind, understanding and forgiving. I value that so much that I will mirror his behaviour and learn to be a friend at his side or at least try my best.

Asha welcomed his comment, and told,

-That is good enough for me. Stop being bitter about it Raph. I beat you to it and that is all there is to it.

They all ate silently after that. Caroline was the first to break the dreary silence as she asked, again with curiosity,

-Do all Angels shed blood tears?

Raphael answered as she saw Az and Ash nodding positively to her question,

-We do, child. However, it is very rare, apart, for the ones with the toughest job, like Azryel. I have seen his often and attempted to dry them and prevent them for an eternity without real success. I tried an approach with him, in order to reduce his deeply sore feelings after each job he had to do as the Death Angel collecting souls, but it proves rather fruitless. I cannot deny that my Angel feels and feels deeply and badly about everything. I cannot protect his soul from hurting, although I desperately tried. Every night I shed my own ones for his sacrificing soul, in the silent solace of the darkness. And if your Bambi shed those kind of tears, we know deep down that she is no heartless monster. She is a sensitive Being and we are determined to meet her and assess her with an open mind. Does this answer your underlying question, child?

She acquiesced with a shy smile,

-It does, uncle. Do you all read minds of humans?

Raphael smiled at her, and replied,

-No. Death possess that gift. As for myself I partially possess it. I read between the lines mainly and behaviours, then put one and one together.

Asha whispered pestering slightly,

-If Az could only read human minds, it would be blissful....

Azryel smirked at him, and admonished,

-Come, come, are you feeling the strain of correctness and righteousness at all times, Ash?

Asha smiled back widely at him,

-Rather the strain of being corrected to correctness, Az. By the way, just to clear one thing up with you once and for all, my friendship was given to you in all honesty with no underlying wish of escaping your constant corrections. If you are my true friend, I expect them just as before with the care that you have that I should survive for another day.

The Death Angel replied wickedly,

-And I shall not fail you upon that Ash, because my wish is to see your friendly face for eternity.

Raphael stood up, and commanded,

-Okay. Stop befriending in front of me you lot, especially when I am not included. Off we go. The helicopter must be waiting for us. I am eager to see the little Being that can cause such a stir in my own house from afar.

Caroline followed them upon the roof of the AA Club where three helicopters had their blades rotating fast. They headed to a black

one, with golden letters upon his long tail, 'Helios'. Caroline read
the red lettered names upon the other black helicopters, 'Selene' and
'Eos'. Undoubtedly a reference to Greek mythology she thought as
she stepped inside 'Helios' helped by Asha and Azryel. She noticed
that Bud had not left the Death Angel's side all morning, and that
the dog jumped inside the helicopter to lay at the Angel's feet
quietly. She sat beside her uncle and was strapped secure by Azryel
before he sat opposite her by Asha. She asked genuinely, making an
upward circle in the air with her index finger, doing so,

-Are the other copters coming with us to the clinic, too?

Her uncle replied to her,

-I know, my child, I am sending my heavy cavalry to Gabriel. He
never asked for help before. He always managed with what came to
him. I knew something deeply unusual happened as soon as he
requested my involvement. He wanted me to fog the trail of one
single human in such a strange way, and he cleverly did so himself,
that I had alarm bells readily ringing in my ears, worried with what
he was dealing with. I can hide something from anyone but none
can hide something from me, especially not with a mind reader like
Death, at my service.

As the helicopters lifted up, one after the other, Caroline looked at
the diminishing AA Club below them, and saw a dozen black cars
leaving the car park all at almost simultaneous time and the three
others that had pursued her the day before. She gazed full of inquiry
at her uncle, who pointed to Azryel,

-My head of security is in charge of all this. He planned it all. There
are a dozen of wrapped packages looking like the one we received
yesterday leaving in those cars from the Club. The helicopters are
going in all directions before heading to their right ones too. The
chasers will not be able to chase any more. They will be
overwhelmed by the options before them and the simplest one will
stare upon their faces. Because, we also increased security at the
Club, in a visible army like fashion, as if we are keeping something
special inside. If it works we do expect a full on attack this evening

at the AA, or in the next few days.

Caroline blinked a few times, impressed by the sheer scale of the operation. She tried desperately to make sense of the logistic of it and asked dimly,

-Well, if our big 'Helios' copter, stops at the heliport above the clinic we will be a bit busted, now, won't we?

Azryel lifted his eyes in desperation to the ceiling by her question, smiling ironically but remained silent. Asha replied to her,

-It will be a little more complicated than that. The helicopters will land at major hospitals. Our contingents will be dispatched in ambulances. Our one will pick up, Walter, en route to the clinic from a hotel, he has spent the night in. The security of all of you, from Micky to Gabriel, is under control, Mademoiselle Caroline.

She swallowed, feeling contrite,

-Will there be a day when I do not have to apologise to Azryel, or feel like shit by him?

Her uncle laughed and seized her hands, enjoined by Asha,

-Welcome to the AA world, Caroline. Whatever you do human, you can never stop to apologise before Death, like all of us. We all have our endless litanies to put to him but it is more than likely than he will carry us all to Hell ultimately. As to feeling small by him, it is an eternal matter of fact that applies to all creatures, supernatural, angelic, human or animal... I am his Master and would not dare crossing him for too long. And he surely can make me feel as shit as hell, whenever he feels like it, which is usually, frighteningly so, when it is needed for one's soul. Without his tough and constant admonishing, I doubt that any angels would still have wings.

Caroline looked outside at the black cars going in all directions, at the three cars in pursuit, one of them, her very first one, tried to follow the trail of the helicopters. But the copters split apart after a few miles heading in totally different ways. Thankfully, the car followed the wrong one. She smiled happily, her anxiety dropping a little, and her reassured eyes met Azryel' s green unfathomable gaze. She acknowledged out loud,

-Azryel Mortimer, head of security, at my uncle's service, I thank you from the bottom of my heart. You might drag me to hell at the end of my life, but I don't give a shit right now. All I care for is a little friendship on your part. The thing that I realise clearly is that I have got nothing to offer you apart from my good smiles once in a while, being all too human. Yet if I was not strapped by a security belt, I would be on my knees by you, begging and apologising endlessly by now.

The Death Angel stroked the dog's head peacefully and quietly, leaving her hoping for his answer for a few minutes before asking, raising a very serious brow,

-Who is in need of help, Mademoiselle? Me or you?

Caroline confessed,

-That would be me and all my family.

Azryel smiled kindly to her and held his hand out to her,

-I love helping. Especially if it is a friend in need, it makes me go way beyond the call of duty, it makes me respond to my own heart. No need for you to beg upon your knees to me human, just shake my hand, my friendship is given most willingly to you, even if all you have to offer is smiles and apologies.

Caroline seized his hand and shook it, with her most childish and truly thankful grin.

Verse 25. COMA, just a stroke not a Final Point.

The 'Helios' landed on the rooftop of a major hospital. His contingent of Angels, Caro and Bud left the building thirteen minutes later in an ambulance in a midst of six leaving the hospital at the same time. None of the ambulances were followed. Their trail was safe. Asha driving in the heavy traffic gave a quick glance to Azryel, winked and told,

-I think your plan worked so far, Az. We are not followed. We lost them.

Azryel Mortimer nodded but warned,

-Just keep your eyes open Ash, we never know how clever they can be.

The ambulance pulled in front of the large hotel, 'The Elysee'. Asha and Azryel jumped out of it pulling an empty trolley. Both dressed up in dark green ambulance paramedic crew uniforms as they rushed inside the reception as if there was a real emergency. The receptionist turned livid seeing them, and replied straight away to the hurried question of Asha,

-Room 601? We had a call.

-Take the elevator. It's on the sixth floor. The eleventh door on your left. I surely hope that it is going to be okay.

She looked quickly upon the register and read for herself with curiosity,

-601, 601, 600, Mr W. Workmaster, checked out at 9 am, here, room 601, Mr Marshall Knight, checked in 7 pm last night.

Arrived by room 601, Azryel knocked. The worried face of a young cleaner appeared, checking upon the visitors. She explained tearfully, full of relief at their paramedics attires, and showed them in,

-I found him in the wardrobe. Is he dead? Unconscious? Our first aid man is off duty and no one knew what to do... I took him off the noose because I couldn't bare the sight of him hanged and laid him upon the carpet. I tried mouth to mouth but he doesn't respond.

The young woman broke down and Asha offered his shoulder for her tears. As he did so, Azryel went straight to the man laid unconscious and assessed him thoroughly. Walter Workmaster was out of it big time, he thought, a proper coma, yet his heartbeat was there beating in a contradicting fashion, one suggesting deep sleep, and the missing one suggesting death. His angelic knowing fingers could feel the influence of two powerful beings upon the man's health. The so called Beast's influence was there sustaining the life of the man throughout, while the angelic one was dangerously affecting him in spasmodic sequences bringing Walter close to death's doors.

Az ordered Ash to take the cleaner outside and to call the cops as the man they were dealing with, 'Marshall Knight' would probably not survive, that he had tried to take his own life, so far with success.

The young cleaner bursting into a flood of tears followed Asha outside the room. Azryel, once alone, recalled Workmaster to some sort of consciousness, just enough for him to know more about the situation.

Walter's blue eyes woke and lit up at the recognition of Azryel. Although dazed, he couldn't hide his relief. Straight away he hugged Azryel. The henchman cocked his brows in surprise, and asked full of irony,

-What deep shit are you in, Sir, for such demonstrative effusion? So you do remember me after all.

Walter gave to him a welcoming smile, and nodded positively putting his hands up in a surrendering fashion, then he tapped his answer in Morse code upon the carpet making no noise doing so,

-I don't believe I am in any shit at all, but Gab said I was, well, he actually told that all my family, himself and I were in danger, just because I found a poor girl which happened to be a supernatural Being of some sort at P's bunker. I was rather impatient to see a familiar face. Gab told me to wait for Raphael's men. From them lot, I think I know your fists and their impacts pretty well and most of all; when it was not the ear pulling, that is, or the taking me in and out of jail. How could I forget Azryel Mortimer, the right arm of Raphael, with the cleanest nails and maybe the dirtiest hands? By the way, I believe the place is bugged.

The henchman grinned sardonically to the human and decided to not play fools with him at all. He sent him his reply by telepathy, invading Walt's mind, to warn him of what he was now stepping into,

-You'd better start believing in what Gabriel is saying, Workmaster. Finding the Beast puts you in danger, and by extension all that comes into contact with her. As for 'Raphael's lot', we are all supernatural Beings of the highest order. We are what humans have dubbed Angels. I have no time to expand upon the matter right now, but I will fill you in, thoroughly, later. I am honoured that my hands and name marked your memory, in such an impressive way. I only wish you knew the reasons behind my actions yet they are beyond records. Let's get you out of here quickly. What made you think the place is bugged, human? Don't bother typing your answer in Morse, I read minds, just think it.

Walter complied and expressed himself fully within his mind,

-Well I'll be damned! Angels. Blast, have you all got a licence to kill rather than a licence to love? You read minds like the Beast can, shit... Does that make you relatives in a Super Being genetic tree of some sort? Basically, I witnessed the room 600 being invaded after my duplicate, the agent passing for me left this morning at 9 am. Gab told me to be on the lookout and to keep my ears open until my deep sleep kicks in to pretend being a suicidal case.

He pointed to a wardrobe before continuing his thoughts sending,

-Like ordered by Gab, I hid in the wardrobe. It has a lock on the inside and is bullet proof. Those two rooms are frequently used by the CIA for different secret purposes I understood. The wardrobe has a spying hole to room 600. They were only three to come and check the room out. I drew their likenesses upon my pad. One took samples of fingerprints throughout the room. They will only find mine there and a few of Gabriel's, as the agent was wearing gloves at all times. The make believe that we were there. Gabriel left the hotel at 11 pm, last night. The other took samples of dead skin cells and hair upon the bed, which can only be mine as I slept there, only to hide in 601 by a secret path five minutes before 9 am. The last one touched furniture in a way that made me think, he was putting mics all over the room. They left fifteen minutes later, and only three minutes before the cleaning staff arrived to do the bedroom. No one checked this room and I have been wearing gloves in here and have stayed in the wardrobe most of the time, following Gab' s order almost to the letter.

Azryel looked damn serious, nodding his head in slight disapproval, making a series of signs with his hands, he ordered Asha to sweep the room clean from any tell-tale traces of the presence of the human. Then he asked the human in a silently scolding telepathic query,

-Almost? You do know Walter, that I do not like the sound of that. Either you follow orders, or you don't. What did you do in there which we need to clear-up?

Workmaster gave him an hilarious grin, batting his eyelashes to him, and answered within his mind,

-Nothing that the toilet flush couldn't clear for you. Come, I am only human. I can follow orders up to a certain point. Basic needs, my dear Angel, basic needs.

Azryel hissed between his teeth in a low voice, looking at his silver Rolex and showing it to the man,

-What are you, a bloody toddler? Nine till twelve thirty. When we say, you don't move from one spot that is what you will do, and you will wait until the relief comes.

Walter shrugged his shoulders and teased in a whispering pestering tone,

-Right, if that please you better, next time I will let you find me with my arse dipped in it's own shit.

The Angel smiled wryly, replying by telepathy,

-That would not be the first time, Workmaster. You have quite a reputation among Us as a shit maker and stirrer, the ace of it. But with me stepping in, my dear human, the order of the day is going to have no laxity whatsoever. Whatever you want to do, you will have to hold it until it is right by me.

Asha came in front of Azryel and gave him an all clear signal. However, the Death Angel ordered him, in the angelic tongue,

-The human used the bathroom once. Skin cells, any hair, have to be removed. Be thorough.

As Asha went to inspect the bathroom, the henchman asked Walter with a certain authority, within his mind,

-Upon that trolley, now, Workmaster. We are going to make a move. I am afraid I have to revert you to unconsciousness a little until we reach the ambulance where I can revert all what has been done to you. It means you will be suffering a little longer under my dirty hands.

Walter could not help seizing Azryel' s hand and sent a wild request to the Death Angel's mind,

-As long as you explain yourself to me fully one day, like you said I will forgive you all your misgivings and your very dirty hands.

The Angel smiled cruelly as he sent the man back to his coma with his reply,

-Workmaster, you are a very weak man with a God syndrome. You are no one to be able to forgive on the big scale of things. I come without explanation. I come with order and fate. I come without forgiveness. I do not need forgiveness for I am the unforgiven one.

When Asha was by his side they wrapped Walter in a body bag and put him on the trolley. Within minutes they were back in the ambulance and heading to the clinic.

As soon as the ambulance doors were closed, the Death Angel opened the body bag under the worried gaze of Caroline and Raphael. He explained quickly,

-The man is in a coma. But he has been badly messed with by Gabriel. Somehow Gabriel tried to imitate the Beast and her powers. He failed. The only given safety net he got was from the young Beast. I need all my skills to bring him back fully and healthy with us. Walt is in danger at the present.

Raphael put his hands upon the chest of Workmaster and told in tongue,

-Death, use me to annihilate any effects of them both upon him. Save my nephew, my so much nephew in law.

His eyes glowing of pure gold, Archangel Raphael was ready to channel all his strength in order to give a better chance to Walter Workmaster. The Death Angel grabbed his Archangelic hand and teased in tongue,

-Isn't that man so peacefully quiet and asleep right now? We should embrace a minute of silence for the miracle it is... peace at last.

Raphael grinned knowingly but confided,

-I love his cacophony. It keeps me upon my lawful toes.

Azryel channelled the Archangelic power to recall Walter totally from his dangerous coma. A blue light surrounded the human for a few seconds before the eyes of the wondering and worried Caroline which held Bud. When the Death Angel had finished, he sat back with Raphael, and told reassuringly,

-Workmaster will come around now. Give him a few minutes. He will be okay.

When Walter stirred and finally opened his eyes, Raphael's concerned look vanished to be replaced by a wicked smile as he could not help welcoming the man,

-Here he comes, Trouble is awake.

Walter tried to sit up upon the trolley but was pushed back in a laying position by Azryel, who ordered him,

-Not yet, give your body a rest, you've been badly messed with.

The man grinned as he replied,

-Not that I am already so messed up that I would never have thought that such instances would occur...

The Death Angel cut him short,

-Workmaster I can assure you, with the kind of trouble that you raised to Gabriel and our attention, that there are great risks that such instances could occur more often and dangerously worse...

Raphael clapped sarcastically his hands and jousted to Caroline,

-Trouble raising up an even bigger Trouble. What do we live for? Eh, not bad, I warned you my child that marrying that man was like embracing an eternity of trouble. He raised the Beast from some shit hole and is planning on raising the young Antichrist. Sweet, somehow I cannot help worrying, knowing 'Wreck-Man' Walter, that all is going to turn Apocalyptic upon us.

The man started laughing on the trolley irresistibly,

-Someone should rewrite the future of humanity to fit our present bill. It would not be the first time nor the last time it was done. As I am talking to Angels shitting themselves upon their Apocalyptic fate, I think I could be the mad man in charge of rewriting history and the future with love and peace instead of hatred and wars. I would abolish any Apocalypse in my scriptures and write about Earth becoming a walking paradise of freedom and democracy instead.

The Death Angel and the Archangel Raphael looked at each other in desperation and nodded in agreement to their telepathic talking,

-I could have made him sleep rather than wake him up, Wrath, now it's going to be hell in the back of that ambulance until the clinic. I hope it is not going to give you a case of Workmaster's claustrophobia.

-A sleeping Workmaster is surely a nice thought but a shit stirrer like him is always needed once in a while to wake everyone up about things that are wrong, things that we grew complacent about and accepted as home truths rather than rectifying them and put them right. I want and need him awake and alive. If my Angels do some brainstorming about his stance then the brainstorming itself shows that something was amiss somehow and therefore was overdue.

-Surely you do not want Workmaster as a Scriptures writer... that would be... that would be....

-Disastrous and apocalyptic. It can't be. Because the man plans to erase all that chapter and skip to the lovey-dovey time. Could we provide him with a real flash-forward?

Death failed to reply as his internal brainstorming started. How could the Angels of Actions prevent a World disaster and help humanity forward?

Verse 26. Raphael's heavy Cavalry.

As soon as the ambulance pulled in the car park of Dr Purallee's Clinic, Azryel was on the lookout for his men and sent them the telepathic order to show themselves. Ten black suited incarnated Angels stepped out from waiting cars and approached the emergency entrance where the ambulance stopped.

Asha opened the back of the ambulance, Azryel and Raphael pulled the trolley out carrying the large body bag and rushed into the emergency room, followed by the ten henchmen.

There Gabriel Purallee welcomed them. The tall Doctor gave an unfathomable look to Raphael before presenting him his hand to shake. Raphael refused the hand, his eyes incandescent and told,

-Honesty is what I ask from everyone. Asking for my help and lying about the subject puts you in the worst of terms with myself and my heavy cavalry right now. Not only that, the human in your care has been messed up badly by 'your' intervention. Death and I had to intervene to not make his one untimely. Workmaster is mine as much as yours, I will not tolerate him and his health being played with by incompetent hands. The powers of the Beast and Death were not given to all for good reasons. Do not play the apprentice sorcerer Gabriel, and raise without order. The Powers will destroy you before you know it. And I would be given the supervision of the task. All my given tasks come to completion. Did I make myself clear, soldier?

Gabriel fell upon his knees before him and pleaded,

-Wrath, I was worried about your reactions because of my initial ones. I did not mean to harm Walter. I just wanted him to play a believable dead for the plan to work. I knew Az could revive him easily. How is he?

The offended Archangel argued as he pointed to the trolley,

-You cannot assume one's reactions upon yours. If you are born racist, a religious extremist, homophobic, and a killer of hate, not all of us are. We use reason and higher moral laws based upon respect and love to guide us, where hate has no place in it. Gabriel if you assumed me as a killer and lied to me because of it, yet dared to beg for my protection, you are in very serious trouble as an Angel. I do not lose my Angels. I deal with them. Consider yourself warned. As for Workmaster, it involved the channelling of my Archangelic powers to save him from yours and your dangerous 'fiddlings'. He is a VIP in this world and the next, you do not mess with his life, you protect it with your own life not secure his untimely death.

As Asha opened the body bag, Walter and Caro were smiling at each other, all snuggled up and intertwined within it. Caroline whispered,

-This was exciting, being rolled up to the A&E.

Walter replied as he lifted himself up from the bag,

-Indeed, my cock is in plea for a relief. Raphael, you torturing me with the very proximity of my ex-wife will not do. I love your niece to bits and she drives me crazy because she is going to give me none of it later. What's up with the big talk with Gab? He is a wicked bastard slash Angel but a good one in a righteous sort of way.

Azryel Mortimer grinned widely and mentioned with a slight cough,

-And that would account to forgiveness being given from the injured party. Let's free his poor dog. Walter, you can't keep Bud yet, I will look after him for a while. He had a transformation, just colour wise so far.

The Death Angel pulled the dog from a tray and blanket under the trolley. He revealed the tied animal.

Workmaster jumped by his side and asked the Death Angel,

-Was he badly messed up too, or not?

-Not. The Beast is careful.

Walter asked out loud his own worries,

-Is it good and reassuring or bad and unsettling?

Raphael, Gabriel and Azryel all answered the man in a same voice,

-This is what we need to find out.

Gabriel added in a matter of fact tone,

-And she is hearing all of us as we speak.

But he added through telepathy to Raphael, Azryel and Asha,

-She said she could not read my mind and found out I was an Angel very early on, maybe because of it. She read every human mind and hears every conversation spoken from miles around her, even through walls. She knows all languages to men and beings but also has a mastery of codes which is baffling. Telepathy between us is the best way forward but she does practice it herself. She can invade my mind at any time to talk. In one word I would advise you all to CAUTION in her presence and far from her.

All the Angels nodded in a common understanding, while Raphael enjoined,

-Let's meet the Beast.

He left the emergency room with Asha, Azryel and his ten Angels in toe. Gabriel told Walt in a hurry, before rushing out to follow,

-It would be better for you two and Bud to miss the meeting between uncle Wrath and Bambi. Deep shit going on, Brother, big shit.

Workmaster mentioned out loud,

-Deep shit is where I seem to always belong, I am coming. Stay there Caro, and keep Bud with you, we do not want him to start eating all the Angels of Uncle Raphael.

He left the room hastily following Gabriel.

Caroline looked at the dog and whispered all alone,

-Hay, Bud, fancy having some Angels for tea time! Let's go and protect Bambi.

She walked out of the building with the dog and went around the building to the quarantine area. A window opened itself and she stepped within the room as the dog jumped in. The window locked itself behind them.

Bambi looked fast asleep upon her bed.

The dog went to lay across the Beast's bed. Caroline sat by and waited for the heavy cavalry, extremely anxious for Bambi.

As the receptionist saw the thirteen suited men emerging from the A&E room to head straight to the quarantine area of the clinic, she left her desk to stop them and stood opposite Raphael.

-This is a quarantine area you must not go in there.

Raphael smiled and muttered between his lips,

-Stating the obvious. I know. I have to go there. We have been called as contingency. We are trained pandemic Doctors coming to contain a potential fatal one for many.

Liz looked unsettled by their appearances and told,

-I haven't been informed upon the matter. We have only one case of Meningitis here, well contained in the quarantine area. You shall not enter until the clearance order of the upper management and your IDs checked out. Doctors do not come in suits but usually in lab coats.

Gabriel stepped in and said,

-All clearance is given Liz. They are US emergency state Doctors, specially trained for major emergency. I called for their help to contain our one properly. A lab coat doesn't make the Doctor, Liz, you know that as well as I.

Liz stood sideways letting the thirteen men pass, as one of them, Azryel sized her up in an all encompassing sideway glance and offered her an approving nod. Gabriel and Walter closed the march into the quarantine room. She whispered for herself,

-What's the ache? Meningitis, I thought we got it sorted...

Verse 27. Greet & Meet/ Great & Meat.

Raphael stood in front of the man made lock of the quarantine room and blinked to Gabriel for an explanation. Gabriel shrugged his shoulders,

-If it is not safe by man's mean, my dear uncle, just enter the room.

The Archangel swallowed the energy around the door knob and entered the rightful code at once,

-3-1-3 Nice and easy, change this code at once. Six digits minimum with a required mix of letters, numeric, capitals, lower case and punctuation. Every human is starting to know that. Lagging behind Gabriel.

Uncle Raphael stepped into the room, followed by all his Angels, Gabriel and Walter. He noticed the presence of Bud and his niece already within the room, and the Beast appearing fast asleep. He looked disapprovingly again at Gabriel, scolding him out loud,

-What kind of quarantine room have you got there Archangel Gabriel where a mere human can step in uninvited by climbing in from the unlocked windows? Security is gone by the window in your establishment making me wonder if you should remain in charge of the safe keeping of the Antichrist. As for you my dear niece, tom boy-ing your way in with that dog could have raised dangerous suspicion from any outside observer. Az, send five to scroll the area around the clinic. Now Caroline any of your sensitivity nor the one of Workmaster will be appreciated in the matter at hand. But I will keep you dangerously in for you two to learn a good lesson about what we are dealing with.

Caroline bit her lips half annoyed with herself for having created a risk and half with sheer anxiety for the young Being before her. She revealed,

-The windows are all locked from the inside, I sent a mental plea to be let in, and I was. One opened to let me in with Bud.

Five Angels left the quarantine room whose door was locked carefully by Azryel. Asha stood by the door within the room on guard.

Gabriel turned to the two humans,

-I told you two to stay out of here for the initial meeting. I do not want any of you to be hurt by your human erratic moves. Stay put and avoid to getting involved.

Workmaster coughed and smiled apologising,

-And that I cannot do my dear Gab. I am involved and if what I see displeases me I can assure you that I will not stay put.

All the Angels turned to him eyes blazing, and warned in a common voice,

-You will get hurt if you do.

Walter shrugged off their warning, yet impressed by the fire within their eyes and their synchronised moves and voices,

-Let's see shall we who will cause me more pain.

The teenage girl opened her eyes at once upon the room. It was not her human green ones but her fully black and demonic ones. Yet her all appearance remained human. An outer voice spoke from her,

-No pain is to be inflicted to Walter nor Caroline. Turn all your violence to me, but never to them, never.

Raphael gazed at the Being before him and announced himself in tongue to It-666,

-Good Afternoon Bambi, your call for an Archangel who is not led astray did not go amiss. I am here. I have no intention to hurt my own family but to teach them an observing lesson upon a subject which should not be dealt with by humans but by other Beings.

The young girl smiled sadly and whispered, almost singing,

-'Hello Darkness my old friend, I come to talk with you again.'

The Archangel swallowed his own breath and answered,

-You are mistaken Beast, I am Light, I am not your friend and never was. You are talking to me once and most probably, for all.

Bambi's eyes closed again in painful sorrow,

-I knew an Angel once. He made me cope. He made me hope. Somehow I hoped he was you. I am mistaken. Please, annihilate me for I have no chance without him.

Raphael was intrigued by the identity of the Angel, the first one that dealt initially with the Antichrist. Did he turn the Beast to do good and only good or else?

-I am afraid to displease you, Beast. I am only Archangel Raphael.

At his name the Great Dane, jumped from the bed and came growling by him, its mouth foaming.

Bambi called out,

-No Bud, no. I want, I seek death. Down, boy, down.

The dog sat and then went down in front of Raphael, howling in a sad manner.

Raphael told his Death Angel to come forward and both took the hands of the teenager in front of them. A long silent ensued as blue light passed to and fro. When the Archangel released her hand, he knew that what all feared had been incarnated. He saw the girl upon the bed crying blood tears, and turned to his Death Angel. Azryel stood tall in full Death regalia with the silver scythe, becoming the scary shadow of his incarnated self. Death spoke in the angelic tongue to the Beast,

-Asking for me, begging me to you, Being. How dare you? How dare you flaunting the orders of all time and fate?

It-666 looked at him fearless and replied by a heated plea, pointing to Walter and Caroline doing so,

-I dare because I have a heart. I dare because I am a time bomb for humanity. I dare because I care for humans, him, her and all of them. I dare because if I am born to be used to do a massacre upon Earth then I would rather simply die. I do not want to cause hurt, pain and devastation. If it is my fate to bring the Apocalypse, I have been fatally flawed with a heart, and I intend to use it and not be used by others to bring Evil.

She stopped talking suddenly. Her bed rose above the ground before crashing itself against a wall with extreme violence. All the Angels came to circle the bed and the damaged It-666, great light emanating from them. All of them singing the soothing song in tongue of the Beast, enjoined by the Archangel Gabriel via telepathy. It was to no avail as the walls started bleeding profusely all around them. The teenager looked at them, shaking to and fro. She mustered in shock,

-Something bad is happening right now, right now. I know the very men. They were all my torturers. Gabriel, Gabriel, they have Micky. They are killing a man by him and a girl is being beaten up thoroughly.

The Beast closed her eyes and threw up in front of them.

Raphael looked at Gabriel with retained anger and asked him,

-Did you send our little boy to school this morning, instead of keeping him by you, Angel?

-I did. I sent him under the protection of a CIA agent who was also supposed to pick him up from school with Cecile, the Au pair girl at three.

A quick look at the wall clock confirmed their worst fear. It was fifteen minutes past three.

Uncle Raphael saw the despair and anguish in the eyes of his nephew. He ordered,

-Az, send the five immediately to the rescue.

Putting his hand upon the shoulder of the Beast he demanded,

-Share those visions with me right now. If you know more about the situation, speak.

The girl held his hand, green light went through him and bestowed him with her powerful all seeing sight momentarily. She spoke in tongue,

-I read their minds. It's an abduction for P. It's Tit for Tat. They are aiming to touch directly Workmaster who removed me from P's hands and his bunker. They will request an exchange, Micky for my return. Everyday that will go past the little boy will be tortured, body parts sent as warning. P intends to use his young blood to wake up the darkest evil and mine. He will put the boy in my shit hole, below the pentagram. We have to stop him. We have to recover Micky at once. He has no clue that he is a budding Archangel, and of the damages his type of blood could do.

Stopping herself, she realised that all the remaining Angels in the room had their hands upon her. She saw their energy passing through her body. She looked at Raphael worried and asked, although she felt a growing calm within her as her mind was becoming extremely collected,

-Pray, Archangel Raphael, what are your Angels doing? I do swallow energy, as I do swallow pain from all around me. Touching me as powerful Angels might be misguided in my case. Sometimes I do not know how to deal with situations I see or feel, like just now seeing visions of the abduction, I went crashing to a wall.

Azryel lifted her chin and replied,

-We are handling you right now, Being. We have just been reading and assessing you thoroughly, in order to know how to deal with you. We can provide you with the control you seem to lack. However you did extremely well at just age sixteen with your type of powers. Your plea for your death has been checked for its truth and validity. I am also rejecting it as well as Raphael here. If you do not want to bring Evil, we can offer you to fight it in our corner. You can start now by helping us recover Micky from the clutches of P.

Raphael enjoined the young It-666 further,

-The all encompassing vision has been given with an extreme rarity as the handling of it is not for the faint hearted. Death before you is the only one possessing it for an eternity, until you came along. These type of powers could be used to protect and fight for good. All your powers could be turned beneficially if we show you how, and for that you shall remain within my Army of Angels. You gave allegiance to Gabriel, I want you and Gabriel to be guided, controlled by the only Angel with similar powers to you, the Death Angel. He has an eternity of Mastery behind him to help you through and forward.

Gabriel who broke the news of the abduction to a distraught Caroline and Workmaster, turned at the mention of his name. He walked forward to the group of Angels surrounding the young Beast, and knelt before Azryel Mortimer bowing his head down,

-I accept. Help us forward. Help us to retrieve young Michael. My failures are calling for guidance to correct my path. Only your intransigence Azryel can drive back a soldier to his best.

It-666 gave her solemn reply to Raphael and his Death Angel,

-My Master has spoken. I bow to you both, Azryel servant of Archangel Raphael. What is the plan to get back Archangel Michael? What can I do to help?

Raphael replied with glowing eyes,

-Just fight with Us Bambi, just fight.

Verse 28. About Embracing Death. TrUsT

The young It-666 looked piteously at herself but offered a smile and proposed,

-Fight, I can't do much with my human shell right now, Gabriel said it will take three months for me to recover and be able to walk. However I have other ways to fight, which are a bit drastic in a poltergeist sort of way.

Raphael cocking his brows intrigued quizzed her,

-Pray would you mind demonstrating your way of fighting? For the bleeding walls and the flying bed were already quite a tasty appetiser.

Gabriel stood up straight away and intervened,

-No! No demonstration, no main course, especially in my clinic. I know what she can do roughly and let's not try that at home nor anywhere. I will not enjoy a freak show right now, knowing that Micky is in danger and we need to retrieve him fast. I say let's go immediately to P's bunker and break all their necks before they lift a finger to remove Micky's ones.

Azryel Mortimer grinned sarcastically commenting,

-Look whose talking! If it is not the very Archangel who let his very Archangelic little nephew down by giving him the security to be walked to school by a mere man and a young Au-pair girl. Did it come to his mind that what men do most easily is die? No of course not, for Archangel Gabriel likes using mankind in his dealings to keep a little away from being checked thoroughly by his own Angelic kind. It gives him the liberties to keep unusual lab rat like the quote 'Freak' to study and to experiment for himself his discoveries about the freaking powers that do exist, which he would like to possess, by trying them out on mere human Guinea pigs, with devastating effects. Someone should not be called Archangel, nor Angel but a fallen one and should have his wings cut. For Gabriel, going into P's bunker all guns blazing, is not a good idea. Shall I re-educate you upon being a clever Angelic soldier, one that uses his brain rather than gut instincts? Gosh, I have my work cut out with you. I can't believe how easy it was for you to bow to me my dear Angel. However looking at your soul right now, I know how lost you are and feel.

Gabriel's head drooped, he sat by It-666, and brushed off a blood tear appearing in his angelic golden eyes. He admitted out loud, losing the Angelic tongue exactly like the Angel of Death, now his Master, did,

-You would be right Azryel as always.

Death smirked, and scolded,

-Not 'would' Gab and you know it. As your family, Caroline and Walter need to hear this. You fall under me and therefore Raphael from now on like your Beast, and we will provide you, Bambi and them extreme protection. Humans, you are under my angelic orders from now on. I can keep you alive in what will unfold. Stray from my orders and I will have to pick you up to 'Neverland' against my will. Unfortunately for you two, you have just stepped in to the worst scenario which could happen upon Earth soon. Yes, Workmaster, that would be the word you hate the most and want to obliterate from any religious books, the Apocalypse. Archangel Raphael's Angels of Action will do their utmost to advert it if not postpone it. And, most importantly, I want you two, to be our soldiers, my soldiers, the beacon of humankind and shine through it all and help others do so.

Caroline took the hand of her ex-husband, went by Azryel Mortimer, and knelt by him,

-I am your soldier. I have faith in you, Az to retrieve my son and help us through it all.

The Angel of Death's face softened at once and helped the woman up, and whispered,

-I will never defect a friend in need.

Caro hugged him and just cried upon Death's shoulders.

Walter stood there a little annoyed by the hug and told,

-I am not very good at kneeling especially to someone that Caro finds in her to hug, a very someone called Death...

He cleared his throat, breaking the embrace doing so then carried on,

-I will remain my own man and listen to my own heart rather than orders. See, if someone says to me kill that guy, I will not be able to do it. I need reasons, valid ones and upon the death sentence, I would say it may send someone to unworthy glory by that swift punishment where they could claim an undue martyrdom, which as murderers of hate, they absolutely do not bestow. Let them rot and chew their sins with a long time in jail, and teach them to be human all over again and to use their hearts rather than religion to explain their atrocious deeds, dead and wounded. How can they use a fair god to be unfair? God upon our understandings needs love rather than hate. To kill mentioning his name as a reason is the worst crime of all. It assumes God wants blood and fight, when it is the opposite. It is a lie inciting others to be murderers. Soldiers! Don't make me laugh. A blind bomb which attacks women, innocent men old and young, and children, teach nothing about being at war but all about cowards attacking people rather than in a proper field fight with the opposite armed force. It is the easiest way, the terrorist with no balls way, it is callous, vindictive, inhuman, heartless and God forbid, it is very much so paradise-less. Therefore I will be my own soldier and listen to my own heart rather than obey blindly to who dares to speak of so called God's murderous will in front of me. For I know I will not be forgiven if I do so.

Azryel Mortimer presented his hand to the man to shake and stated,

-That stance makes you a sound man and a good hearted one by my standards, I will protect you as long as you follow your heart, human. I will even soldier by you to make sure your stance stays alive and well.

Walter blinked with surprise yet held his hand out, shaking the Death Angel's hand and confessed,

-I thought I would be crucified for not kneeling by you, Az.

Death smiling wickedly answered,

-Some bestow the Ultimate Passport. It is only acquired with a sound heart and the use of it. Now, soldier, I need to gather my troops to get your son back. I have a plan which will keep you and Caroline safe for as long as I can and it involves you Puppet.

He turned his whole attention to It-666, who blinked at him totally insecure.

Workmaster grew worried in nanoseconds voicing his concern,

-Now, going from nicknaming her Bambi to downright Puppet scares the shit out of me a little especially talking to a Super Being dubbed the Beast. She fears being used and the name calling implicate just that.

The Archangel Raphael smiled with a little cruelty to the man stating,

-Do you want your son back safe and sound Walter, or in little pieces? Your quote 'Super Being', our young Antichrist has found the perfect Puppet Master in the Death Angel. She fears being used for Evil, We will use her for Justice and Good. If she strays with Us, we acknowledged her want and desire for death and we will grant it.

Workmaster looked at the injured It-666 in despair. He said out loud,

-Your quote 'Puppet', is all broken up by others who tried to use and abuse her for her powers. She lays there because of her non violent heart. Are you going to use her as a killing machine for all Evil doers? How do you recognise one of them in a crowd? Will she be Evil and wicked because she refuses to kill? Will it be deemed as being astray? Will she be granted death because of her pacific ways? She is scared of her own powers for Christ's sake! How can you reassure us and her that it will be safe for her to use it, even if she uses it for good? Anyway she is too broken to be used for the time being and she therefore has three months to think about it. Raphael, don't involve her in the retrieval of my son. I know your men and I trust they will get me back Micky. Maybe the all guns blazing on P's bunker of Gabriel is the best way. But just shoot their knees.

All the Angels coughed loudly within the room, smiling at one another deeply amused, looked to the sky in false desperation, then laughed heartedly.

Raphael tapped Walter's shoulders in a friendly way and teased him,

-We love you Workmaster. You are so human, the all package with the human heart, eyes and scope. You see we Angels have mysterious ways of dealing. It does not involve officially or non officially, killing, mass killing or just shooting the knees... I will not explain our ways to a mere human but in time you will give me and my quoting correction, 'Angels', the benefit of more trust hopefully leading to the full variety. As for Puppet, my leading Angel, Azryel has a plan of action for her. He is taking her on as a soldier but her heart will be fully respected whenever it decides to show itself. As for her decision she already took it, Walter. Anyhow three months of indecision in your human eyes is far too long for our Angelic ones. Puppet can retake her decision now if she wants to.

It-666 had followed the whole exchange with her full attention. Reading the mind of Walter she understood fully well all his concerns and where they came from. However she could not read any Angelic minds within the room. She could not know for sure if she would be fooled and abused or not. She had to rely on what she was lacking, like Walter: Trust. Just trusting others was a big ask providing her past, let alone the bigger ask of trusting herself. She stuttered at first in an awkward human voice, yet her voice grew stronger and stronger as she spoke,

-I will be no Puppet nor Bambi. I will be who I want to be. I will not fulfil your labels of Beast aka Antichrist. I like the quote Super Being in reference to myself until forward slash if I turn bad. I will have no name apart from It, until I dub myself with one I like and choose. I will guard myself against bad use like I always did. I will use my own heart in that matter. I am young, erratic yet not stupid. I can stand on my own two feet once they are healed. I do not seek protection for myself. I seek protection for others from myself or Evil. If all stand to 'if I can be used for good' then my heart is only willing and saying to you Angels, show me. If I feel I am used wrongly or if I feel I am turning into the so-called Beast then my heart will say so. Death I will sent you my inner warning and kneel by you for the slaughter. My reassurance will be just this and depends entirely upon it for it will prevent what we all fear with certainty.

The Archangel Raphael and the Death Angel looked at each other for a long time before Azryel replied in a solemn voice,

-Granted, although it will defy the Powers.

It-666 nodded downcast,

-Well they should listen to mankind's minds more often, like I do. I will bear the grunt. I care enough for human's hearts to listen to them all and wanting all of them safe and well from It all.

Raphael had the final word,

-Maybe in grand scheme of things, 'It' was supposed to be flawed and be made like any human with a heart, and bestowed with free will, just maybe, so that everyone could have the hope of a better future. Azryel, make that soldier fit to stand and fight in my corner.

Verse 29. Speedy Recovery Company...

The Death Angel obeyed Raphael's orders and went by the young It-666. He held her shoulders strongly and poured great energy within the teenage body of the injured Antichrist.
Within minutes, before everyone who was present within the room, 'It' was able to stand and walk. Yet she knelt by the Angel who carried on filling her with powerful Angelic strength. Just her bold head remained, without scars yet without hair, tell-tale sign of her dreaded past. When she stood before them, her eyes shined an aquamarine beam upon the room and said,

-Let's recover Micky.

Workmaster and Caroline held each other's hands while the Great Dane Bud went by the young It and laid by her. Archangel Raphael asked his Death Angel,

-What's the big plan now? Spell it out.

-Speedy Recovery. 'La piéce de Resistance'. My orders are sent. Gabriel you will stay here and look after the humans in your care. Raphael, It and I are going to recover little Micky.

Gabriel's emergency buzzer startled everyone by its noisy beep-ing. He stood up, checking its message,

-The ambulance bringing Cecile the Au-Pair and the security agent just arrived.

All the Angels regained their human aspects apart from Raphael who ordered,

-Gabriel, go to them. Azryel, go along and get information from the humans if you can. Come back ASAP for the recovery mission.

The two incarnated Angels left the room followed by Walter eager to know more about his son's abduction.

In the emergency room, Gabriel told his staff to leave and closed the door behind Walter Workmaster. Azryel went to the suffering Au-Pair girl, Cecile. He applied a cold compress upon her tumefied cheekbone and asked in French,

-Cécile, ma fille, dis moi ce qu'il s'est passé? Gabriel is a good Doctor. He will tend to your injuries. You will make a full recovery under his hands. Speak, my girl, speak for his nephew is in danger right now.

The girl started crying and pointing to the hospital bed of the killed CIA Agent told,

-They got Tango Charlie. They killed him, the three of them. He had no chance. I was battered until I released Micky from my protection. Meagre, the space of my arms, they broke them. One, a tall bold man, put a chloroform tissue upon little Micky who fell unconscious immediately. He took him in a white van with 'Electricity E & E' written upon it. The cropped blond haired guy gave the final blow to Charlie and jumped into the driver's seat of the van. While the Mexican one with a Santa Morte tattoo gave me a blow to the cheek that sent me miles away counting birds in Feather land.

Az asked further,

-As tu entendus leur noms? Their names, my dear girl?

The French girl shook her head, replying,

-Code names. No real names. Tattoo guy is known as Santa Morte. The blond one was called the Aryan and the bold one was named '3'.

Azryel ordered,

-Gab, stop doing a post-mortem on Tango Charlie. Cécile is alive and needs your full attention to get well: two broken arms, contusions, a cheek bone fractured, one eye is almost lost and in need of immediate attention.

Walter who stood by Azryel silently all along, put himself across the door as he saw him about to leave the room, and asked,

-What about Tango Charlie?

Az answered bluntly,

-Flat and dead. It was his time.

Workmaster shook his head negatively,

-It wasn't! He was killed by the will of three men and their Mastermind. Do not tell me that their wills rule fate and the World and that whatever they decide to do will go past unchecked. Do not tell me that their murderous will is granted as fate and accepted. For all can murder at will and fate does not exist but only free will. Bring that man back to life, give him back his chances, you and I, know that you can. Az, bring Tango Charlie back. He is a good solid man. Please, I beg of you to consider him.

Raphael's henchman smiled ironically and muttered to himself, then out loud,

-Working upon Workmaster is an impossible task. Charlie Tango is a weakest link. His time did come. The man will be dead in any future endeavours. He has no future. Listen if you can, Walter.

Walter shook his head and pointed to the dead CIA agent,

-That man died for the life of my son, I want him alive and well. What about the rewriting of the Scriptures? My re-writing of them? It starts right now. If you cannot deflect one man's life course, how are you going to preserve the whole of humanity from Evil and the

Apocalypse? Are you going to do fate upon us all and bring Evil to pass as if it was said from high above and set in golden letters that cannot be changed? Or Are you going to use your own free will Angel and re-write it all with Us?

The Death Angel stood by the door shaking his head in a negative fashion before walking to the dead Charlie Tango. He put his hands upon the dead man's chest, recalling him to the living. Cécile' s eyes blinked amazed before Gabriel sent her to a level of unconsciousness in which her recent memory would be erased. As he started to tend to her broken arms, he enjoined Azryel with a wicked smile in the angelic tongue,

-Workmaster' s way, where will it lead Us? I can take care of those two humans and Walt. Make sure you get to little Micky ASAP. Beware of Bambi. She is a hell of a girl. She seemed tamed but I do not know how tamed she is, or if she really is. But she is the real thing, I have her blood sample in my lab. Get to know the slab before going to get little Micky.

Azryel nodded, pulled Walter out of the room with him and asked,

-Happy? Charlie Tango will make it for another day.

Workmaster queried,

-Just a day? I thought your powers were great. 'Apocalypse Now' it is, then.

Death turned to him and scolded,

-Walter, the man is due. Charlie Tango will not last long whatever I do. There are things your mind will not comprehend. The leeway to work upon them is very slim. I know the leeways but cannot abuse them. I abused one for Charlie Tango for I need to move on to fetch Micky before it is too late. Come, stay behind and look after Caroline, she is very distressed right now, and will be until I bring her son back and alive. I will secure Bambi throughout, do not worry about it. Raphael will make sure all of us, Micky, Bambi and I will come back in one piece. He is coming forward. In Angelic terms, it means he will reveal himself to humans. It also means he is the first warning.

Walter kept the fast stride of the Death Angel and asked worried when he reached It-666's containment room,

-First warning?

Azryel smiled to him sarcastically,

-Not now Workmaster. Long explanation to a human mind, yet alone an Atheist one. I will be there all night and I am needed elsewhere. Long kiss good night, wish me luck, wish that your son has not bled a single drop yet.

Walter grabbed the hand of the Angel and wished,

-With all my heart, go. I just wish what you are wishing. I do not know any better, Az. I will keep an eye on Caroline and provide her the shoulder she needs right now.

The Death Angel disappeared saying to him,

-Good man.

As Workmaster looked inside the room, he saw It-666 and Raphael vanishing from sight too. He gave a worried look at his ex-wife who held his Great Dane Bud tightly.

She crumbled before him, and confessed,

-We have to trust them. It's our only option. Micky is very very important for them for he is one of them in the making, an incarnated one. They chose you and me somehow, to carry Raphael's Archangelic line forward. Micky will become Archangel Michael.

Drawing his arms around her, Walter cradled Caro to and fro and reassured,

-Azryel is on the case, very focused. He will see it through, Babe. We will see our Micky back in no time. CIA man is alive again because of him.

In the forest, a few miles away a white van labelled 'Electricity E & E' stopped by a bunker, P's bunker. Three men and a child stepped out. As they went by the secured door, their enter code would not work upon the digit pad. The more they entered it the more a warning flashing light came through highlighting the whole keypad. In desperation, 'Santa Morte' keyed a single letter and the door opened to P's henchmen and torturers, telling them that the place had been hacked and to be on their guard. They brought the child as fast as they could to the main room of the bunker, the one with the pentagram.

With clear orders, the Mexican henchman drew the blood of little Micky, slashing his wrists above the pentagram. Then he was ready to hide the child below it opening the trap door. As the blood dropped, slowly but surely, It-666 appeared in her cage and burst from it. Her shoulders covered by the blood of the child, she stood strongly within the room. The very room started bleeding thoroughly from every wall. When she opened her arms, hellish figures sprouted out of her attacking the three henchmen. The child was released in the commotion and captured by a very ready Archangel Raphael who made him disappear from all sight.

As the henchmen of P were fiercely attacked by dark shadows, Death appeared into the room in his all dark regalia, spreading his black wings. Lifting his scythe he called out,

-Aryan, Santa Morte. You are called upon. Come with me.

A swirl of his scythe made the two heads roll upon the ground.

The last man standing ran to the door, but could not get it open. When he turned back to face the room all had disappeared but the bleeding walls. The pentagram on the floor was gone. Full of fright and dismay he could not believe his eyes of what just happened. He went to open the trap door to check if It-666 was hiding within. Rats and mice came pouring out of it by the thousands, attacking him. He ran away, managed to get out, and ran very, very far away from the bunker, in shock and breathless.

He will have to report to 'P' the situation and did not look forward to it.

Verse 30. Re-Cove-Ry

The Archangel Raphael carrying the distraught little Micky within his arms appeared before his parents within the quarantine room of the clinic. His first words were orders,

-He needs immediate attention. Both of his wrists were slashed open. Walt, get Gabriel, now. Caroline, talk to Micky. What he saw was distressful, what he went through horrendous. I need him fully here with us.

Walter left the room running to the A & E room to fetch Gabriel. Caroline helped Raphael putting her son upon the hospital bed, reassuring him as much as she could,

-You are going to be alright, Micky. We got you back. Gab is coming, he will look after your little arms, mend them. It is all over, my baby, all over.

Great light poured into the room, as Azryel and It-666 materialised within it. Raphael glanced at them worryingly yet before he could say one word, he saw the young teenage Beast walk to the bedside of Micky. She enclosed both of his wrists between her hands and whispered a reversed incantation. Before their eyes the child's deep cuts sealed themselves closed. She kissed his forehead gently, saying,

-You will sleep now and forget about it all, Micky, for it was all a bad, very bad dream. You are safe. It is all over like mummy said.

The child blinked a little then fell asleep, safe, sound and healed up. Raphael picked up his little hand and checked his wrist thoroughly, assessing the child's bodily functions doing so, he confirmed to Caroline,

-Micky is going to be more than fine. He will not remember what he lived and saw. Nothing happened but school today for him, now. He does not need any intervention from any healing Angels regarding his blood loss either, for right now it is fully re-established. Caro, your child has just been healed thoroughly by It.

Caroline fell inside her uncle's arms and cried,

-Thank you, thank you all for bringing him back, for tending to him, for healing him, thank you so much. I am indebted to you.

Azryel came to check the child as Raphael did, but more thoroughly so. He nodded his confirmation to Raphael and Caroline. Micky was healed, safe and sound.

As he glanced back at It-666, she was far from alright. He could see both her wrists bleeding slowly. She had swallowed the pain and the ordeal of the child and took it upon her. 'Swallowing Pain' was one attribute of the Beast but a dangerous one. The digestion of pain was a process very much unknown to many Angels and the ultimate result could mean worse than what was absorbed. Death looked worryingly at Raphael and told,

-I have one soldier to tend to, I am afraid.

He went to It and asked her gently,

-Hold my hand and be off.

The young girl held his hand firmly, half collapsing upon herself, and disappeared with him from the room.

Raphael closed his eyes painfully and reverted to his human form. He shook his head and confessed to Caroline,

-Bambi got damaged. The blood of Micky reached the pentagram. It means that she may have been raised. Well the Evil within her. It can take all shapes, forms, it is cunning and manipulative. Death will assess her and deal with her if needs be. She was brilliant. She pulled the scariest tricks out of her bag. We kept her away from slaughtering. For this is Az's formal orders, eternal tasks and will remain so. Out of three miscreants of P, two were called by him to the after-world. One was left alive to tell the tale to P. The one called '3', will be sent to an asylum soon afterwards, believed to be mad, for he saw an Angel, Death and Demons, within the same room and all disappeared very neatly leaving no traces.

Gabriel and Walter ran into the room full of anxiety. Caroline went to her ex-husband and reassured him at once,

-Micky is safe, Walt. Uncle Raph has been updating me upon the situation. Bambi may have been damaged. I saw her take upon herself the pain of Micky. She did her swallow thing. Her wrists were bleeding afterwards and Micky was like nothing happened. She healed him and wiped away his memory from his ordeal. She was taken by Death to be assessed, they disappeared.

Gabriel who was checking the child turned to Raphael and said,

-He is fully recovered and saved. I can feel her powers all over him, very healing, soft and soothing. Where is Bambi?

Raphael nodded and told,

-By Death. He is appraising her. She got damaged on her first mission. She fulfilled what was asked of her to the letter and attended to Micky as soon as she stepped into the room without any orders. She delivered more than we could hope for. Yet, her life is now in the balance, as something happened there, which put her life into question again, and much more. I want to fight by her again and hope she makes it by Death's standards.

Verse 31. The Tutor.

Deep in the cool damp darkness of an autumnal forest, the Death Angel reappeared, having taken It-666 by the hand, through space and time. The teenage girl turned around, humming the air, a single blood tear slowly pearling in the corner of her blue-green eyes. She faced the Angel and told,

-I know this place. This is the very woods of my childhood, my feral years. May I die here, Master?

Azryel' s black wings spread, as he smiled wickedly to her, demanding,

-You may, all in good time, It. First, show me your wrists. Second, tell me the reasons for them, all your reasons. Third, we are here in the past inside the Black Forest to find out more about you, my dear, for you are a very powerfully peculiar creature.

She bowed her head down, sadness piercing her voice when she replied, presenting her bleeding wrists to the Angel,

-Azryel, I will not lie to you, ever. I took on what happened to little Michael upon myself, swallowed his ordeal, removed his pains and hurt for two reasons. First it was for his total recovery, for we cannot allow any child to suffer. Second, it is another of my attempts to get rid of myself, that, quote 'very powerfully peculiar creature' which stood below a pentagram, in the worst position for her as the blood of the child, not any child, an Archangelic one, was drawn above her. The precious blood went through the dark magic circle and covered my shoulders. The hate I felt at that moment for the World and what was happening was hard to control when all I wanted was to prevent any harms to Micky. Yet I could not do so, for I was too late to prevent even the worst.

She stopped as she knelt by Death, before making her plea,

-The worst will be me. I know it for the tremendous hatred I felt within. I know it for being covered by his specifically Archangelic child blood, and under those circumstances, it worked as the anointing of my Being as a gate for Hell. I exercised that right to help us save Michael. You witnessed it too. I released demons just by opening my arms. It gave the right commotion needed. I felt in great control of them all the way through. They will do any of my biddings with no struggle. I have a ready hellish army to answer my wishes. It terrifies me. The possibilities if I let the hate which I felt come out, will spell an end for this World. Dying is my only option before it is too late. This will properly re-write everything and save everyone. I beg of you to let me do so. To expire within this forest, where I grew a love for everything I hold dear, would mean a lot to me, for the woods are where the beasts live, should stay, and perish.

Before the Death Angel could say a word in reply, a voice sang a very sad, powerful and peaceful lullaby. Azryel scrutinised his surrounding, yet could see nothing. It-666 was up on her feet at once, joy passing through her aquamarine eyes, where resignation reigned before. She took the hand of Death, inviting him to follow her,

-He is here! Come, meet my Tutor. Come, I know where he is, very close by, where he taught me many things...

Azryel ran with her intrigued to finally be able to discover the face of the Angel who took on the young Beast. They reached a small clearing with a great oak tree almost in its centre, and below it stood a Being glowing powerfully. The young It left his hand to run towards him. The Death Angel considered the whole scene. When the teenager reached the Angel, she knelt by him, putting even her head upon the floor, she obviously had a relationship with him that could not be described by simple words. He truly believed at that moment, that It-666, the Beast, the due Antichrist was worshipping her 'former' Tutor. But who was he? The question was crucial as if he was worshipped by It, it also meant his influence upon her could be great. This could pose problems to Raphael, Gabriel and him in the guardianship of the young Antichrist.

The first words of the Being teased gently It-666, as he stroked her cheeks in the most gentle and kind manner,

-Here, here, brave girl, you are doing well. I never thought my instructions would impress you so much, my little Beast in the woods.

Az could not help but be impressed by the awe which clinched him deep down by the side of that Being. He was no Angel, for that he was sure of, he was something else, something else but what? Who? Death stood full of suspicion and asked It,

-Bambi, too much effusion. Stand up, by me and do the presentation.

She smiled at him in a childlike manner,

-Azryel Mortimer, Angel of Death, meet my Tutor.

He grinned a little annoyed replying with slight impatience,

-And your tutor has a name, I suppose?

The Being gazed upon Azryel attentively as he replied instead of It calmly and firmly,

-It, chose 'It' to be her name for the time being, until she finds her own one, not a satirical one given by others. As for Ours We have many.

The Death Angel felt a little unsettled. The Being was not a vision of the past even if Azryel had travelled with the young Antichrist to her past. They were supposed to walk her past trail, relive her memories of time gone by in that forest and meet shadows of things and beings that were. However the so called Tutor was very much real, very much aware of the present and things that had been going on since. Therefore he had travelled back to her past as well.

This meant a very higher Being of some sort. Azryel apologised,

-I am sorry to have offended. We are rather protective of It. Bambi is her pet name among Angels, I am concerned by her, and calling her back by her pet name comes out of care and caution.

Death looked at It-666 watching him intensely as he gave more explanations to her Tutor,

-She is a very special girl. So much so that she will be overprotected by Us to make sure she does not fall under the wrong hands. It implies a worry upon whoever makes a connection with her, deep or not. It also implies assessing every single contact she had since her birth. Hence, It and I are walking through her past.

The Tutor stopped stroking gently the chin of the teenager, and made a ordering move with his head. It-666 got up straight away and went back to stand by the side of Azryel. He then levitated above the grass commenting,

-Apologies are not necessary with Us, Azryel, for like you We have a tendency not to forgive. It is nice of you Angels to show such caution and care regarding It, to give her a code name, rather than a pet one, which indicates your level of involvement with such a special Being. It is all in the angelic elongated pronunciation of our poor 'Bambi', or more likely 'BAAmbi': Beast. Antichrist. Apocalypse. May be. Imminent. That is a straightforward looking after, to care or to kill. It already chose the answer for herself.

The Angel of Death could not help being impressed by the level of intimate knowledge the Being had. It also meant that he would be an extremely hard one to assess. His great aura and presence unnerved him for the first time in his whole entire eternal life. None the less he decided not to show his deep worries, as he spoke again,

-Many Names, nothing is as straightforward as it seems to be. 'It' is sweet sixteen with a whole mess of a future in front of her, a damned good heart, and an horrendous past behind her to digest and grow out of. She can write her own future for she was given her own loopholes. The first consists of a heart, which as weak as it seems or as powerful as it is, has kept her in check for so long despite tortures and pressures of all kind. The second is that she was incarnated in human shell. Hence she bestows the true free will that was bestowed to human kind. 'It' can achieve devastation perhaps but also write up her own story to her own liking, to greatness from salvaging everyone, to using her good heart to her full potential. She has the power to tidy up her own so called 'fated' future, making sure she is part of it all for the good of everyone. It's answer is the one given frightened by her experiences, uneducated by how we can help her deal with the powerful Being she is. It has learnt and within reason, to trust her own self and no others. Belonging now to an Angelic Army, she will now be shown Universal Love and the Trust behind it which will let her use her heart to the full for the better. It will be taken great care of. She will be educated and developed in Our way. I am Death. When her heart stops working towards the Universal good I will know and only then her death wishes will be granted.

The eyes of the Being in front of Azryel glistened like fireballs. The Tutor glided towards the Angel and patting his back told,

-As you have her heart's best interest, Az, let me guide you through her past connections. We will have to start a little earlier than where you landed. Let me show you her arrival in the Black Forest.

The Tutor simply clicked his fingers together. The clearing became en-snowed in front of their eyes. A great deer jumped in the background running away from hunting shots. Hunters came in the clearing, turned around and could not see the animal, they looked for tracks but could find none in the deep snow. One ventured that they had lost the track of the beast and to go home before darkness fell upon them.

The Tutor smiled knowingly,

-We are invisible to any eyes. We are the 6th of December 1996. It is about 3 pm. The time when 'It-666' entered the forest unannounced. A strange thing happened then, unexplained: all beasts in this woods failed to make any marks upon the ground until 'It-666' was taken away from it. It was eight bad years for hunters, and thriving ones for beasts of all kinds. It repaired the ecosystem of that part of Europe for a long while. Follow me.

Death followed the gliding Tutor across the clearing where he pointed to him the path of the great deer. An untouched snow was glistening under the last rays of the cold afternoon for him to acknowledge. Walking behind the fast moving Being, Azryel was eager to discover more. Soon they reached a little log cabin in the midst of the wood, the Being pointed to a nun and a priest carrying an infant in his arms, walking silently in the snow towards the cabin.

The Tutor announced to It and Azryel,

-This is the arrival of It-666. She is just six month old. The priest holding her tight is Father Arthur Williamson, and the nun is Sister Theresa Da Priera. Both were there at the birth of the child. Take a closer look at It. Remember, none but the baby can see you.

Death approached to be at arms distance only from the priest and watched in wonder. The baby was extremely beautiful with a head covered by lovely blond curls, like a cherub, yet as she opened her eyes staring right at him the perfect picture was immediately destroyed. She had deeply black and braising demonic eyes. She blinked a few times, smiled at him then waved, blabbering,

-Az, Azry, Az.

The priest thrust her back more closely into his chest, telling to the Sister,

-She is seeing things again. Let me warn you Tess that you will never be completely alone with her. Spirits, demons and ghosts will be surrounding you at all times.

To which the nun replied shrugging her shoulders,

-Well any entities better be warned I will not suffer their presences around the little one. I will exorcise them all.

The Tutor put his hand upon Death's arm recalling him,

-Let's move on to another chapter of It's childhood. The child saw you somehow. You don't want to be exorcised, do you bad spirit?

Azryel smiled sarcastically, as he answered,

-How would you know if I was a bad spirit? Anyhow I cannot be erased for I do the erasing in every World.

The Being smacked his hands together bringing the three of them to a new scenery after mentioning,

-A self satisfied spirit can be a plague and also a plague to deal with. Ask Raphael, he will tell you the same for he knows.

Verse 32. Soulful Singing Lark.

Azryel, the Death Angel was by now annoyed with the Tutor for he seemed to know far more than him. Transported to another moment in time in the childhood of It-666, three years forward, he wondered if he would be able to gather the identity of their guide. Death enquired,

-You seemed to know me very well yet I did not have the privilege of your acquaintance. Do you personally know Archangel Raphael?

The Tutor beaming blinding light throughout his entire entity replied nonchalantly, ignoring the fact of how disturbing he was at that moment,

-We made a point to know all. There is no bright side nor dark one that are escaping Us. We know you Azryel Mortimer very intimately and so do We know Archangel Raphael.

The Angel shook his head in an helpless fashion before raising it with a sarcastic smile,

-Many Names, either you are the most pedantic Being in the whole World, or you are the sum of all spirits to adopt the universal 'we' speaking of yourself. Which is it?

Winking at the Death Angel, the Tutor replied pointing at the three year old It-666 running happily in the forest,

-Take a wild guess. You are getting closer. Now, pay attention and watch. You will see the young Beast, care free, at play and learning to be. You will see Tess tending to her welfare and her tuition but more importantly what It as a toddler makes of it all. This is what fuelled her heart, the initial spark. It is important for it will help you with her. It will make you and all Angels understand her fully and where she comes from experience wise. 'It' although here has no knowledge of our conversation, Angel. We obliterated that part from her.

Azryel nodded. The Being was keeping some things away from the young Antichrist's knowledge. He needed to know if the Us the Being was referring to was the same that he knew about, the universal union of all and Angels, or something else. He watched the past before him, It-666 by his side not losing a minute of it.

They witnessed the special toddler as she found a lark lying lifeless on a layer of leaves. Carefully picking the little song bird up within her baby hands, she considered it attentively. A few pokes from the child had no effects. She kissed tenderly the feathers and ran back towards the cabin with her new found feathery treasure. She showed her find to the Sister who was cutting wood into logs with a large axe. The nun Theresa rose her eyebrows and scolded her,

-No, child, you cannot bring every dead thing in the house. We have a garden now filled of those dead animals. If you ever bring me a live creature I may let you keep it as a pet, but that would imply you looking after it and caring for it, it's entire lifetime and at three, I doubt you are up to it right now. Did you kill that one or find it like that?

The toddler blabbered away,

-Like that. I heard it sing. In the morning. Every morning singing song. Nice. I want the little bird back.

Theresa dropped her axe by her side and held the child's hands together, enclosing the lark within. She stated,

-The little bird flew away into the spirit world. Maybe it was it's time, maybe it had an accident. The wind was powerful last night. Who knows? Feel it's cold breast, it's little heart has stopped. It means it's life is totally over and will not sing anymore, despite us wanting it to do so. It passed away to our great sadness but maybe it made babies this year, who will sing next year.

The little It-666 started crying gently her baby blood tears, and mumbled,

-I wanna hear his babies but I wanna hear him too. I wanna hear his little heart again. I wanna have him all back and alive.

The Sister took back her axe, lifted it and told,

-Cry all you want, child. It is life. With life comes an inevitable death. And all your wants and 'wanna' can do nothing about it.

The young curly blond girl pouted. She shook her head, spoke in tongues for a minute then reverted back to the human language for the benefit of the nun, in her strangely odd voice,

-I can do something. For all I want I can. Heart means life you kinda said. Watch.

Theresa dropped her axe at once and her hands went to join the ones of the toddler upon the bird, giving her a most disapproving look. She scolded,

-Think before you do anything, child. A heart can beat with its spirit gone. Without its spirit the lark will be a living shadow. Its songs will ring into our ears every morning soulless.

It-666 smiled brightly at the nun. She stroked the lark upon her own heart and whispered,

-I can feel what you mean. It is not far away. I can catch it back too. I got it. I got it right there with the heartbeats.

She opened her hands to release a living lark. The bird flew to a tree nearby, sang beautifully before flying back to the child landing on her shoulder. The Sister muttered to herself,

-I will be damned, the child Antichrist can make miracles, age three.

Death looked at the Tutor for answers yet he was enjoined to keep his whole attention upon the scene,

-It is far from over.

Azryel saw the toddler running to the garden plot by the cabin. There she dug and unearthed dead animals. One by one she raised them all from their dying state back to the living. When all were running happily around her, she laughed out loud and tried to reassure the deeply worried and baffled Sister,

-They are all good. They are all okay, they all got their souls back too.

The teenage It-666 commented upon the scene having watched her childhood self with certain pleasure,

-It was one of my happiest moments. I learnt that day about heart and soul. Before I could only pick up dead things upon my path. After I could make them better and live once more.

The Tutor announced,

-Lets go to the following crucial moment when her powers reveal themselves to be able to cause death as much as being able to raise anything and anyone from their graves.

He snapped his fingers and the scenery changed once more all around them.

Verse 33. Tess's death.

Death felt the teenage It-666 holding his hand as the infamous scene of her past appeared. He could feel her hand trembling within his. She confided to him,

-Azryel, I don't know if I am ready to see this part. I might get upset all over again and react. I may need to be contained.

The Tutor turned to her, his voice soothing and strong reassuring her at once,

-My little lost beast We taught you how to contain your own self, your wrath and desire of retaliation. We know you can do it for you are Our brave one. Be confident as you have shown great restraint which honours your every action ever since that event. You can rely upon your own self forever, remember that as a fact. You can win your own inner battle yourself. Never forget that. Never. You are stronger that the rest of Us. You cannot give your own responsibilities to anyone great or small for it will wreck them all. Remember your own internal turmoil, its your own to deal with, it has been given to the most powerful Being ever for good reasons. It cannot be shared. It can be dealt with, by you and you only. We are counting on you to do so. We will walk by you all the way to help you support your ordeal. You can count on Us to not let you fail. What you are about to see, you have grown out of it. You have become the courageous individual We always knew you would be. Against all odds, you made it to the AA Army as their newest recruit. And for all you are, It, they need you more than you will ever know in the future that is unfolding as We speak.

The Death Angel felt the hand of It-666 becoming strong and firm. Her trembling disappeared during the arousing speech, he had noticed. Somehow he wished he had told her all those exact words at that moment in time. Somehow he wished that someone could care enough of his own self to come up with spurring words like those to carry on his own eternal task or the courage to give it up. He looked bereft upon the Tutor who was beaming bright like a beacon within the Black Forest. By now Azryel knew who was 'Many Names', the Tutor of the Beast and he could hardly believe it. Was The Most Superior Being of All truly there for all creatures?

The murderous scene of the Beast's past, unfolding before their eyes, seemed to be the attestation of that fact.

The 6th of June 2001 looked like a normal quiet day by the cabin in the wood. It-666 was five years old and nowhere to be seen.

The Tutor moved his hand in the sky and opened a window showing the whereabouts of It to the Death Angel. Az then saw the young girl, her bare feet inside a small river, her hands holding a fresh water fish still moving helplessly. He saw her apologise to the poor shiny creature,

-Nun Tess has not eaten well for four days now, I am so sorry little fish, so sorry. I will bring you back later, all of you back, flesh and all, for I will keep your bones, like a treasure, little one. You will come back, cross heart and all.

The Tutor smiled knowingly to Death and commented to his mind only,

-How could I not be there for 'Playing Death and life' little sweet heart It? She was feeding herself and the nun so sparingly, with a care of her surrounding that was very touching. Although five, she ruled the woods. She loved her animals, feeling close to them and they loved her back. It runs deep within her body. She is the born Master of the Animal kingdom of Our days. Remember this, Azryel, Solomon's gift is a great one to bestow, and It-666 has got it fully.

Azryel focused back upon the scene as he saw Sister Theresa opening one window of the cabin happily, humming a joyous air. Death recognised the 'Do-Re-Mi' tune of the 'The Sound of Music' film and sadly shook his head when he saw the doomed human putting a strawberry cake to cool upon the window sill.

He whispered to the Tutor,

-The strict nun loved the child. She was celebrating her fifth birthday. I understand they hardly had any food yet she managed to get enough to bake a cake and finish it off by using strawberries from their small garden.

The Beaming Being replied,

-They looked after each other. The 'child' remained the child for the nun. Sister Theresa did not enforce upon It-666 a monstrous identity. She treated her as a child first and foremost, a special one that needed to be told upon not to make zombies in the garden patch. Yet she tried to educate her too, like any child to read and write. She realised soon enough the 'child' already knew that, and more frighteningly so she knew it in all languages, alive or dead. Tess exorcised the child every evening since she was one. It worked like a favourite bedtime story to the young impressionable Beast. It made her fight her own evil every night before she could rest peacefully exhausted. Fight against Evil was impressed upon the child first and foremost by Tess. In the young It-666's heart, Sister Theresa is her mother, adoptive and all encompassing of her all specialness. Yet Theresa failed to name the child as she dreaded the day, she would be snatched from her. She expected it to happen. She always thought she would never survive the grief of it. She did not. Watch.

Four men ran within the woods towards the small cabin, fast and fully armed.

The young Beast in her river lifted her head up, shivered all over, the fish within her palms was charred to death. She ran as fast as she could towards the cabin.

When she arrived upon the scene, Sister Theresa had a colt pointed to her head, with four men harassing her. She could not stand the rib cage battering inflicted upon her guardian and shouted to the aggressors,

-I am here. Come and get me.

One stayed by the nun as three went to grab the child. Although It-666 went straight to the man holding the colt and no one could stop her.

Theresa pleaded,

-Run away, child. Do not fight. Run away from it all.

The man shouted to the nun,

-Shut up, Bitch! No running away on my watch.

He pulled the trigger of his colt.

Tess closed her eyes, blood pouring from her forehead and whispered her last words, before falling lifeless in front of her,

-Run, far and you will see One's way. Run far away.

It was not to be so, as when the child reached her she enclosed the Sister within her small arms and cried out,

-No...............

The man holding the gun met her braising black demonic eyes just once before bursting into a living human flame. As she turned around to run away, It met the three others, and her straight look within their eyes sent them bursting into flames likewise. She ran past them further and further away from the fire she was leaving behind her. Her eyes were covered by blood tears, she could barely see her way forward. She started shivering all over as she jumped streams and bushes, as an understanding reached her that she had burned those murderous men alive just by looking at them. The more she trembled, the more she felt the ground below her tremor. It was getting worse the further she went. The sky was dark at three. An electrical storm flashed lightning by her path, splitting trees, until she reached a clearing where the sun seemed to be there despite it all. Breathless she ran to a Being sitting peacefully upon a dead log. He opened his arms wide and received her. Patting her back, he started singing to her something she had heard before. It soothed her slowly but surely. The quake by her feet ceased altogether as she fell upon her knees by the Being. She asked him breathless,

-Are you the One? I need to run a bit more if not.

The Being stroked her cheek gently, answering,

-You will always be a runaway, child. Tess called me to look after you, to keep an eye on you for a while longer and forever.

She smiled to him and just collapsed at his feet.

The Tutor clapped his hands recalling the Death Angel and the teenage It-666 to their previous point in It's past. He enjoined,

-Azryel, take her back to the present she saw enough to recall her goal and you saw enough to know what she is about. Both of you are needed right now for all is moving forward very fast.

The Death Angel held the teenager's hand and guided her back to the present.

Verse 34. House of Cards.

Raphael smiled wickedly as an annoyed Workmaster took his watch off and put it upon the hospital bed by a lot of other items like his leather wallet, designer sunglasses, and a zippo. Gabriel walked inside the hospital room with test tubes filled with blood, gave a quick glance at the two engaged in a fierce poker game and scolded them out loud,

-Honestly Raphael, are you not ashamed of fleecing the human of all his valuable belongings? He already has not a lot, I can assure you of that. When will you stop humiliating him? When he is stark naked? And you, Walter, when will you learn and agree that there is no point competing with an Angel, let alone an Archangel, especially of the calibre of Raphael. When will you curb that senseless human pride that you can beat him at a stupid card game? Hmmm, when? You are both wasting your time. Any signs of Azryel and Bambi?

His uncle looked at him and coughed forcibly,

-Warning, the walking kill joy is in the room.

Gabriel shrugged his shoulders, came to the Archangel, pulled three cards hidden from his suit jacket, and put them in front of a disgruntled Workmaster, and just stated,

-Just the mobster I always knew. Game over. You do not know how to play games in an honest way.

Walter swore,

-What the bleeping hell, Raph?

Raphael put his hands up with a look of pure innocence, explaining himself,

-Why play fair when I know all the ways to always win? Why have so much knowledge and not use it? Honestly Gabriel, why would I dumb myself down to Walt's level? We are talking about Wreck-Man here. He is a born loser, remember, he would not have known the difference.

Gabriel went to his lab ignoring his uncle yet shaking his head disapprovingly while Workmaster stood up and picked up his belongings, visibly annoyed. Walt vented,

-May I be allowed to wreck someone's winning smile?

The Archangel crossed his arms upon his chest, and teased the man,

-Go on, just try. Give it your best shot. For if you don't, you will be very, very sorry. I have a talent to humble everyone in my path. Do you want to eat a bit of humble pie Walter?

Gabriel put his head outside his lab and warned,

-Workmaster, don't even think of taking on the bet. I don't want to have to pick up your human bits everywhere with a little spoon. Uncle, don't encourage him, for Christ's sake! And where is Bambi? I am worried sick. Was it a good idea to let Azryel look after her? He has a tendency to cut everything short, from smile to life passing by conversations and apologies.

He had barely finished his last sentence when the Death Angel appeared in the room glaring at him with incandescent eyes, the young It-666 alive and well by his side.

Gabriel gulped an apology. Walter ran to the teenager checking her out. Raphael stood up at once and went to Azryel,

-Finally, I thought I would die of boredom one hundred times over rather than by your dirty hands, my Death Angel. I can see that you spared and repaired the little one. What's the score? Can We take her again on outings?

Death knelt by Raphael and invited,

-Take my hands and know all for yourself. We walked in her past. We were guided throughout and sent back to the present. You might find our Guide very interesting, he is answering our prior questions. He is the one that took her on.

While the Archangel read his henchman. Gabriel took It-666 in his lab, a worried look upon his face. Walter followed them, asked,

-Pray, It, put us out of our misery we were worried sick about you.

The teenager sat upon the stool presented by Gab, giving them her kindest smile,

-Azryel is fearsome but fair. I explained myself to him. I begged for my own death.

She looked sheepishly at them both, apologetically so, as Walter nodded with comprehension,

-My dear girl, you saved my little boy. You cured him beyond any means. He is now safe and sleeping in his own bed at Caro's, like nothing ever happened to him.

Gab commented,

-Begging for death to me was not a good idea, It. Begging for death to Azryel is a thousand times worse. He does not take any prisoner. Yet, you live for another day, how come?

The young girl answered gravely,

-My decision upon my life was ruled out by two powerful Beings, my Tutor and Death. I have much to learn. I am a soldier, however new, I am needed to sort out what is to come. I cannot have an early exit. Gab, give me a blood test. I have concerns that its structure did change slightly. Hope you will know what to make of it if I am right and show the results to Azryel, to let him know how to deal with me in the future.

The Angel smiled and reassured,

-Learning that you are not alone anymore, surely must soothe your tortured heart. You have been found by Us and We don't let go easily of anything or anyone without due consideration. Now, after all my work on the previous samples, I need to put myself back at 'It', it seems. Will it give me another sleepless night? Will a drop of it falling upon the floor, burn a tiny little hole a few inches deep like the former one?

The Death Angel stood nonchalantly at the doorway smoking a cigar replied sarcastically for the teenager,

-Gab, now you will have a crater. The child swallowed Archangelic blood through her skin. Be prepared to get your whole clinic fixed up at some point.

He threw a little of his ashes down before continuing with worried brows,

-Where are Caroline and Micky?

Raphael standing behind him stated confidently,

-Safe and well at Caro's home, guarded by Asha and the three. Cécile is there with them. She should make a full recovery with the good work Gab done with her. I have all my cards in hand, Az, do not worry. Our plan worked. P has lost track of It-666. That mother fucker of a politician cannot draw a valid hand anymore. He lost the game.

Verse 35. Playing P.

In Boston, within the large mansion of famous politician Paul Peterson, the night was not going according to any plan. For no plans went well for the last few days, and the infamous 'P' was seated in a narrow control room watching over and over again the CCTV footage from his bunker. He asked for the hundredth time to the last man standing, the torturer called '3',

-And the entire bunker vanished? Demolished by vegetation, rats and mice... And the Beast was there but disappeared, and so was the 'Real' Santa Morte with a big silver scythe and all, and some large winged creature took the child, Workmaster' s son, away with it into the air... In my honest opinion, Mister 3, you just went bonkers.

The man stuttered helplessly, and pleaded,

-Lets watch it all again Sir, it must all be there, it must.

Peterson lifted his hand with impatience, as he ruled it out,

-My bunker is gone and I have a mad man as an only witness who does not make sense at all. I am very upset right now Mister 3. All my plans to regain the Antichrist relied on the exchange between Walter Workmaster' s son and her. Now I have nothing left, not even the place to keep my Antichrist. Indeed, Mister 3 I am very, very upset. I shall not watch again that fuzz of a CCTV footage. I shall cut your damn tongue and relieve the headache of the bad news it caused by doing so.

Mister 3 cried out,

-Everything went fast forward. The destruction of the bunker was a natural one if it was left a thousand years to the elements and the environment yet it happened within seconds. We need to slow the footage right down and look at it backwards, like when we listen to evil tracks. Then we will see the Beast in action.

P's smile grew back,

-Interesting concept. Yet it came from one who was the first to see the rise of the Antichrist. I think we should give it a fair try. What do you think BigBrother4?

A large coloured man in charge of the control room, nodded positively, moving switches upon a panel,

-Let's give it a good go.

All of them sat back in awe as the screens revealed the actions which went on within P's bunker from Z to A. They replayed the actions once more slower and Peterson remained utterly silent throughout, while BigBrother4 commented,

-The fast forward destruction does look like a natural process. The rats and mice trick is very freaky. We are talking about thousands there. The kid is gone with some kind of blurry figure who's got four wings. For 'Santa Morte' well, if it is who we think it is then, the Antichrist has the help of the Grim Reaper to do her dealings. Watch those heads roll. Serious, that is the part which scares me the most, he is fucking calling out their names. How did he know them if he is not for 'real'? And then, our girl just revealed herself as the real thing too. Those demons pouring out of her, that is phenomenal, I would have shite myself, pardon me to be crude, Sir. No wonder 3 has gone mad.

Peterson was transfixed upon what he saw and asked for it to be replayed, then asked BigBrother4 to stop at one precise moment,

-There, look at the eyes of that kid when the blade of the knife is slashing his wrists. Pause it. Just there, pause it, I said.

3 and BigBrother4 stated at once, together,

-Fire balls. There's fire burning in his eyes.

Paul Peterson laughed out loud,

-And how many kids do you know with those kind of eyes? None, I am sure, that is because we stumbled upon Workmaster' s one, and he happens to be a very special one which got rescued big time with paranormal creatures. 3, you have seen enough, lived enough, your time with me has ended.

Mister 3 looked in disarray, pointed at the CCTV's and begged,

-But you saw what I saw.

P stood up as he answered, pressing a red button upon the panel,

-I know and for that very same reason I do not need you anymore. However I will be magnanimous with you for you shall live yet unable to communicate.

Two henchmen stepped in the room within seconds, as P ordered,

-3 is to lose his tongue and fingers. Get rid of all his identification papers and release him into the wild, far from here. May God take him into his tender care and grace.

The man panicked and tried to run away from the room yet he was tasered to the ground before he could reach the door. P looked down to the paralysed Mister 3 in disgust and left the control room to head to his office within the mansion.

The politician walked hastily, deeply annoyed by the destruction of his bunker. It had been his most secure place to perform human sacrifices to the Devil and a very bespoke place to keep an Antichrist. He had the girl all along for the past eight years, and now that she came out of her shell finally releasing hell demons upon Earth, she was out of his grasp and impeding him. He stopped by a hallway rococo mirror, pushed a strand of his straight black hair away from his forehead, thinking he was the one supposed to welcome and cater for It-666. The girl slipped from his hands somehow, however injured and unable she was to do so, just because a mere human opened her cage. 'Mere' was an understatement, for the human in question was Walter Workmaster. That former human rights lawyer had been treading upon his trail for far too long. Peterson spat in a fruit bowl by him, he despised Workmaster. The fruit spat on, a bright yellow banana with a smiling bend to it, disappeared to thin ashes, within a faint puff of smoke. Paul swore to his handsome reflection,

-I will damn the man before he knows it. His life will be hell on Earth. I will have my Antichrist back, one way or another. He undermines, I will undermine him big time. He will lose everything. Ashes to ashes. Dust to dust. Amen. A man will be gone and dusted.

A call came buzzing from his pocket. The politician barked,

-What's up?

-Well, Sir, the siege is over. There is no point. We cannot get in. The place is so protected, it is unbelievable. There is a bullet proof shield at work all over the building. Rocket proof too, tried and tested. Can I be hologram-ed to you, Sir? I need to de-brief and consult you upon our next plan of action.

Peterson rushed in his office, locked the door and put his mobile upon a cradle. There, his main henchman, Colt, appeared before his eyes, projected within the room. The tall bold man standing before him was hurt. His right shoulder was shot through, bleeding badly as the man spoke,

-Sir, the place is overly protected and I have a strong belief that project 'A' definitely was, maybe still is or will be harboured again within those walls.

The politician turned around the man with pure unabated wrath, and raged,

-How come my project appeared in the bunker, sprouting from her cage at about 4-ish this afternoon, releasing demons, rats and mice by just opening her arms, annihilating two of my henchmen with a lookalike Santa Morte prop, and taking my bargaining tool, Workmaster' s kid from my grasp by a four winged creature? How come, if she was held in that AA club all along? De-brief, please do so!

The man nodded taking the information in. He replied undeterred,

-The place under our scrutiny is the AA club, as you know, Sir. It is not your standard club, on the contrary. You may laugh outright or you may sigh. The owner of that club is very scarcely seen at any one time, yet has been referred to with great respect as Uncle Raph. W.R.A.T.H. He is said to bring the wrath of God upon Earth. If one has a valid grief, he may be shown to him. The result is always untold but newspapers headlines warn the grieving party that something usually gruesome was done about it. The Uncle is the leading Mobster this part of the USA. His powers are reaching very far and lasting very long. He is called upon. Some say, he is protected from far above. Some say, he is an undercover USA agent. Some say, he is a Universal secret agent, working for higher powers. All I can say from my men's observations of the compound that 'Project A' was handed to him. I can also say that the helicopter activity showed that the in and out were regular and often. That whatever Uncle Raph is doing right know is impossible to know. The protection of his compound leads me to think it is his base and 'Project A''s base from now on. It is the most secure, my wrecked shoulder is a damning proof of it.

P, his closed fists stammering upon his desk, shouted,

-Helicopter activity, can't you be more precise? Why did I hire you? I want the exact time for lift off, I want to know where and when those copters land. I also want a full biography on Uncle Wrath. If he is my new enemy on the scene, I want to know who I am dealing with exactly.

The henchman bowed down,

-I cannot fulfil you for this afternoon yet at 11 am this morning three copters left the helipad of the AA. One has reached Washington, one is in LA and the other landed upon a general hospital. If 'project A' was seen in fighting form, I would investigate the hospital, Sir.

The politician calmed down, stroking his chin, lost in his thought for a few minutes before he replied,

-Her recovery was far too fast to be associated with standard hospital care. However Workmaster has obvious hospital connections, and went to run head first with our project 'A' to the clinic of his ex-wife and her brother. I need to understand why she would then transport 'A' to Uncle Wrath. But also Workmaster seems to have disappeared from the scene altogether. Maybe realising he just stole my pet project from under my nose would grant him a swift death sentence, he just took off cowardly. Yet Walter although he has never been the brightest man on Earth, killing himself slowly with alcohol, so deeply entrenched in his loss and sorrow, has never shied away from a stand off. He craves it. So why be a coward now? It does not match the Walter I know of. Something is up. Investigate every single connection of Walter Workmaster and dig him out, his death is due. His son is also rather special... He would make a perfect offering.

Saluting P, the henchman resumed it all,

-Will do, Sir. Workmaster is to be brought to you, dead or alive?

Peterson smiled cruelly as he answered,

-Alive of course... We reserved for ourselves the pleasure to make him pass. He has been such a hindrance for the past ten years or so that he has earned himself the slowest and most painful torturous death I could ever conceive. I am sure he will be a joy to erase. As for his son, this time I will be in charge of the abduction. It is official, my henchmen lack subtlety, craft and a certain 'je ne sais quoi'. On the other hand I do not lack 'finesse' and 'doigté', I can bring something up and make all the rest fall apart. You may now leave us and go about your tasks, Colt. Remember one thing from now on, be thorough as the Beast is on the loose.

The hologram of the henchman disappeared from the room as the call ended.

Left alone Paul Peterson sat upon his black leather chair in front of his desk. His hands reached for his skull which he grabbed and massaged in a horrendous manner. As the cranial skin moved below his nervous fingers, P swore out loud,

-Who thought of incarnation? Pest and plagues on Earth! How do I plan the retrieval of an Antichrist on the loose? Her time, her perfect timing should occur in 17 years from now. Her coming is far too early. It totally jeopardises my own coming, my incarnated reign of 15 years.

A call cut his rant short. Peterson answered,

-Speaking.

-It's me Sir, the Worm. I think I got warm today. I followed Workmaster with my team. He spent his night in a hotel, a posh one if I may say, Sir, not one the guy would have chosen for himself. He is a tent and B&B type, you know, atypical and friendly. Well, the Doctor, his brother in law, stayed with him until 11 pm last night. Workmaster headed to the airport in the morning. He flew off, Sir, to Australia, right down under. Information from his landlord confirms this to be a fact. His flat is going to be rented for a while until he decides to come back. There was something else, Sir, very intriguing, which may interest you.

The guy fell silent. P ordered at once,

-Fire away!

-Well, Sir. There was a girl on the same flight as Workmaster. They booked in at separate times however their allocated seats were next to each other. The girl appears to be sixteen and she, kind of made an impression on the airport staff, for she was bald. Her passport details showed that she was named Cherie Leanne Pie, born on the 06/06/1996 in London. She travelled on her own, told she was abandoned at birth, had chemotherapy for her cancer, hence her baldness, and she explained cuts on her scalp as being a messed up self harming teenager. She was selected as a human guinea pig to try state of the art cancer treatment in Australia. I enquired about the Australian Cancer project. It does exist and their selection of Cherie dated back to three weeks ago.

Peterson fell into a dumbfounded silence, before begging for more information,

-Are their ultimate destination the same? Can you enquire further about Cherie? I need to know her whole past. Yet I need you in Australia tracking both down every day from now on and report.

The Worm replied,

-Workmaster has been booked as a Guinea pig too for the same experiment. He has cancer of the throat yet he did not tell anyone. Only his best friend the Doctor knows. The girl and him will be located in the same hospital compound. I will enquire further about Cherie, Sir. She sounds damn interesting.

P shook his head as he commented,

-Yes, she does. She confuses everything.

Verse 36. Of Sucking Parts, Blood and Lives.

Midnight struck within the Boston mansion of Paul Peterson. The twelve long strikes echoed in the air, drumming in the depth of the night the start of a brand new day.

P's head shook with disbelief upon his black silky pillow. For the first time in his incarnated life he had failed to come. He did not do failures. He was re-known for his impeccable timing. If someone was at fault it would be anyone else but him. He looked in desperation at the mirror ceiling, canopy of his extremely large bed, saw his well muscled body spread like an eagle, and within his legs the 'failure'. She was his fling for the past six days and nights. Her mouth was hard at work, working too hard and missing the whole point of pleasure. Could he be bothered to teach a human the whole point? He smiled wickedly to himself, thinking that to send her to hell first was a better idea. He grabbed the blond hair of the woman at once, pulled her up upon his broad chest, and stated in a smooth silky voice,

-Failure to launch, Babe. You are so under-performing, it's pathetic to watch. You cannot make it to day seven I am afraid. I am deeply unimpressed so much so that I am going to let you go your own way tomorrow.

The woman curled her legs upon his, and wrapped herself like a kitten who could not let go, she purred,

-We both need a rest. At the rate we went on all week, a dry one was meant to happen.

Paul whispered within her ear softly,

-Sweetie, this is the problem. You need a rest and I do not. I can go on forever and you cannot. I do not do dry ones and failures. I do not accept mediocrity, I move on. So tomorrow your bags are packed, little Marie, and my driver will take you back to your home. Do not fight this fate, Sweetie, and do not follow me for you cannot, for obvious reasons. Love you and leave you is the best I can do. I am going to let you rest in peace and sleep tight, now, for I am going to have a shower. Do yourself justice, do not follow me, Marie. Tomorrow, your parents will be glad to have their runaway daughter back, at long last.

P left the room and a helpless Marie upon his large bed. She could not believe that her dream was over. She looked at her beautiful figure upon the ceiling mirror. Nineteen, fit and one of the best students in her university, yet the politician she was dating just labelled her as a 'failure'. She was not ready to pack her bags, she wanted to bag him as the biggest catch of her life and show him off to all her friends and proud parents. She thought she had the right youth and beauty. She could make it work, somehow she could...

Within the black marble bathroom, P went straight to the shower. The water trickling down offered him a cooling respite for a few seconds, yet the mirror panels of his shower surrounding him did not. Fire seemed to surround him from every angle, P laughed half-heartedly, knelt and pleaded,

-Not now Master for I cannot answer.

A dark figure appeared within the mirrors laughing louder than P, within the embracing flames,

-You can beg your whole life away it would not work upon me... How good are you as a guardian remind me? Did my very child, the Antichrist run away from your hands? She is my gateway to the World and you lost her. Failure springs to mind. I do not do failure, follows suit. The dealing of failures is called upon. I want them all. Now.

P stood up and replied,

-I am the major one in this instance, I must admit. I failed to recognise your daughter and therefore to treat her appropriately. I thought I had her but yet I doubted for she was unwilling to use her powers and show her true self all the while. She conned me onto a wild goose chase, which took my attention away from her for a few weeks. It was enough for that bastard of a human, Walter Workmaster to take her away from me. I am on his case, and I will retrieve the Antichrist, I swear.

The dark figure within the mirror brought the blaze to another level and stated,

-Not good enough. Do you want to end me for your gross negligence suggests you do? I want to come forward. You are not helping me in any way. Your mistakes are hindering my path. Why shall I allow your coming, when you cannot fulfil my very own one...? I need more blood, more parts and lives. I am starved to death. Feed me or I will feed on you and all my other hell demons. If my daughter is unwilling, I have ways to make her be my doorway to Earth. She seems to have grown a liking for humans, a little like you P. I can correct that for infinity.

P defended himself and stood up within the hell fire of his shower,

-I never grew a liking for humans unlike your daughter. I love abusing them but that is another story which pleases you and me endlessly. She grew up strangely, I do not know how to deal with her. She is pure. She cannot be read either. She is just instant manifestation. She played the dull and dead being with my men for 8 years. I need your help with her. The nun that raised her, must have influenced her somehow in goody goody ways, for It-666 to show so much restraint over her powers. At the end I believed I had the wrong person. Now, she reappeared this afternoon within my bunker, releasing hell demons and all sorts to save a child. She destroyed the entire place, wiped it to oblivion from the surface of the Earth.

One of the mirror shattered into thousands pieces, the glass of it flying and lodging itself deep into the skin of the knelt incarnated

Demon P. The voice within the mirrors vociferated in tongue, the dark figure exhibiting pure wrath,

-What do you expect? You tortured my child in that damn bunker! Did you want her to leave you a thank you note? 'By the way thanks for having me, 'P', it was the most enjoyable eight years of my life.' Jeez... Now, you made me swear. Of course she is going to rescue a human kid after what she went through. Sympathy, sympathy for human causes and pleas, that is what you gave her, taught her without knowing, by your eight years of fiddling with her trying to guess if she was the real thing by torturing her. Yes, of course she would wreck your place so you cannot use it any more. She has been there and you made it like hell, not like a hell princess would be treated, but like the scum of the human kind, the worst criminals, would be. If you have damaged my daughter irretrievably so she hates the dark sides of where she comes from, you are an ancient Demon which was meant to rule the Earth for a while which will be destroyed to oblivion, by no one else but me.

The Demon stood up bleeding from his every wound of mirror shards as he pleaded,

-Master, I beg of you to give me time. I will sort out the whole conundrum of It-666. She is now a fully revealed hell princess, the Beast, our Antichrist. We will retrieve her. If she is talking to the wrong kind, too many humans and especially Walter Workmaster, that can influence her badly in the most righteous way possible, the human right ways, then we just need to re-establish contact with her in the most powerful way possible. We will make sure she is in direct contact with Hell at all times. It can only give your daughter choice, and more perspective, much much more, as we know it, for humanity is doomed. Who better than her own Father, the ruler of Hell, himself, to sway her to get back onto her fated track? Who can teach her better than all but her Father?

The dark shadow stood still as he enjoined the Demon to carry on,

-Pray, P, how would you make this happen?

P smiled thoroughly back to his Master and replied,

-By gathering all the human parts needed to perform the feat. I have already a few which I was going to offer you as a feeding gift. Now, the parts will play a much more important role. Communication, all what they were intended for. I am missing some which I expect to come forward within a few minutes. The last piece will feed you well for three days.

The figure laughing loudly asked,

-Have you got something under your sleeve?

The Demon replied with a knowing smirk,

-Human stupidity and vanity as usual Master.

As he finished his words, a small knock resonated within the room, a weak voice tried her luck,

-It is only me, Dumpling. I heard a bad noise. Are you alright?

The dark shadow corked his eyebrows,

-Dumpling? Interesting. My gift, my feed, I suppose?

P replied quickly in a low voice before answering to the knock loudly,

-Yes, Master. An infatuated little posh goose, beautiful and clever, which believes her belly button can make the whole world turn. You will love her blood, fresh, healthy and young.

-Go back to bed Sweetie. I knocked a mirror moving badly. Nothing sensational. Remember what I said to you. Bed. Now.

Marie replied opening the door straight away,

-Aww, poor thing let me make it all better for you.

P shook his head disapprovingly, stated in a low voice for his Master's benefit,

-Here we go, human sheer stupidity. Is it lack of understanding or insolence? I keep wondering as it never fails.

Marie stood in the bathroom and shouted at the sight of her bleeding politician lover. He moved forward and silenced her swiftly. The young woman fell unconscious upon the bathroom floor tiles.

P turned to his Master, with a wicked self satisfied smirk,

-Feeding time, the meat is fresh. Now, I have all the human parts required, ready for the communication ceremony.

Verse 37. The Calling. Hell Control to It-666

The procession walked in line, one following the other, in the deep darkness of the woods. The Autumnal night sky was clear of clouds yet seemed devoid of stars. Ahead of the procession P was tracking down the emplacement of his erased bunker. He could feel the ground below his feet trembling the more he approached the doom centre where he had performed so many human sacrifices. His elaborately sculpted ebony shaft within his hand started pulsating the rhythm for a new dark ceremony. The wooden snake upon the shaft awoke to life and slowly slithered to reach P's hand encircling it firmly upon the staff.

P paused, turned upon himself halting the procession, and stated,

-Our Lord Satan is with us. No secrets can be hidden from him. Nothing stolen from him cannot be found and retrieved. Here is our grounds. Here is his Earth.

The incarnated Demon thrust the tip of the staff upon the earth below him before waving it in a circular motion around him in a very precise manner. A huge pentagram made of blood lines appeared upon the ground as the vegetation above it disappeared into ashes. He smiled to his followers, showing off the five pointed star, then told,

-Praise be to Satan to find what was lost. Praise be to Lord Satan, for although you failed him, he allows you to worship him still.

The black adder moved from his hand to return upon the tip of the ebony shaft, where it curled upon itself whistling into P's ear. The Demon looked at the people gathering around him, taking their position in a neat circle. All of them were cloaked in black leather capes, and hooded in a fashion which disguised the identities of the bearer. He knew them all by heart and once again they did not fail to turn up. Some were politicians, some were celebrities, some were pure incarnated demons just like him. He engaged six members which held precious boxes to come forward, as all but him started to sing in a strange language the Satanic praise.

The first person, a famous and beautiful actress, knelt by him, presenting her small box made of Ukraine black granite. Opening the lid, in a grand manner, P exhibited its content to the Satanic congregation, a pair of feminine human ears complete with understated but real pearl earrings. He told the actress,

-You may be thanked by our Lord.

The woman trembling presented her hand to the snake. The adder sank her teeth within it drawing her blood. The actress closed her blue eyes feeling faint, her heart pulsating madly. When the adder released her hand, P took it and kissed it for a long while, licking it and sucking the poured blood. When he gallantly let her hand go, the actress could see nothing but the two red dots of the snake bite, her hand appeared to be healed and her stammering heart rate returned to normal. She took her place back in the circle smiling with a strange satisfaction. The incarnated Demon deposited the box in the centre of the pentagram, singing louder than any other present in tongue. The adder swiftly dropped from the tip of the shaft to the opened stone box, where it swallowed slowly but surely the human offering. When P finished his incantation, the snake's shape shifted and the humble adder became a black rattlesnake.

The second individual stepped forward to present his gift. He did not kneel by P, he shook his hand firmly for he was a powerful ruling politician. He opened himself the lid of the precious opal coffret to exhibit his present, a human tongue cut only hours ago. He deposited the box at P's feet and went on to stroke the rattlesnake. The split snake tongue licked the hand of the man before, the 'Crotalus horridus' rattling his tail moved to the newly opened box. There, it swallowed the whole tongue as the Satanic songs rose to another level, and there it transformed into a smaller Silver snake.

The third to come forth was an elderly lady, which could barely be seen within her large leather cape, which contrary to all others had a silver lining to it, instead of their carmine satin one. She looked frail yet she walked to P strongly and as her predecessor did not bow to him. The casket she handed to the Demon was made of pure gold. She revealed its content with a wicked smile, and whispered,

-I can still see them moving. Swift and diligent they were. Not only that, they were the most loyal I ever knew. It is definitely a parting.

P knelt by the human, took the golden casket from her hands and presented her with the silver snake. The reptile entwined itself around her arm like a Roman bracelet. It wriggled strangely for a few minutes, before leaving the old lady and heading for his new box. The woman turned around so her back only was seen and flashed her thin white hair to the crowd as they became thicker and dark silvery grey. She put her hood back on and stated,

-At this rate I will go on forever.

P commented swiftly,

-This is what happens to amazing humans.

The snake ate his gift of fingers greedily. At the end of it, the reptile grew to a huge golden Thai python to the amazement of the black mass singers.

The fourth man to come forward flaunted the anonymity as he lowered his hood and showed his face to the whole assemblée. He stood before P, proudly, handsome as hell, and handed him a transparent glass box beholding a few human eyes. He then knelt and kissed P's hand with devotion. The Demon smiled wickedly and ordered,

-Deliver the gift, Pet. Be reverent and off upon your glorious glowing way.

The man opened the glass box and lifting the golden python with the utmost care, took it to his novel feeding ground. The python swirled upon his neck three times before digging into the man's main artery. The snake drew so much blood than the man was about to die. The python left him slowly pushing the human with its strong tail towards the incarnated Demon, as it headed for the eyes within the glass box.

P gathered the man in his arms and put his lips upon his neck wound. It was slow and tender as he brought life back to the famous model. When the man opened his eyes, he asked confused,

-Am I back?

The Demon answered,

-You are, Pet. You are looked after. You gave a real good feed. We are thankful to you. We won't let you go. Now, shoot off like the star you are.

The man sprung upon his feet healthier than ever, gave the Demon a peck on his lips before disappearing in the worshipping crowd.

The fifth came forward as soon as the incantation resounded back into the air of the night. Small, smiling peacefully, the man knelt humbly by P. His black leather cloak covered badly an orange toga. He deposited a wooden casket made of walnut by P's feet, then left without a word in the deep darkness of the woods. The Demon's eyes glowed, following the path of the human within the forest. When he could not see the man he opened the walnut lid of the casket, to reveal the brain it contained. It was old, very dead, and very clever. The Demon could not help stroking the grey matter before him with awe. The greatest scientist brain to be stolen was by his feet, as an offer to his Master. He giggled as his green eyes searched for the horizon, then looked upon the new snake. The golden python was now a smaller cobra, very much aware which headed straight for the opened walnut casket. No brain was too big for its mouth. Swallowed it was finally taking longer than any operation... The snake shedded its skin straight away to become a larger than life Coniophis.

The sixth person was led by a leash. She was the young hooded Marie, blinded and gagged by thick leather strips. Stunned and scared, she recognised P's voice and tried to plead at his feet, yet her words died within the gag not reaching out to anyone,

-Give me a chance, just a little one, please.

P said solemnly, ignoring her plea,

-Our human box contains the ultimate gift. Let us unwrap her flesh. Who will be the first tin opener?

His human Pet, the famous handsome model presented himself and knelt by his Master who handed to him the sacrificial knife. He took the girl by the hand and told,

-There is no hope for you, Sweetie. You failed to understand and follow simple specific orders. Do not fight it anymore, just lay. You were given many chances, more than what is required.

The young woman lay by the male model's feet and kept pleading without being heard,

-Please, help me.

Only the demon replied to her,

-He can't, for you doomed your way all the way.

P added and ordered,

-She did damn herself and is ourselves to take. Do it Pet for your Master. Cut her throat, I have heard enough from that useless and proud human.

The Pet cut the throat of the nineteen year old above the pentagram with no further ado, and gave the knife back to his Master. The Demon stood above the dying woman and thrust the knife into her chest, digging out her beating heart. He presented it to the crowd before pouring the blood out of it above the pentagram.

As the young woman died below his feet, P offered her precious organ to the snake, which took it all slowly, still pulsating slightly.

He called out in tongue through the darkness of the night, accompanied by the evil pray of his followers,

-It, Dear It-666, Control panel to you. Major Hell princess on the loose, your great Father is calling you and forever. Listen, listen, you can only listen to your Father.

Miles away, the sleeping It levitated upon her bed within Purallee's clinic at that very moment. Archangel Raphael stood up straight away, worried,

-What's up now?

It-666 floating within the room woke up. Her demonic black eyes opened upon the room and stared into the darkness as the surrounding walls started bleeding.

Gabriel slapped by his uncle woke up to witness the levitation of It-666 and asked wildly,

-Who did upset the damn girl?

Raphael replied,

-She is doing it by herself. I swear. She was sleeping nicely a minute ago. And then, she went all levitating. Something is up, Gab. Where is Az when you need him?

Azryel came at that very moment and stood by the door extinguishing his cigar upon the door frame. He watched intently as the levitating girl awoke and started speaking in tongue. He swore,

-Great, we have her Dad on the line. He made a bloody connection to It...

Gabriel looked at him very worried, asked,

-How can he? The girl was trashed by him for dead for her past sixteen years.

The Death Angel replied strongly,

-He never trashed her, she was abducted at birth by a fervent priest and nun who aimed to protect the World. He tried to find her via P and he just did. He is talking to her right now. The feat took the death of a fair few humans. It-666 will never be the same again. She has direct contact with Hell from now on. She is going to be a Hell Baby to deal with, of that I am certain... Are we sure about raising the girl?

The End.

Finding It-666: The Beast

Book One of the teenage Antichrist years.

Born on the 06/06/1996 in London, the young It is a sweet sixteen supernatural Being of a special kind, one meant to bring the end of the human world: the Beast incarnated, the Antichrist.

Fall 2012, the Beast was found. From the deep darkness of her hole, she is raised up to the light. From her closed caged below a pentagram made of blood, she is freed. The human who found her, Walter Workmaster, is a firm atheist, a private investigator and former human rights lawyer who becomes her staunch advocate. Adopting the lost It, the man released her to his world to make her face humanity and unknowingly much more... The advent of the Beast has started. Step one, she is found.

Coming Soon:

The Compendium of Characters of Cordelia Malthere.

Take a guided tour in the It-666's saga and the Author's fantastic stories' world. Switch gears from Earth to Hell to the unknown... Meet the characters, their pasts, their presents, and maybe their futures... This Codex is the ultimate companion to Cordelia Malthere's universes.

Raising It-666: The teenage Beast

Book Two of the young Beast years.

Adopted by the human Walter Workmaster, the Beast is being given a fair chance to live and learn almost like a normal teenager. 'Almost', for normality does not apply when It-666 is concerned. Trained to be a Soldier by the Angel of Death, monitored by Archangel Raphael and looked after by Archangel Gabriel, It is raised as a Being with the open opportunity of her own heart, which they will protect. Trips to Hell and fighting demons make her earn her true colours within the Angelic Army raising her up in their midst.

By the same author:

Hair Rising, Heir Raising, Erasing.

By Cordelia Malthere.

A vibrant beyond the grave tale which will chill your bones while warming your heart. When the deadly serious is delightfully hilarious, you will know you have just been acquainted with Abraham Wilton-Cough. His skeletal hand will drag you from grave to grave, under the moonlight of the night where many dead are rising... Could it be the apocalypse?

www.ingramcontent.com/pod-product-compliance
Lightning Source LLC
Chambersburg PA
CBHW061609170626
46811CB00001B/366